"No, Stacey, I didn't kill your father," Clay said. He relaxed his grip on her shoulders and looked into her eyes. "Stacey, you do believe me, don't you?"

"I . . . I don't know what I believe," Stacey said. She suddenly started struggling again. "Go away, Clay Conway. Go away and leave me alone. I don't want to listen to you anymore."

Clay again grabbed her arms to subdue her struggles. "I'll leave," he said, "but not until I have done this."

He leaned down and kissed her with hot, hungry lips. The impact of the kiss took Stacey's breath away. Her head started spinning, as she felt his tongue, first brushing across her lips and then forcing them open.

Sensations so overwhelmed her that for the moment she forgot her struggles. His hands moved gently across her smooth golden skin, spreading fire wherever they went, and though now Stacey had renewed her struggle, it was as much against her own feelings as against Clay.

As he thrust himself upon her she gasped and raked his bare back with her fingernails—whether in a burst of passion or a last effort to fight him she couldn't be sure. He moved his mouth over hers, stifling her cries with smothering kisses. Then, with all pretense gone, Stacey gave herself up to him. She felt the breath leave her body as she was lifted to the stars, there to become a blazing comet, exploding in golden ecstasy that went on and on and on.

Later, as he rested quietly beside her, the realization overcame her: she had just made love with the man she believed killed her father. His words had not convinced her, but her body had betrayed her. . . .

Other Pinnacle Books by Paula Fairman:

In Savage Splendor
Forbidden Destiny
Storm of Desire

The FURY and the PASSION

Paula Fairman

PINNACLE BOOKS • LOS ANGELES

THE FURY AND THE PASSION

Copyright © 1979 by Script Representatives, Inc.

An original Pinnacle Books edition, published for the first time anywhere.

First printing, August 1979

ISBN: 0-523-40569-3

Cover illustration by Bill Maughan

Printed in the United States of America

PINNACLE BOOKS, INC.
2029 Century Park East
Los Angeles, California 90067

This book is for
Mike and Joanie Wells
who have restored to
Sky Meadow
its original excitement

THE FURY
AND THE PASSION

Chapter One

It was midspring of 1881. The cold rain had begun before dawn and continued to slash down on the small, weatherbeaten house which perched precariously on the edge of Wells Canyon in the Cascades of Oregon. The back door of the house opened then slammed shut, and someone hurried through the dark and the rain to a barn which stood some thirty yards distant from the main building.

The house served as a stagecoach way station and alongside the building, looming blackly in the night, was a large green Concord stage, with yellow letters proudly proclaiming the carrier: Wells Fargo. The letters also indicated the point of origin, Winchester, and the destintion, MacAllister. The stage was a fine looking piece of equipment. It had rolled into the station at nine o'clock the night before, pulled by eight prancing horses blowing fog in the cold night air, and driven by a driver who wearily pulled the big team to a halt.

There had been six passengers on board the stage, four men and two women, and they left it exhausted and grateful for the sparse comfort offered by the way station for the night. Their luggage remained in the tightly lashed leather boot, dry and secure despite the rain. The window curtains, however, did little to keep out the rain, and already the hard leather seats were cold and wet.

The hurrying figure moved gracefully across the distance and slipped into the barn. Sure hands removed a match from a waxed, waterproof box to light a kerosene lantern. When the flame was turned up, a small golden bubble of light cast long shadows inside the barn, and at the same time illuminated the face of the lantern holder. It was only then that one would have noticed that it was a girl. One also would have noticed that here was no ordinary girl, but one of uncommon beauty. She had hair as black as a raven's wing, and it fell softly to her shoulders from beneath the felt hat she wore. Her eyes caught the reflection of the yellow flame and their natural amber color took on an even brighter hue. Her skin, now rain washed, was olive complexioned and without a blemish. She was slim of form, but well enough rounded so that the boy's clothes she wore did little to hide her gender.

The girl's name was Anastasia Pendarrow, though if anyone had asked she would have said her name was Stacey, as that was what she preferred to be called. Stacey was seventeen years old, and the daughter of Seth Pendarrow, a Wells Fargo stage driver and station agent for this way station, where they lived. The station was known as Sky Meadow, and Stacey helped her father run it. In fact she often went along with him on the Sky Meadow to MacAllister run, helping him drive. She had a light, sure touch on the "ribbons," as the reins were called, and played upon them, four in each hand, one rein for each horse, with the skill and virtuosity of a master violinist.

There were those who argued that such work was ill-becoming for a young woman, and they chastised Seth for the arrangement. The most vocal of these detractors was Pricilla Prescott, Stacey's maternal aunt. Aunt Pricilla, who was Mrs. Tobias Prescott of the Denver Prescotts, had begun petitioning Seth to allow Stacey to live with them from the moment Stacey's mother had died.

"Stacey likes it up here on the mountain with me," Seth had insisted. "And I would miss her more than I could bear if she were to stay away too long."

"Anastasia is a lovely young woman now," Pricilla had replied. "It is only right that she get away from horses and wagons and the ruffians who abound near such places, and come to Denver to live with us. We will arrange introductions with all of the proper people, and see to it that she meets qualified young gentlemen of means."

"I'll think it over," Seth had promised, after being relentlessly bombarded by Pricilla's demands.

Stacey was fully aware of the battle going on between her father and her mother's sister, but she had already resolved to stay right here regardless of the final outcome. She was born to this kind of life and she loved it. She thrilled to the sound of the stage driver's trumpet as the stage approached the station. She liked the smell of leather and cured wood, and the feel of power when she held the reins of eight spirited animals. She liked to see the daily parade of passengers and guess about their backgrounds, and wonder if they found life as exciting as she did.

Stacey walked over to the first of the eight horses that would form the hitch for the coach. She leaned against the horse and began stroking his neck. Add to the bouquet of leather and cured wood, the smell of horseflesh and the aroma of hay, she thought. For these smells too were pleasant to her.

It was warm and dry inside the barn, though the sounds of the wind and the rain outside were testimony of the cold, wet beginning of the new day. In a way there was something sensuous about the protected isolation of the barn, and Stacey let her mind wander, directed by the delectableness of the moment, until she recalled the dream.

The dream! It had been both frightening and shameful, and had occurred in that last hour before awakening. Despite the fear and the shame, there was also, disturbingly, a pleasant aspect to it, as it evoked feelings of hidden desires and untested passions.

There had been a man in her dream, nameless and vague to be sure, but a man nonetheless. He was created by the growing demands of her body for gratification of the puzzling concupiscence which seemed to lie just beneath awareness.

In the dream the nameless man's hands had touched her breasts and caressed her until her nipples, like tiny budding blooms, rose in response. The same hands explored her smooth skin to the dimple of her navel, and then moved further down across the curve of her thighs and into her most private part. There, knowing fingers played upon eager flesh until that which consciousness would have denied burst upon her in sleep, awakening her to exquisite delights.

Stacey had lain awake for a moment, drifting with the slowly receding sensations and listening to the rhythm of the rain beating against her window. Then, to her utter shame, she suddenly realized exactly what she had done, and she quickly withdrew her hands from the cleft of warm, wet flesh that was the cause of her rapture. The resultant flood of shame and guilt quickly washed away the last ripples of pleasure, and Stacey hastily got up from bed to attend to her morning chores. Thus it was that she now found herself in the barn with the stage horses.

The horses moved expectantly toward the trough to await their morning meal of oats.

"Good morning, animals," Stacey said, forcing herself to put the dream out of her mind. "Did you sleep well?"

Stacey began scooping oats into the trough and continued to talk to the horses as if they could understand her. In fact, Stacey had such a way with horses that there were those who believed she really could speak with them.

"Listen to the rain, horses," she said to them. "Doesn't it feel good to be warm and dry inside, with the rain coming down outside?"

"It feels very good," a voice answered her.

"What?" Stacey asked, gasping.

A young man suddenly sat up from the straw of one of the empty stalls, laughing. "What's the matter, miss? Did you think perhaps the horses were talking back to you?"

"Sir, you should have made your presence known!" Stacey gasped.

"I'm sorry," the young man said, still laughing. "But the opportunity was too good to pass. You should have seen your face when you thought a horse had answered you."

"I did not think a horse answered me," Stacey insisted.

"Oh, yes you did." The stranger brushed at the straw that was the same yellow color as his hair, until the last piece of it was removed from his clothes. He walked over to Stacey and looked at her with his smooth, boyishly handsome face. Handsome he was by any standard, but Stacey was still too angered by his rude intrusion to notice.

"Who are you? Where did you come from?" Stacey asked.

"My name is Clay Conway," the young man said. "I arrived on the stage last night."

"No, you did not," Stacey said. "There were only six passengers on that stage, I know that for a fact."

"Oh, ho, you're so smart," Clay teased. "But, for your information, I'm not a passenger. I'm riding as the shotgun messenger."

"Shotgun? But you're just a boy."

For a split second Clay's eyes lost their humor, but the humor returned as quickly as it left. "When a gun is fired, it doesn't make any difference how old the finger is that pulls the trigger."

Now it was Stacey's turn to laugh. The remark about his age had a telling effect, just as she hoped it would. In her mind it evened things up for his startling her. She decided to press her advantage further. "You are a bit touchy over your age, aren't you? But then, boys always are."

This time Stacey overplayed her hand, as something in Clay's face told her. But she saw it too late to react, for he reached for her, grabbing her by the shoulders. "I'll show you who's a boy," he said. He pulled her to him, crushing her lips against his. His arms wound around her tightly, pulling her body against his. At first she struggled against him, both out of anger and out of fear. But the harder she struggled the more determined he became to hold her, until finally she abandoned the struggle and let herself go limp in his arms.

Then a strange thing began to happen. The surprise changed to surrender, the fear to curiosity, and then to sweetness. A pleasure not unlike that which she felt during the forbidden dream began overtaking her. Clay's lips opened on hers and his tongue pushed into her mouth. It was shocking and thrilling at the same time, and involuntarily a moan of passion began in her throat. Her blood felt as if it had changed to hot tea, and her body was warmed with a heat she had never before experienced. The kiss went on, longer than she had ever imagined such a thing could last, and her head grew so light that she abandoned all thought save this pleasure. Finally, Clay broke off the kiss, and Stacey was left standing there as limp as a rag doll.

"Now," Clay said insolently, "is that the kiss of a mere boy?"

Stacey looked at him, her senses reeling. Finally, sanity returned and she realized with a start what had happened. Her cheeks flamed in embarrass-

7

ment, and she felt a rush of anger. She slapped him, hard.

"How dare you do that to me?" she demanded.

Clay laughed easily. "Now I reckon I had that comin', miss," he said. He rubbed his cheek with the back of his hand, and studied her, never losing his smile. "But then again, I reckon it was worth it."

"Ooooh, you are impossible!" Stacey cried. She whirled about angrily, then strode quickly out of the barn and hurried through the rain to return to the house.

Chapter Two

Clay laughed softly as he watched Stacey hurry angrily through the rain. The taste of her kiss was still on his lips, and he touched them lightly with his fingers, as if permanently sealing her kiss there by that action.

"Horses," he said quietly, speaking to the animals, "she's just as pretty as they said she was. In fact, she may be a bit prettier."

Clay had heard talk back in Winchester of the beautiful young girl who lived at the Sky Meadow way station. There never had been anything off-color in the talk, but it had persisted to the point that Clay became obsessed with the idea of meeting her. He had a mental image of what she might look like, and he composed the speeches he might use if he ever met her. In his mind and in his fantasies, she had become a beautiful fairy princess.

Clay had decided that she would always be that to him—a fairy princess known only in his imagination—when the opportunity to meet her presented itself. Of course, the opportunity wasn't actually to meet Stacey, it was to ride as an armed guard on a special shipment aboard the Winchester to MacAllister stage run. But that was a run which would pass through Sky Meadow, and to Clay, it was finally a chance to meet the girl of his fantasies. So he accepted the offer without the least hesitation.

It was no surprise that Clay was offered the job. He was the best man with a gun anyone in Winchester had ever seen, and though he was only twenty-one and looked even younger, he was a man who had the respect of all who knew him.

Clay had not set out to become a gunfighter. It had been his boyhood ambition to go to sea, for that had been the way of his grandfather, and Clay could still remember the marvelous stories of wondrous far-off places that he had heard at his grandfather's knee. But his grandfather died when Clay was fourteen, and Clay's father and mother, younger sister, and Clay himself moved west where his father opened a general merchandise store.

By the time he was fifteen Clay had come to enjoy the great West though he had not yet given up his dream of going to sea. But all his hopes and dreams ended in one night of horror. It was a night that Clay would never allow himself to forget.

Clay's family lived in three rooms behind the store. They had just started supper one night when the bell on the front door rang as it was pushed open.

"I thought I locked the front door," his father had said in surprise. He glanced at the clock on the wall. "It's way too late for any normal customer. I wonder who it is?"

"Shall I see, Father?" Clay asked.

"No, I'll see," Josh Conway said. He stood up, but had no sooner gained his feet than their small apartment was invaded by four men.

10

"Just sit down, Pops," one of the men said. "We'll serve ourselves." The man who spoke was a big man, with a scar twisting his face into grotesque ugliness. He walked over to the table and grabbed a piece of meat from the platter. "This looks good," he said.

"What is this?" Josh demanded angrily. "Who are you? What do you want?"

"Who I am don't make no never mind," the man said, tearing into the meat with yellowed teeth. "I want some supplies," he said.

"Well, this is not the way to go about it. Come back tomorrow when the store is open."

"We can't do that, Pops," the man said. "You see, we robbed us a bank earlier today, and we got us a posse on our tails. Right now we need some ammunition and some grub to take with us. We gotta hide out for a while."

"Get out of this store right now!" Clay's father demanded, pushing the scarfaced man away from the table.

The man simply pulled his gun and shot Clay's father dead, without so much as a second thought.

"Josh!" Clay's mother screamed, running to her husband's body.

"Well, Snake Eye, lookie here what we got," one of the others said, looking at Clay's mother. "Are you thinkin' what I'm thinkin'?"

"Yeah," the scarfaced man who was called Snake Eye said, rubbing his crotch. "It's goin' to be a long, cold, lonely time up in them mountains. Maybe the lady here would sorta give us somethin' to think about to keep us warm durin' the cold nights."

11

The one who had spoken to Snake Eye grabbed Clay's mother, and ripped her dress and undergarments down the front, exposing her breasts.

"You get away from her!" Clay shouted. He grabbed the meat knife from the table and started toward his mother's assailant, but before he could get to him, he heard the loud noise of a pistol shot, and felt a burning, breathtaking pain as the bullet slammed into his back. He fell to the floor and passed out.

When he came to he saw both his mother and his sister being abused by the four men. He tried to get up, but no matter how hard he tried, he couldn't move. He stared at the four ugly faces, burning their images into his mind so that he would never forget them.

"Let's go," he heard a fifth voice say. The new voice surprised him. He had thought there were only four. Now he tried to turn his head to see the new speaker, but as before, he was unable to move.

"Don't you want to try a little of this, Barney?" one of the men asked. "The young 'un there'd be about your speed, I reckon." The others laughed.

"No," Barney said. "We must leave at once. Unless you wish to see the posse descending upon us through the front door." Barney's voice, unlike the others, was cultured and educated.

"I reckon he's right," one of the men said. "Come on, let's go."

"What'll we do with 'em?"

"Burn the store, that'll take care of 'em."

"Don't be a fool," Barney said. "If you set a torch to this place they'll see it burning for twenty miles.

You might as well just ride into the posse with your hands up."

"Well, whatta you think we should do?"

"Kill them," Barney said.

"The man and the boy are already dead," one of the others said. "You wanna kill the women too?"

"We have no choice now, thanks to your lustful pursuits."

"I don't know, I don't hold much with killin' no women."

"You get the supplies on the horses," the one called Barney said. "I'll do what must be done."

Clay tried with all his might to move to reach the knife which lay just in front of his outstretched fingers, but he couldn't. He watched with horror as Barney calmly shot first his mother and then his sister. Clay never saw Barney's face, but he did notice his hands. The fingers were long and delicate looking, almost like a woman's. Not much to help him identify someone, but it was all he had to go on. That, and the cultured, educated voice.

Customers found Clay the next day, and they took him to the doctor's office. The doctor removed the bullet which was causing pressure on his spine, and after the bullet was removed, the total paralysis which had overtaken Clay was slowly relieved.

Clay eventually sold his father's store but not before he took the finest gun and sheath in stock, along with a large supply of ammunition. He began his search for the five outlaws, all the while practicing his draw, and taking part-time jobs to keep him going. By the time he was twenty, his draw was like greased lightning, and at sixty paces he

13

could put six bullets into a silver dollar in less than three seconds.

It took Clay five years of searching to find the first two men. Snake Eye and the one who had torn his mother's dress were drinking at a bar when he saw them. At first they were confused as to why a mere boy would have the nerve to challenge them, for Clay's face was that of a youth much younger than his twenty years.

"My name is Clay Conway," Clay said. "Does that name mean anything to you?"

The two men looked at each other with insolent grins on their faces. "Naw, kid, that don't mean nothin'," Snake Eye said. "Is it supposed to?"

"Perhaps if I showed you the bullet scar in my back, it would remind you of the time you murdered my father, raped and murdered my mother and sister, shot me in the back and left me for dead. Would you remember that?" Clay asked.

His voice was calm, and soft with the inflection of youth. But his words fell like ice with the impact of their meaning.

The others at the bar backed away then, leaving the youth and the two villains facing one another. Slowly the two men spread apart, putting distance between them, making it difficult for Clay to cover them both.

"I thought you was dead," Snake Eye said easily.

"I recovered."

"Maybe you wasn't hurt all that bad in the first place. Maybe you was just too scared to do anythin' about it," the other desperado said.

"Or maybe he was enjoyin' it," Snake Eye said. "There's those who get their kicks by watchin'."

"You two men drop your gunbelts and come to the sheriff's office with me," Clay said.

"Haw, lissen to that!" Snake Eye laughed. "Kid, if you know what's good for you, you'll hightail it on outta here 'afore we finish the job we started five years ago."

"I'm taking you in, dead or alive," Clay said.

"Boy, you're talkin' like you think you're pretty good with that hogleg," Snake Eye said, pointing to the pistol hanging at Clay's side. "But no matter how good you are, you can't shoot but one of us, 'n the other'n's gonna get you."

"Let's try it," Clay said calmly.

"Dammit, Snake Eye, this boy aims ter kill us both!" the other man suddenly said. "Let's take our chances with the sheriff."

"No!" Snake Eye shouted to his partner. "Fill your hand, you cowardly son of a bitch!"

As Snake Eye called out, his gun started coming up from the sheath he wore tied down on his side. Before his gun had even cleared his holster, Clay's gun boomed and bucked in his hand, and Snake Eye grabbed at the hole in his chest with a look of surprise on his face. Then, through the blue puff of smoke, Clay's gun barked a second time, and the other man fell, firing his gun ineffectively into the floor as he did so.

The smoke from the three discharges hung over the barroom, and its acrid smell burned the eyes and throats of the patrons, but when it rolled away there was the smooth-skinned, clear-eyed youth standing calmly, with his gun once again sheathed, looking at the bodies of the two men he had shot.

Clay's reputation began with that confrontation,

and it grew when two of the remaining three tracked him down. Both men fancied themselves fast with a gun, and indeed, they were known and feared throughout the West as gunfighters. Neither had any intention of fleeing from a mere boy. And though each thought he was able to handle Clay alone, they wanted to take no chances, so they faced him together. They found him in a small California town and called him out into the street.

There were perhaps a hundred people along the sidewalks and in the buildings, looking out at the scene. The gun-wise veterans of the outlaw trail, who had perhaps a score of killings between them, stood challenging a young, clear-eyed boy. They drew first, and one of their bullets carried away Clay's hat, while the other burned a painful but not serious brand across his arm. Clay fired only twice, and both his missiles found their mark in the outlaws' hearts.

Now there remained only the mysterious Barney. Barney, with the woman's hands and the cultured talk, who was forewarned that Clay lived and was looking for him. And to make matters more difficult, Clay's reputation was preceding him wherever he went. That meant that Barney would know Clay before Clay recognized him. But that didn't deter Clay from his efforts to find him. It was while he was searching for Barney and taking jobs where he found them that he got the opportunity to take the job that would allow him to meet Stacey Pendarrow.

"Now I've met you, Stacey," Clay said, looking through the rain toward the house. "The question is, where will it lead?"

Chapter Three

The coffee Stacey had started just before going to feed the horses was done, and its rich aroma filled the kitchen. Her father, who would be taking the stage on to MacAllister, and Jethro Engles, the driver who had brought it in from Winchester, were already in the kitchen and they leaned against the sideboard drinking the coffee they had poured for themselves.

"D'ya feed the horses?" Seth asked.

"Yes," Stacey answered shortly, still angered over her experience with Clay Conway. She opened the oven and tried to remove the pan of biscuits, but she was so angry that she forgot to use a pot holder. As a result she burned her hand, and dropped the biscuits on the table with a shout of pain.

"Honey, it ought not to take too many times to learn that a biscuit pan is hot when it first comes out of the oven," Seth teased.

"It wasn't hot. It just didn't take her long to look at it, " Jethro said; then he laughed uproariously at his own joke. Finally both men quit laughing when they saw that Stacey wasn't appreciating their humor.

"Did you see Clay out there?" Jethro asked.

"I saw him," Stacey answered shortly.

"Is he awake?"

"Yes."

"Then I reckon he'll be in for breakfast without my having to go through the rain to fetch 'im."

"Say, who is this fella, this Clay?" Seth asked. Seth was sliding on waterproof overalls to help fight off the rain, since he would be driving while exposed to the elements.

"His name is Clay Conway," Jethro said. "He'll be ridin' shotgun for you."

"Clay Conway? Haven't I heard that name?"

"I should think you have," Jethro said. "He's the fella that shot them two yahoos down in California last year. You might'a heard of them two: Ben Jones and Johnny Blue."

"Gunfighters, weren't they?"

"I doubt that there were ever two meaner hombres that walked like men," Jethro said. "Anyhow, the story is, they called the boy down, and he faced 'em square 'n proper, then kilt 'em both."

"At the same time?"

"Yep."

"He must be fast."

"Faster'n anyone I ever saw, I can tell you that for sure. You can tell by lookin' at 'im. I mean the way he carries himself 'n all."

He's fast all right, Stacey thought, and I don't mean with a gun. But of course Stacey didn't give voice to the words which lay on her tongue.

The young man who was the object of their conversation came in through the back door then and shook the rain water from the crown of his hat. He

18

stood there looking around, poised, Stacey thought, like a cat, light on his feet, ready to spring. He looked at Stacey, then smiled broadly at her.

"Would you like some coffee?" Stacey asked, looking at him curiously in the light of Jethro's story. Despite what Jethro had said, she didn't think he had the look of a killer. But of course she had never seen a killer and had no idea what one would look like. She knew from his smile, though, that he was thinking of what had transpired in the barn, and she hoped he wouldn't speak of it.

"I sure would like some," Clay answered. "And maybe a biscuit and some of that salt meat."

"I'll have some eggs in a moment," Stacey said.

"This'll do, thank you," Clay said, helping himself to the fare. He pulled a chair into the corner, then tipped it back and held his coffee in one hand and the biscuit sandwich in the other. His rain slicker, Stacey noticed, was flipped back out of the way, leaving the butt of his pistol exposed. Stacey looked at the pistol handle, but didn't see any notches carved in it. She had read somewhere that gunfighters did that to the handles of their pistols, and now she wondered if the story Jethro had told them was true.

"They don't usually send a shotgun guard on this run," Seth observed.

"You don't usually carry as much as ten thousand dollars," Jethro offered.

"Ten thousand dollars?" Seth whistled. "What are we doing with so much money?"

"Wells Fargo is transferin' some funds to the new branch bank in MacAllister," Jethro replied. He finished his coffee and put the cup down. "Well, if you're ready we can go hitch up the team."

"Stacey, honey, if you'll make me up a couple of those sandwiches there, I'll eat 'em after I get underway," Seth said.

"Are you sure you don't want to wait just a minute before you go out there?" Stacey asked. "I can have your eggs in just a second."

In fact, Stacey was trying to prevent them from leaving her alone with Clay, but she knew she couldn't say anything without bringing on unwanted questions.

"No, darlin', the sandwiches will be fine," Seth insisted. He and Jethro pushed the door open and stepped out into the rain.

Clay remained in the kitchen with Stacey. It was strangely quiet, with only the popping noise of the meat frying in the pan, the slurping noises of Clay drinking his coffee, and the seemingly louder than usual ticking of the wall clock. The clock indicated five minutes until five.

"Don't worry," Clay said after a long pause. "You are in no danger from me. I've had my fun for the day."

"That's what you call it, Mr. Conway?" Stacey asked with biting sarcasm. "Fun?"

"That's what I call it, Miss Pendarrow," Clay said easily.

"I do not share your enjoyment of the situation," Stacey said stiffly.

Clay smiled a slow, easy smile. "Now, Miss Pendarrow, that just isn't true. One thing you can't fool a fella on his how you feel when you're kissin'. You

20

were kissin' me back, Stacey, and you were enjoyin' it as much as I was."

Stacey's face burned red with embarrassment. "I suppose you've had a great deal of experience in these matters, sir," she said loftily.

"A little experience, yes," Clay agreed.

"You seem to be experienced in a great number of things. Mr. Engles told me about the men you killed."

"I *thought* you were looking at my gun earlier," Clay said, laughing. "You were trying to see if I had notches in the handle."

"I was not!" Stacey protested.

"Oh, I think you were," Clay said. "I'm sorry to disappoint you, Stacey. I don't believe in such a thing. In fact, I've never met anyone who did."

"Well, I should hope not," Stacey said. "I could not think much of a person who would take pride in murder."

The smile left Clay's face. "It wasn't murder, Miss Pendarrow," he said. "I gave them a chance to surrender, and they chose to go for their guns instead. I feel no pride in what I did, but no shame either, for if ever there were men who deserved to die, it was those men."

"What did they do?"

"They murdered my father, and they raped and murdered my mother and my sister," Clay said.

"Oh," Stacey gasped. "I . . . I'm sorry. I hadn't heard the reason."

"What did you hear? That I faced them down in the street, like some sort of contest?" Clay asked.

"Well, yes, as a matter of fact."

"Unfortunately, that's the part of the story that is

21

spread around," Clay said. "And now I find that I must spend all my time avoiding such confrontations. Until I find the last one."

"The last one?"

"Yes. There's one man remaining," Clay said. "And I'll not rest until I've located him."

"Are you going to kill him too?"

"Or bring him to justice."

Clay met Stacey's amber eyes with his own clear blue ones, and he stared at her without guilt or shame for his remarks. Finally, Stacey smiled at him. "I'm sorry," she said. "I've said awful things to you, but no one has more right to seek out justice than you."

"Well," Clay said easily. "Maybe it's time I did a little apologizing of my own. I'm sorry about what happened in the barn. But I couldn't help it, girl. I never saw anyone in my life as beautiful as you were, standin' there in the light of that lantern."

"Do you . . . do you really think I'm pretty?" Stacey asked, running her fingers along her cheek.

"I think you're beautiful. And I'd like to see you when I come back through."

"See me? Of course you'll see me, I'll be right here," Stacey said.

"I mean I'd like to call on you, courtin', as they say," Clay said.

"I . . . I don't know," Stacey said. She flashed a big smile. "I'm not sure Father would approve of that until I'm eighteen."

"And when will that be?"

"In three more months. My birthday is July fourth. Father says that's why I'm so independent," she added with a laugh.

"Perhaps your father will let me call on you," Clay said. "And when you are eighteen, maybe I can take you out for dinner."

"We'll see," Stacey said. She looked at the clock. "Oh, I'd better start the passengers' eggs. Would you wake them, please?"

"I'll be glad to," Clay said.

As Stacey scrambled the eggs, she looked through the door and into the dark shadows of the great common room where the passengers had stretched out in various chairs to sleep. She could see Clay moving through the gloom, waking them gently. He moved with an easy grace and confidence, and as Stacey looked at him, she could appreciate his handsome features without his knowing it. She was amazed at her reaction to his easy talk of courting. It had reawakened the strange feelings he had aroused in her when he kissed her in the barn, and now she had to fight to keep her hands from shaking as she cooked the eggs.

As Stacey served breakfast to the passengers, she listened to them talk, hoping thereby to quiet the tumultous feelings which stirred inside her. As she often did, she was able to put together enough information on each of them to establish their background. One of the women, young and pretty, was an army wife, traveling to Fort Casey to join her husband, a lieutenant newly assigned to the Western Territory. The other woman was in her late forties, a spinster schoolteacher trying to find in a new location what she had been unable to find in any previous place. There was a farmer, a travel-wise drummer, an out-of-work mechanic and a lawyer named Bramwell Caulder.

Caulder, who was about 30, had black hair and flashing dark eyes. A small, thin moustache was set above a well-formed mouth. He was very handsome and most attentive to Stacey. Partly because she knew Clay was watching, and partly because she found the situation of being paid court by two young men in the same morning pleasantly stimulating, Stacey allowed his flirtations. In fact, it might be said that she encouraged them.

The front door opened and Seth and Jethro returned. Jethro, who now had a rest period until nine o'clock when he would take a stage headed east, bade Seth goodbye, then went into the driver's room to go back to sleep. Seth rubbed his hands together and looked over toward the passengers, gathered around the common table and just finishing breakfast.

"Folks, take one last mouthful, then climb aboard," he called. "We got us a lot of ground to cover."

There was some groaning and complaining but the passengers heeded Seth's instructions and filed out of the house to climb into the waiting stage. The drummer, seasoned by stage travel, hurried to the far corner of the coach to fix himself comfortably for a nap. Mr. Caulder, after receiving permission from the ladies, lit up a cigar, and the others settled in as well as they could under the circumstances.

"Here are your sandwiches, Dad," Stacey said, handing her father a package wrapped in oilcloth.

"Thanks, honey," Seth replied. "I'll see you tonight."

"And I'll be seeing you again too," Clay called

down, hooking his heel over the footboard and cradling the rifle across his lap.

"Hyah, team!" Seth shouted. He swung the long whip out and snapped it over the heads of the eight-horse hitch with a report nearly as loud as a pistol shot. The horses strained into their harness, the great wheels of the stage began to turn, and the coach started down the road. Stacey went back into the house to retreat from the still-driving rain.

It was more than four hours later, after Jethro had already left on the eastbound stage, that the front door suddenly burst open and Stacey saw the bedraggled form of Bramwell Caulder standing there, wild-eyed and dirty, his clothes torn and bloodied, looking for all the world like a visiting angel from hell.

"Miss Pendarrow, there has been a terrible tragedy!" he cried out.

"Mr. Caulder, what is it?" Stacey asked, her voice reflecting her fright.

"We've been robbed, Miss Pendarrow," Caulder said. "The ten thousand dollars were taken. Everyone was killed."

"Every . . . did you say everyone was killed?" Stacey asked, her voice barely audible with horror.

"Everyone," Caulder said. "I'm sorry, girl, but your papa was the first to go."

"No!" Stacey said, screaming in anguish. She sobbed in her heartbreak for several moments, then looked at Caulder. "What about Clay Conway?" she asked. "Couldn't he stop it?"

"Stop it, Miss Pendarrow? Hell, miss, he was the one who did it!"

Chapter Four

Rain was dripping in Clay's face, and he turned his head trying to get away from it. He thought perhaps he was still in the barn and he attempted to burrow down into the straw to get warm and dry, but there was no straw available. There seemed to be only hard wet wood, and he could draw scarce comfort from that.

Wait a minute! If he wasn't in the barn, where was he?

Clay opened his eyes to look around, and saw that he was lying in the well of the front seat. But why? What was he doing sleeping on the job, and why had the stage stopped? He remembered climbing onto the stage to leave Sky Meadow station . . . so what was happening now?

Now Clay was fully conscious, and he could hear the rain drumming into the stage as well as feel it.

A wreck! That was it, there must have been a wreck! But no, the stage was upright and undamaged, and the horses stood quietly in their harness, waiting patiently for the order to go ahead.

Clay pulled himself up and looked on the seat. The oilskin package with Seth Pendarrow's breakfast was still there, but Pendarrow was nowhere to be seen. Where the hell was he? Why had he stopped right in the middle of the road?

"Hey!" Clay called. "Anyone down in the box?"

There was no answer, and Clay climbed over the edge, feeling his head reel as he did so. Once he reached the ground, he grabbed the wheel and stood there for a moment or two, fighting the wave of nausea and dizzyness which nearly overtook him. He was aware of a throbbing pain in the back of his head, and he put his hand there. It came away with blood, and he felt a wound where he had obviously been struck by something. Or somebody. Though he couldn't remember anything like that. His last memory was of riding along in the shotgun seat, thinking of Stacey Pendarrow.

Finally, the nausea and dizzyness cleared enough for him to move, and he stepped back to open the door to the stage. "Folks, what's going on?" he started to say, then stopped when he saw that the stage was empty. There was no one inside, nor was there any luggage or any personal objects to indicate that anyone had even been there.

"What is this?" Clay said aloud. "What the hell is going on?" He pulled his gun from his holster and spun around, looking toward the side of the road. His skin prickled as if he were being watched, and he crouched slightly, staring through the rain into the rocks. Was someone up there watching him? Did somebody, even now, have a bead on him? Could he expect a rifle bullet to tear into his flesh at any moment?

After a few seconds the feeling passed, and Clay returned his gun to his holster, and looked once again at the empty stage. One of the horses snorted and stamped his foot, and the unexpected movement caused Clay to draw his pistol again. When he realized what it was, he holstered his pistol. He walked up to the lead horse and began stroking his head.

"I sure wish I could talk horse talk," he said. "I'd ask you just what happened here."

As Clay stroked the horse's head, his eyes caught something white among the rocks beside the road, and he walked over toward it. It was a piece of cloth, and unless he was mistaken, it had been torn from the dress of the young army wife. When Clay leaned over to pick it up, he looked down into the ravine which bordered the road, and then he saw them.

"Oh, my God," he cried, for down in the ravine, a drop of perhaps fifty feet, he saw the crumpled bodies of the passengers.

Clay returned to the stage and got a coil of rope; then, securing it to a rock, he dropped the end over the edge and climbed down to the bodies.

There were six of them: the two women, Seth and the three male passengers. Three men? Wait a minute, Clay thought. Weren't there four men?

Yes, there were four men, he remembered. The dandy who had been talking to Stacey was missing. Where was he, and how did he get away?

Clay checked each body and discovered that they had all been shot, presumably by the same people who had knocked him out. But who had done it? And why couldn't he remember anything about it?

Clay tied the rope around the first body, then climbed back up and pulled the body up after him. He worked hard for quite a while as the rain lashed against him, and eventually had all six bodies lying alongside the road. He covered them with a tarpaulin, then went over to the stage and sat there for a while, resting from the exertion and from the pain and nausea which threatened to overtake him.

The money! he thought suddenly. He climbed up on the driver's seat and looked for the strongbox, but it was gone. Of course, that was it! Someone had heard about the ten thousand dollars, and the temptation had been too great. But that was why he had been hired. He was supposed to protect the strongbox . . . and the passengers' lives. He swallowed a lump which had risen in his throat. He had failed them, just as he had failed his own family.

Clay heard horses approaching, and he hopped back down and ran to the side of the road, seeking cover behind a rock in case the murderers returned. He pulled his pistol and watched as the riders approached. There were seven of them, including the passenger who was missing from the stage, and Stacey Pendarrow.

"No, Stacey, go back!" Clay called out, stepping out from behind the rock. "You shouldn't see this, it's . . . ."

"That's him!" Caulder shouted, pointing at Clay. "He did all of this!"

"What?" Clay asked. "What are you saying?" Clay suddenly saw six guns pointed on him, and he realized that they thought he was the murderer.

"Drop your gunbelt, Clay," one of the men said. "I know you're good, but I don't think you can shoot us all down."

"Shoot you down? Why would I want to shoot you down?" Clay asked. "Listen, I didn't do this terrible thing! I don't know what happened, but I—"

"We know what happened," the spokesman said. "We've got an eyewitness."

"An eyewitness? Who?"

"Me; I saw it all," Caulder said. "You thought you'd killed me like the others. But after you shot them, and started for the strongbox, I sneaked up behind you and hit you over the head, then made it back for help."

"He's got a wound on his head, all right, look at that," one of the others said, pointing to the blood in Clay's hair.

"Mister, you're lyin'," Clay said.

"Then why don't you tell us your side of it? What happened?"

"I . . . I don't know," Clay said. "One minute I was riding along, and the next I was coming to. I found all of these people dead, down in the ravine. I pulled them up here and covered them with a canvas, then you rode up."

"Check his gun," Caulder said. "See if it has been fired."

"Yes," Clay said. "I'll go along with that." He started to reach for it.

"You just step back," the leader of the posse said. "I'll pick it up."

Clay stepped back out of the way and watched the leader of the posse pick up his gun and sniff at the barrel. Clay looked up at Stacey, hoping for sympathy from her, but she turned her head away from him, and he saw tears streaming down her face.

"You say you haven't fired this gun?" the man asked Clay.

"That gun hasn't been fired in nearly a week."

Clay said. "I plinked away at a few cans about a week ago."

"It smells to me like it's been fired." the man said. He opened the gate and looked at the cartridges inside the cylinder. "Did you reload the gun after shooting at the tin cans?"

"Of course I did," Clay said. "You don't think I would come along as a guard with an empty gun, do you?"

"No, I wouldn't think so," the posse leader said. He flipped the cylinder out and ejected the contents onto the ground. There was an audible gasp from the others as they saw what fell: six empty shell casings.

"What?" Clay gasped, astonished at what he saw.

"That's all I need," someone said. "Let's hang the son of a bitch right here."

"There ain't no tree," one of the others noted.

"Then throw the rope over a rock."

"No!" Stacey called out. "I don't want my father's killer lynched. That's too quick. I want him tried for it. I want him to think about it awhile."

"Stacey, I didn't do it," Clay protested. "You've got to believe that!"

"Shut your mouth, mister, or I'll shoot you right where you stand," the posse leader said.

"How are we gonna get 'im back to town?" one of the men asked.

The leader turned in his saddle. "Well, I reckon we could tie him up, and then throw him in the stage. We've got to get these bodi . . . uh, people . . . in the stage too," he said, softening his statement for Stacey's sake.

"No," Stacey said. "I don't want him riding in the

stag with my father's body." She swung down from her horse. "Put him on my horse. I'll drive the stage."

"You're gonna drive the stage?"

"Look at the road," Stacey said. "Do any of you think you could turn the stage here?"

The men looked at the narrow road, then grunted in the negative.

"Well, I can," she said, climbing onto the seat, and holding the reins while the bodies were placed inside.

Clay's hands were bound behind his back and his empty pistol was put back in his holster, then he was helped up on Stacey's horse. He looked at the girl.

"Stacey, please, you must believe me!"

Stacey didn't answer. Instead she snapped the reins, then pulled the horses into a tight turn.

"Mr. Conway," Caulder said. "I am a lawyer."

"Why are you telling me? Or do you intend to represent me?"

"No," Caulder said. "I intend to apply for permission to act as prosecutor in this case. I am going to enjoy watching you hang by the neck until your demise, Mr. Conway."

"Demise, listen to that purty word," one of the men said, laughing. "I tell you, Bramwell, you're so educated you make dyin' sound almost dignified."

"Lookit that, the girl's got the stage turned. I don't think her daddy could'a done a better job on it. Come on, let's get back," the leader said.

As Clay looked toward the others, he suddenly noticed something which gave him hope. The rope that was used to secure him was wet with rain and failed to hold the knot. With just a little maneuvering, Clay had his hands free. He chose a moment when everyone else's attention was diverted, then spurred the animal he was astride. He pulled it around and started at a full gallop away from the posse. For the first few yards he had the advantage of having the stagecoach between him and the posse, and that masked their fire. By the time the posse galloped around the stage, he had opened up enough distance between them so that only the best marksman could have hit him, and Clay instinctively knew that there was not a crack shot among them.

It was clear to Clay that Stacey's horse was the fastest of the lot. The horse ran easily along the winding mountain road. The trail became rocky and rough, necessitating a decreased speed, but that also affected the pursuers. Finally the road leveled off, stretching out across open meadow land. There Clay was able to let the horse out to a full gallop. Clay was light and wiry and the horse was strong and fast. His pursuers were, for the most part, bigger men, thus burdening their horses with additional weight. Clay's advantage told clearly after a few miles, and by the time the open meadow was crossed and he gained the trees on the other side, he had completely lost the posse.

He dismounted to allow his horse a chance to regain its wind, and breathed a sigh of relief. He had made good his escape.

But now he was a wanted man, wanted for killing Stacey's father. And the worst blow of all was that Stacey believed Clay was the killer.

Chapter Five

Seth Pendarrow had been a very popular man. As stage driver he was also the mailman, so he knew all the citizens of Winchester and MacAllister and nearly everyone in between. Because of that, and since a funeral was a social event as surely as a wedding or a spring dance, there was a great crowd at the MacAllister graveyard when he was buried.

Reverend E. D. Fears, who had been preaching in MacAllister for twelve years, had never seen such a crowd, and he bristled with pride and preached his best sermon at the graveside. It was entitled "Jesus, the first pioneer," and it was particularly appropriate for the pioneers of western Oregon. He thought it went especially well, and was pleased by the number of wet eyes he saw, for a moment forgetting that the tears expressed sorrow over the death of a fine man, and thinking instead that they had been moved by his words.

Stacey stood at the graveside for a long time, even after the others had gone, and looked at the pile of dirt that covered her father. She had wept bitter tears of grief for the past four days, but now her eyes were dry and her sorrow was numbed. There remained only anger at the brutal and sensless murder, and deep inside, Stacey vowed to get the man responsible for her father's death.

"Anastasia, dear, we must be going soon if we are to make it to Medford in time for the train." The woman who spoke was in her late thirties, very pretty and perfectly groomed, dressed all in black.

"Very well, Aunt Pricilla," Stacey answered.

"Your Uncle Tobias has hired a fast team and a carriage. The roads are quite good, I'm told, so we should make it with little difficulty. I must say, too, that I shall be very glad to quit this place; it is most depressing."

"Funerals always are," Stacey said.

"Of course the funeral is depressing," Pricilla said. "It was sad to have to say a final goodbye to my dear, late sister's husband. But I didn't mean that. I mean this whole place is depressing. The squalid little towns, the dreary mountains, the unending rain. I must admit that I was pleasantly surprised to see that the sun had come out for your father's funeral. Well, thank the Lord for small favors."

"I like it here," Stacey said stubbornly.

"I know dear, you made your point perfectly clear to the judge when he issued the order remanding you to my care until your eighteenth birthday," Pricilla said. "But I know that you'll love Denver even more. We have so much more to offer there. Beginning, I might say, with places in which to buy you some decent clothes. It was most fortunate that Mrs. Tanner was able to make that dress for you in time for the funeral, otherwise you would have had to come in men's pants. It is absolutely scandalous the way your father allowed you to dress."

"It is difficult to drive a stage in a dress," Stacey said.

"Yes, to be sure," Pricilla answered. "Oh, here comes Tobias now. If we start right away we should make the train in plenty of time."

Tobias was a man in his early forties. He was broad across the shoulders and narrow in the waist, and he had big arms and hands, products of his work as a lumberjack when he was young. Tobias had brains as well as brawn, and while the other lumberjacks spent their money on whiskey, Tobias bought timberland and sawmills. By the age of twenty-eight he was a wealthy man. He moved to Denver and managed his business from there, but he was not above going into the woods or even climbing to the top of a Ponderosa pine to top it off if need be. Though welcome because of his wealth in the finest homes in Denver, Tobias Prescott still looked and thought like a lumberjack, much to the chagrin of his wife.

"Stacey, I see you stood up to the funeral all right," Tobias said, running one hand through his prematurely silver hair, and holding the reins with the other.

"Of course she stood up to it," Pricilla said. "What a foolish thing to say."

"Ah, I just don't like funerals," Tobias said. "They are brutal affairs, and I swear if you give me one, I'll come back to haunt you. Climb aboard, ladies, we've got to hightail it on out of here. Stacey, honey, would you like to drive?"

"Tobias!" Pricilla exclaimed. "It is unbecoming

37

for her to drive. And I have asked you not to call her Stacey."

"But I prefer to be called Stacey," Stacey said.

"Yeah," Tobias said. "And it might be unbecomin', but if we want to make that train we're better off with the girl drivin'. You know damn well she's a much better driver than I am."

Stacey took the reins from Tobias and clucked to the horses. They leaped into their harness and the carriage was off at a fast clip.

The graveyard at MacAllister was laid out on the lower slopes of a mountain. High on the mountain, looking down over the scene, a lone rider sat. He leaned forward in his saddle when he saw the girl leave the graveside, and watched her climb into the carriage and drive away. The rider was Clay Conway, and he had come to pay his last respects to the man he was accused of having killed. He had to stay up on the mountain, because he knew that if he showed himself he might be gunned down before he even had a chance to speak.

As he thought of that possibility, he pulled a paper from his shirt pocket and looked at it. He had pulled it off a tree, just out of town.

WANTED
DEAD OR ALIVE!
CLAY CONWAY
Reward:
$1500
Contact Any
Wells Fargo Agent

38

There was also a likeness of him, an artist's drawing, but Clay didn't think it was a good enough likeness to give him away to anyone who didn't already know him. That was the trouble, however. Because of his reputation as a gunfighter, Clay was already well known, and there were few towns he could enter without being recognized. With a dead-or-alive warrant out for him, Clay knew that nine out of ten people would shoot first and ask questions later. And for fifteen hundred dollars, even the most cautious person might be tempted to try to bring him in.

Clay had thought about his predicament for the last few days. He considered turning himself in, but he knew that the circumstantial evidence was too strong against him. And with Bramwell Caulder, a respected lawyer, as an eyewitness against him, Clay knew that he wouldn't stand a chance in court.

Bramwell Caulder, Clay knew, wouldn't have lied about seeing Clay kill the others, unless it was Caulder himself who had done it. And, Clay reasoned, that would make sense out of the rest of it. Why did he not see the robber approach? Because the robber was already on board the stage, that's why. Clay was convinced of that, because there was no other way to explain what had happened.

He was able to piece it together now. Caulder had simply climbed out of the passenger compartment and up onto the top of the stage. Clay, meanwhile, was studying the terrain, figuring that any danger would come from there and not from within. Caulder then knocked Clay out from behind, took Clay's gun and shot Pendarrow before the older man had time to react. He halted the team, told the others that there had been an accident or something and got them out. Then he quickly shot them, one at a time, as they stood there helpless and unsuspecting.

Clay was convinced that it had happened that way. But how was he to convince anyone else?

Obviously, he could not. He was a wanted man, and he would be shot down before he could even approach anybody. And even if he survived long enough for a trial, who would believe him, a known killer, over Bramwell Caulder, a lawyer, a man who was smooth with words? Nobody, that's who.

Clay knew that the part-time jobs he had held in the past would no longer be available. It was too risky to try to work anywhere, because there was always the chance that he would be recognized. That left two choices for him to consider.

The first was to leave the area completely. Just fork his horse and ride away, maybe down to Arizona, or over to the coast to sign on as a seaman. The second choice was to stay around, but that meant living on the dodge, always running from the law and anyone else with greed and an itchy trigger finger. It also meant, in all probability, that he would be forced into a life of crime in order to survive.

Clay abandoned the first idea completely. He had no intention of leaving the area until he had located Barney, the last surviving member of the gang that had killed his family. And now, along with Barney there was Bramwell Caulder.

That meant Clay would stick around. He made a vow that he would harm no one, unless his own life was threatened. And he would wage a personal war against Wells Fargo, for they were the ones who put the warrant out on him.

It was two days after the funeral before Clay committed his first job. He chose a secluded spot in which to wait for the stage to Bend. There was cover and concealment beside the road, a clear stream running nearby, and a stretch of road which would see on average only one traveler a day, besides the regular afternoon stage.

There were wild flowers growing in the meadow near Clay's hiding place and to pass the time he gathered bunches of the red, yellow, purple and white blooms. Then, just when he had a full, luxurious bouquet he heard the stage approaching.

Clay climbed to the top of a rock overhang, and crouched down out of sight. It was his plan to descend upon the stage by dropping to its roof from the overhang. That way he would be able to get the drop on the driver and guard with less possibility of gunplay. Clay did not want gunplay if it could be avoided.

The stage approached steadily, and he waited until it was right under him. Then he leaped down, landing lightly on his feet just behind the driver's seat. He pulled his pistol and called out to the driver and guard.

"Stop the stage!"

"What the—? Who are you? Where did you come from?" the driver asked, looking around in surprise, for so lightly did Clay land atop the stage that they neither felt nor heard him.

"I know who it is," the guard said. "It's Clay Conway."

"That's right," Clay said. "Now stop the stage."

"Right away, Mr. Conway. Just please don't shoot us like you did the others," the driver said, pulling the team to a halt.

When the coach was at a complete standstill, Clay vaulted over the side and pointed his pistol toward the passengers. "You people in there, get out!" he called.

There were one woman and two men inside, and they quickly climbed out as ordered. One of the men started to reach for his inside coat pocket, and Clay cocked his pistol and pointed it toward him.

"I'm just going to give you my money," the man said in a frightened voice.

"You people can keep your money," Clay replied. "I'm only interested in the Wells Fargo money. Driver, open the strongbox and toss me any money you find there."

"I don't have a key."

"Then throw the box down here," Clay ordered.

The drive flipped the box over the side, and it landed at Clay's feet. He shot the lock off, and as he started to open the lid, realized that he was still carrying the bouquet of flowers. He smiled, thinking what a ludicrous picture it must make, him standing there with a pistol in one hand and a bouquet of flowers in the other, robbing a stage coach.

"Here, miss," Clay said, handing the bouquet to the lady. "I think these are very pretty, don't you?"

"Yes," the woman said, flustered by Clay's action. "Yes, they are quite lovely."

"I thought you might enjoy them," Clay said. He dropped to one knee and rifled through the contents of the box until he found a large brown envelope marked Wells Fargo. He opened it, looked inside, and saw a stack of bills. He smiled as he stood up again.

"Well now," he said, "Yes, I think this will do nicely. Would one of you gentlemen be so kind as to hand the box back up to the driver?"

"You're gonna let us take the box back?" the driver asked in surprise.

"Of course I am. There's no more Wells Fargo money. Besides, there might be a letter from some cowboy's sweetheart in there, and I would hate to cause him to miss it."

Once the strongbox was in place, Clay indicated that the passengers should board the stage again.

"You mean you're just gonna let us go, like that?" one of the men asked.

"Just like that," Clay said.

"Then why didn't you let the others go? Why did you kill all of them?"

Clay sighed. What was the point in telling them that he didn't do it? He knew that they wouldn't believe him, and it wouldn't do him any good if they did believe him. Finally, with a wave of his pistol he ordered them back on.

"And be quick about it." he added. "Or I might change my mind."

The passengers boarded quickly, and the driver, with one last look at Clay, snapped the whip over the head of his team and the stage resumed its journey.

Clay stood rooted to the spot for a while, watching the stage roll off into the distance, followed down the road by a billowing cloud of dust.

Finally, when the stage was out of sight, he allowed himself the luxury of taking the money out of the envelope. There was a small packet of bills, wrapped in a paper band. When Clay counted the money, he found that he had exactly $138.00. Not very much money with which to launch a life of crime. But then, this wasn't a vocation he chose willingly, so it really didn't matter. All that mattered was that he had enough for a little food and supplies. After all, he wasn't asking for much. Just enough to keep body and soul together until he located Barney. That was all he wanted. After that, he'd see to Bramwell Caulder.

Chapter Six

The table in the Prescott dining room was larger than any Stacey had ever seen before, larger even than the great common table at Sky Meadow, and that one could accomodate all the passengers from two stagecoaches, should two arrive at the same time.

Stacey wondered when she first saw it why anyone would have a table so large if they had no intention of turning their private dining room into a restaurant. But that question was answered for her the second week she was in residence with her aunt and uncle, when Pricilla gave a party to introduce Stacey to all of the "correct people," and to one young man in particular.

All of the "correct people" were there that night. In fact, the guest list read like a Who's Who of Denver society. The most important guests were Mr. and Mrs. Upton Tremain and their twenty-two-year-old son, Marcus. The Tremains were in banking and railroads, and Marcus, recently graduated from Harvard University, was ostensibly in business with his father, though in fact and by his own admission he was living off his father's generosity. Marcus was handsome, but with a jaded face which rarely showed interest in anything. Until tonight, that is, when Marcus displayed a decided interest in Stacey.

Mr. and Mrs. John Sinclair were also present at the party, with their eighteen-year-old daughter, Yolinda. There were two other girls the same age as Stacey: Mary, the daughter of Mr. and Mrs. Edward Beeson, and Cynthia, whose parents were Mr. and Mrs. Sidney Lyons. All were wealthy, though none were as wealthy as the Tremains. The Sinclairs, Stacey had already decided, were the biggest snobs. There were other guests, but Stacey had already forgotten their names.

There were four beautiful silver candelabra on the table, each with eight graceful tapers burning brightly. The soft golden lights of the candles were reflected in the silver, china, and crystal. The meal consisted of marvelous French dishes, served to the diners by a parade of servants who moved in a steady flow from the kitchen to the dining room.

"Mrs. Prescott, this is a perfectly marvelous meal," Upton Tremain said.

Stacey had never seen people so elegantly dressed as those here tonight. Despite her initial reluctance to abandon the pants and shirts she loved , she had to admit that it gave her pleasure to be wearing a dress as beautiful as that worn by any of the other women.

"Thank you, Mr. Tremain, I will tell M. LaMont. I am certain he will be pleased."

"I must say, you had singular good fortune to acquire M. LaMont from the Marshall House. Their dining room has not been the same since he left their employ."

"Mr. Tremain, I wouldn't think you could even consider patronizing the Marshall House now," Pricilla said in a shocked voice.

"Why?" Mrs. Sinclair asked, her eyes lighting up at the possibility of learning some new gossip.

"Oh, my dear, you mean you haven't heard?" Pricilla answered, her voice registering her displeasure. "They have hired a female piano player to 'entertain' the guests."

"You don't say," the woman answered, reflecting Pricilla's shock.

"But she is quite a good pianist, actually," Marcus Tremain put in. "I think it makes for a rather pleasant evening," he added, looking directly at Stacey, almost as if inviting her to go with him.

"Nonsense," Pricilla said, missing Marcus's obvious play for Stacey. "The place for that kind of thing is in the theatre, for then a person is forewarned, and prepared to be scandalized."

"Oh, I wouldn't go so far as to say that the theatre is scandalous," Upton Tremain protested mildly.

"Now a bawdy house, perhaps," Tobias put in with a chuckle. "I must confess to having heard some really fine piano playing in a few of those establishments in my wild youth."

"Tobias, really!" Pricilla gasped, absolutely shocked and livid that her husband would make such a remark.

While the men laughed, the women stared at their plates in embarrassment—all except Stacey, who had trouble stifling her own laughter. Pricilla was so prissy that the remark served her right.

Prissy, Stacey thought. Yes, that would be Pricilla's secret name from now on. Aunt Prissy.

"I was just making a small joke, dear," Tobias said easily.

"I must say that the joke was in extremely poor taste," Pricilla said angrily. Then because she realized that to carry her anger any further would have been a social *faux pas*, Pricilla fixed a smile on her face and looked at the others. "You will have to forgive my husband," she said. "I think sometimes that the rowdiness of those ruffians who work for him is infectious. It is unfortunate that one must come in contact with such people in the pursuit of honest business."

"Yes, my dear, that is certainly true," Mrs. Sinclair said, making a show of agreeing with Pricilla, though actually carrying on the conversation merely to prolong Pricilla's discomfort. "I know I simply cringe when one of our people comes to the house to see John on a business matter." Mrs. Sinclair said the words "our people" possessively, patronizingly. "And I keep Yolinda out of sight, for the freight drivers are so uncouth."

"You're hitting the nail on the head on that point, I'd say," Stacey pitched in, glad that the conversation had finally reached a subject with which she was familiar. After all, she was certainly more qualified than any of the others present to talk about freight drivers. And how was she going to satisfy her aunt's wish to meet the others on equal terms if she never spoke a word?

"I'm quite sure," Pricilla said, rather stiffly.

"Please, do go on, dear child," Mrs. Sinclair said, delighted at this sudden turn of events. Mrs. Sinclair saw Pricilla cringe at the prospect of this wild young mountain girl making a fool of herself. But,

Ellen Sinclair thought, it would certainly serve to show the Tremains, and Marcus in particular, that there was really no choice between the Sinclairs' daughter Yolinda and the Prescotts' niece, when it came time to think of a marriage partner. Yolinda was obviously the better choice.

"Anastasia, I'm sure no one wishes to hear—"

"Oh, but we do, Mrs. Prescott," Yolinda said, suddenly, along with her mother, seeing the potential of the moment.

"Well," Stacey said, pleased that she seemed to be making a hit with her aunt's guests, "I've known quite a few freight drivers. And for the most part they are a bunch of drunks and whoremongers, if you know what I mean. Now the stage drivers, why they aren't like that at all. Oh, they'll turn the air blue with their cursing all right. In fact," she smiled, "I've handled a few teams myself that wouldn't respond to any other kind of command. But the stage drivers are generally sober, honest, family men. I imagine it's because stage drivers have the lives of their passengers to be responsible for, whereas freight drivers haul rope, or feed, or something like that, and they just don't take the same pride in their work."

"Anastasia, please!" Pricilla hissed.

Stacey noticed the strain in Pricilla's voice and was puzzled by it. What had she done wrong? After all, she had finally joined in the conversation, and she had agreed with the woman who spoke. That was only being polite.

"Tell me, Anastasia," Yolinda said, leaning forward and smiling with a secret sense of superiority that Stacey didn't perceive. "Can you really drive a stagecoach?"

"I hope to smile I can," Stacey answered proudly. "Of course, I've never been an official driver, mind. But I reckon I can handle the ribbons about as well as anyone."

"Ribbons?" Yolinda replied, puzzled by the remark. "What are ribbons?"

"Oh, excuse me, I forgot that you wouldn't know what I was talking about," Stacey explained. "The ribbons are the reins. There are eight of them, of course, for an eight-horse hitch."

"Eight?" Sidney Lyons said. "My word, how could one handle eight reins at the same time? I must confess that I'm not all that comfortable with two reins. That's why I hire liverymen for my rig. Then I just tell them where I want to go."

The others laughed at Lyons's remark.

"Oh, but it's simple," Stacey said. "Well, no, not all that simple really, but I mean once you get the hang of it you can do it." She began gathering up the array of silverware which lay beside her plate. "I was wondering what I could do with all this," she said. "Now it'll come in handy."

Stacey began lacing the knives, forks, and spoons through her fingers as if they were the reins of the horses; then she held her hands out, showing them to the others. "Now all you have to do is keep the horses pulling even," she said. "Because if you don't, you are likely to get one that's a bit lazy and he'll slack off and let the others do all the work. You can tell by the pressure on the reins who's doing his job and who isn't, see, like this." She moved her fingers to show that she could control each rein individually.

"Anastasia, please! I have never been so mortified in my life!" Pricilla said. She got up from the table, and left the room dabbing at the tears in her eyes.

Stacey was shocked by her aunt's reaction. What had she done? Why was her aunt so upset? She looked at the others, hoping to gain a clue to the reason for her aunt's strange behavior. Most of the others were staring at their plates, as if embarrassed. She thought, however, that she detected a small smile on Yolinda's lips. Why? Because she found the situation amusing? Or because she enjoyed having brought discomfort to Stacey? And if she did enjoy Stacey's discomfort, why? Stacey had never done anything to her.

Tobias cleared his throat. "Mrs. Tremain, would you lead the ladies into the parlor? I believe M. LaMont has a dessert for you there. And Upton, please take the men into the study for brandy and cigars. I'll join you shortly."

"Of course, Tobias, I'd be glad to," Mrs. Tremain answered. "Come along, ladies."

The dining room cleared in just a few seconds, except for Tobias who sat at the far end of the table, and Stacey, at the opposite end, next to where her aunt had been sitting.

"Mr. Prescott, will you require . . . ." one of the servants inquired, sticking his head through the door. Tobias dismissed him with a wave of the hand, and once again the two were alone. There was a moment of quiet, and tears began sliding down Stacey's cheeks.

"Honey, don't worry about it," Tobias said gently.

"But Uncle, what did I do?" Stacey asked, her voice nearly breaking on the last word.

Tobias got up from his chair and walked over to her. He put his hands on her shoulders. "You didn't do anything, dear."

"But I must have. Aunt Prissy was so upset. And Yolinda was smiling, as if . . . as if she enjoyed my discomfort."

"Prissy?" Tobias said, laughing. "You call Pricilla, Prissy?"

Stacey smiled through her tears. "I'm sorry, it's just sort of a nickname I made up for her."

Tobias threw his head back and laughed out loud. The laughter seemed to do more than anything to relieve the discomfort Stacey felt, and she laughed with him.

"I think that's a marvelous name," he said. "Simply marvelous."

"I'm glad you approve, Uncle Toby," Stacey said, using for the first time the nickname she'd given him.

"Approve? Yes, but I'm not sure how Pricil . . . that is, Prissy, will take it." he said. "Perhaps we'd better keep it our little secret for the time being. Do that for me, and I'll accept my nickname without fuss," he offered with an easy smile.

"All right," Stacey answered. "It's a deal."

"Now, Miss Stacey Pendarrow," Tobias said, helping Stacey from her chair. "Dry your eyes and go in for dessert. And do me a favor, will you?"

"What?"

"Just stare Yolinda down. I'd be willing to bet

she's the kind who can't meet a good, honest gaze head on. You try that for me, and she'll be laughing out of the other side of her mouth."

"I'll do that, Uncle Toby," Stacey agreed. She started out of the room, then stopped and looked back at her uncle. "Oh, and it's good to see that I have a friend here."

"You've always had me, darlin'," Tobias said easily. "And you'll have me all the way."

Chapter Seven

As Tobias had promised, Yolinda would not return Stacey's honest gaze. But Yolinda hid her mouth behind her fan and whispered with Mary and Cynthia, and the three young girls giggled and shared secrets that excluded Stacey. Or at least she thought that was what they were doing, and the effect was just as devastating to her, so that after a while she got up to leave the parlor, making the excuse that she didn't feel too well and needed some fresh air.

The Prescott home was a huge, two-storied brick house which sat in the midst of three acres of landscaped lawn. The parlor opened through French doors onto a veranda which completely encircled the house, and once outside, Stacey strolled along the flagstone deck until she was behind the house. There she kicked off her shoes and climbed up on the waist-high, wide-topped stone fence that guarded the edge of the porch. She sat there, leaning against one of the many pillars that rose to support the roof, and looked out across the gently sloping lawn and into the clear night sky.

There was a quarter moon that night, so its brightness didn't obscure the stars, and Stacey enjoyed their diamond shine, scattered across the sky. They were the same stars she could see from Sky Meadow, and somehow looking at them made her feel close to home. And to her father, whom she missed terribly.

As she thought of her father her sorrow was replaced by a deep hatred for Clay Conway, and she remembered her resolve to make him pay for what he did. She pulled her knees up and when she did so, her dress fell back so that her legs were exposed from her knees down. She wrapped her arms around her legs and rested her chin on her knees. The position was comfortable, and the cool breeze felt good against her legs which were too warm because of the dress and all of the petticoats she was forced to wear. She smiled to herself because she knew the pose was probably unladylike, and Aunt Prissy would have a fit if she saw it.

"It's a beautiful night, isn't it?" a man's voice said.

Stacey looked toward the sound and saw Marcus Tremain. He was smoking a cigar, and the ash on the end glowed red as he took a puff.

"Yes, it is," Stacey said. She made no effort to cover her legs or change her position. She knew that that was probably the proper thing to do, but she had had just about enough of the proper things for one night. She turned to look at the stars again. "That star is my favorite," she said, pointing to a bright orange light. "It looks like a gold nugget that someone just hung in the sky."

"That's Arcturus," Marcus said.

Stacey laughed. "You named the star?"

"No, I didn't," Marcus said. "The stars were named many years ago."

"Are you serious?" Stacey asked. "You mean all those stars have names?"

"I wouldn't think all of them have names," Marcus said. "There are too many."

"How many?"

"Oh, about nine thousand can be seen with the naked eye," Marcus said. "Though we can't see them all from the northern hemisphere."

"How do you know so much about the stars?"

Marcus stepped up to the porch rail beside Stacey and ground his cigar out, then flipped it over the edge. He looked at Stacey and smiled. "That, my dear, is a result of one of the many wasted classes I took at Harvard. It dealt with the heavens, and was called astronomy."

"Oh, I wouldn't think that would be a waste of time," Stacey said. She looked back at the stars. "I've always loved the stars. I'd like to know more about them."

"Perhaps you'll allow me to teach you," Marcus offered.

"Oh, would you?" Stacey asked, her voice bubbling over with enthusiasm.

"It would be my pleasure," Marcus said. "In that case the class could well prove to have been a blessing and not quite the waste I thought it was."

"What's that star? The one just above Arcturus?"

"Spica," Marcus said. "You are a very beautiful young lady, Anastasia."

"Stacey," she said.

"What?"

"I prefer to be called Stacey."

Marcus laughed.

"What is it? What's so funny?"

"You are quite remarkable, did you know that? You're a breath of fresh air. I tell you you are a beautiful young lady, and instead of huffing up and acting scandalized as proper young ladies are supposed to, even though they never really are, you just correct me on your name."

"I suppose it's obvious after tonight that I don't know how to act like a proper young lady," Stacey said, matter-of-factly.

"Then I hope you never learn."

"But I must learn," Stacey said, "if I am to make what Aunt Pricilla calls a favorable impression."

"You've already made a favorable impression on me," Marcus said. "But I'm not altogether certain your aunt would approve of that."

"Oh, you are the one she most wants me to impress," Stacey said. "You're rich, aren't you?"

Marcus laughed again. "You do have a disarming candor which is most refreshing," he said. "Yes, I suppose I am rich. Or rather, my father is, and as I am his only heir, that makes me rich as well. I've done nothing to earn it, though. In polite circles I'm known as a ne'er-do-well. Except in those families who have marriageable daughters; there I'm held up as a sterling example of young manhood. You probably noticed at the dinner table tonight how Mrs. Sinclair tried to make me notice the attributes of her daughter, Yolinda."

"So that's why!" Stacey said, realizing for the first time why Yolinda and her mother had so obviously enjoyed her discomfort.

"Ah, so you see the light now, do you?"

"But surely they see no competition from me!" Stacey said honestly. "Yolinda is so beautiful, and so . . . so proper."

"You know, if anyone else had made that statement, I would swear she was fishing for a compliment," Marcus said. "But from you, it rings with the truth. I think you honestly don't realize how desirable you really are."

Stacey ran her hand through her raven-black hair, then looked at Marcus with confusion in her amber eyes. "But I'm just a mountain girl," she said. "What do I have to offer?"

Marcus turned his head toward her, and his face was bathed silver in the sparse moonlight. The jaded, almost hard face she had seen at the dinner table was now soft and sensitive, as if he were showing her a most intimate part of him which he allowed no one else to see. Something in Stacey responded to it, and she moved her face toward his. Their lips met, and she felt a tingling, pleasurable sensation run through her. The kiss deepened, and Marcus put his hand behind her head and pulled her to him while he ground his lips against hers, until finally the kiss ended.

"I . . . I'm sorry," Marcus said, after he pulled away.

"Why?"

"Why?" Marcus laughed. "Why indeed? I'm not sorry, I rather enjoyed it actually. But one must always apologize after such a thing."

"But I wanted to do it too," Stacey said. "Doesn't that count for anything?"

"Oh, you had best be careful, dear girl, for such

honesty is not known in polite society, and I fear you might be hurt by it."

"My father used to say that the truth never hurt anyone," Stacey said. "And he was a pretty smart man."

"You thought a lot of your father, didn't you?" Marcus said.

"Of course I did," Stacey replied. "Doesn't everyone love his father?"

"There are, I suppose, degrees of love."

"Don't you love your father?"

Marcus put both hands on the wide stone fence and leaned over it, staring up toward the stars. Finally, with a sigh, he answered.

"I don't know, really. I do respect him, but as I have been such a disappointment to him, I feel that he doesn't love me. And that makes it very hard to love him."

"A disappointment? How?"

"I told you I was a ne'er-do-well," Marcus said. "Oh, I've tried various things—managing banks, working as a railroad administrator, puttering around here and there—but I've shown a talent for none of the things my father has spent a lifetime building."

"How do you occupy your time?"

"It turns out that my one talent lies in gambling," Marcus said. Stacey noticed that a strange new excitement came into his eyes. "I have fantastic luck with cards. I can almost feel the hands the other players are holding, and odd as it may sound, I can even feel what my next card will be. I've no doubt that I could make it as a gambler if I had to. Of course, such a vocation would be unheard of for one of my station. I must confine myself to friendly matches, or else play under an assumed name in the gaming houses over in Chipville."

"Chipville?" Stacey said. "Where's that?"

"It's a collection of gambling houses which have grown up about five miles outside the Denver city limits. They moved out there to avoid the do-gooders who are constantly trying to shut them down in the city. People like my mother, Mrs. Sinclair, and your Aunt Pricilla."

"What's it like in Chipville?"

"Like? Oh, there's an excitement that you can feel the moment you step inside one of the establishments," Marcus said. "Poker, faro, roulette. And," he laughed, "even the piano playing that upset your aunt. Plus dancing girls. It's a gay place all right."

"Do you go often?"

Marcus rubbed his chin and smiled a conspiratorial smile at Stacey. "A bit more often than I should, I'm afraid. One of these days someone there is going to recognize me, and when they do, there'll be hell to pay."

"Why? You're a grown man, aren't you?"

Marcus laughed again. "Yes, I am," he said. "But if my father chose to be obstinate, he could change his will to insure that I would never get my inheritance except in small, doled-out amounts. No, it would be best for me to present at least the facade of respect for Father's ideas, if not the substance."

"When are you going to go again?" Stacey asked.

"I don't know, really, I hadn't thought about it," Marcus said. "If I didn't know better, I'd say you wanted to go."

"Oh, yes," Stacey said. "Please, Marcus, would you take me?"

"Hold on, here," Marcus chuckled. "I've got enough trouble protecting my own identity. If I took you, there'd be twice the chance that we'd be recognized. Besides, there's always the possibility that I could convince Father of my genuine repentance if I went alone and was found out. But with you? No, I'm afraid that would generate a scandal that neither you nor I would be able to live down."

"Oh, please, Marcus. You've got to take me."

Marcus ran his hand through his hair in exasperation. "Why? Why would you want to go?"

"You were at my aunt's dinner tonight," Stacey said. "You saw how well I fit in with Aunt Pricilla's friends. There has to be something better than this. Maybe your gaming houses are."

"I don't know. I'd have to be responsible for you."

"I'd behave just as you wanted me to," Stacey promised. "There won't be any trouble. You'll see."

"All right," Marcus said. "I'll do it."

"When?"

"When? Well, I don't know. We'll have to work something out."

"There's an art exhibition next Monday night," Stacey said excitedly. "It's in the city library, and Aunt Pricilla has suggested several times that I should attend it. We can say you are taking me to see it."

"I don't know. Your aunt may insist upon a chaperone."

"She may," Stacey said, "but she also wants me to

make a good impression on you. If I tell her you won't hear of a chaperone, she'll give in."

Again, Marcus laughed. "Very well, Miss Pendarrow," he said. "I shall call on your aunt and uncle tomorrow afternoon, at which time I shall request the pleasure of your company for the art exhibit next Monday."

"Oh, thank you, thank you!" Stacey bubbled. "You won't be sorry, Marcus, I won't be any trouble at all, I promise you."

Chapter Eight

As he had promised, Marcus took Stacey to one of the gaming houses Monday night. Stacey had never seen anything like the Golden Pigeon. It was many times larger than the hotel ballroom in Mac-Allister, and much more beautiful. She counted at least ten huge crystal chandeliers that, along with the clusters of lanterns on the walls, provided a brightly lit interior. There were tables covered in green felt around which men and women sat playing cards, long tables where they cast dice, and her favorite, the roulette table where a wheel was spun with dizzying speed and the object of the game was to guess on which number the little ball would end up when the wheel stopped. She also saw balconies, spaced at intervals along the walls, where guards armed with shotguns kept watchful eyes on the players.

"What do you think of it so far?" Marcus asked, after he had shown her through the place.

"It seems terribly exciting," Stacey said. "I can see why—oh, my goodness!" she suddenly said, putting her hand to her mouth.

"What is it?"

"That girl, Mark," Stacey said, using the nickname she had given him. "What has happened to the front of her skirt? Someone should tell her. Oh, the poor thing will be so embarrassed." Stacey pointed to a beautiful young woman who was carrying a tray of drinks. The front of her skirt was gathered up above her knees, and the red garters on her legs were clearly visible.

"It's supposed to be that way," Marcus said. "Don't worry about it."

"Supposed to be that way? Whatever for?"

"She works here. That's part of her costume. Wait until you see the dancing girls, if you think this is something."

"Oh, yes, I'm looking forward to that. I've never seen dancing girls, but I have heard about them."

"You are about to see them," Marcus said, "for I notice that the stage is being prepared. Would you like to take a table and have a drink while we watch?"

"A drink? You mean whiskey?"

"Sure, if that's what you want."

"I don't know," Stacey said. "I've never tasted whiskey before."

"Why don't you let me order for you?" Marcus offered. "I'll pick out something you might like."

Marcus spoke to one of the girls wearing a cutaway dress, then escorted Stacey to a table near the stage. A moment later the drinks came, and Stacey saw that hers had a slice of orange and a cherry in it.

"What is this?" she asked. "I've never seen fruit in a drink before."

"It's a house special," Marcus said. "Made especially for ladies. I think you'll like it."

"Mmmmm," Stacey said, after taking a sip. "You're right. It tastes better than lemonade."

"But it isn't lemonade," Marcus cautioned. "So be careful."

Three men came to sit at the table next to theirs, and Stacey noticed that they looked her over pretty thoroughly. Finally, one of them leaned forward and, tweaking his moustache, spoke with Marcus.

"Tell me, sir, where did you find such a beautiful young lady?"

"She's a . . . uh . . . friend," Marcus said. "An old family friend."

"Perhaps you'll be so kind as to introduce us to your . . . family friend," the man said.

"Very well," Marcus said. "Her name is Stacey. Stacey, these three men . . . ."

"Wouldn't 'gentlemen' be more appropriate?" one of the men interrupted.

"These three *men*," Marcus said with emphasis, "are Jack and Billy Miles, and Lorin Keefer."

"Perhaps you would like to join us?" Jack invited. Jack had been their spokesman. He was around twenty-five with a handlebar moustache and black, slicked-back hair. Billy, his brother, was a younger, smaller copy of Jack, while Lorin had red hair and a pale, rather unimpressive countenance.

"Thank you, no, we wouldn't care to join you just now," Marcus said.

"Perhaps just the lady?" Jack asked.

"Certainly not!" Stacey snapped. "And I consider it rude of you, sir, even to suggest such a thing."

"Oh ho," Jack said to his partners. "The lady's got spirit. How did she meet up with someone as gutless as Tremain?"

"Mr. Miles," Marcus hissed. "You are forgetting your end of the bargain, sir!"

"Oh, oh, yes," Jack said. "Shhhh," he whispered to the other, placing his finger across his lips. "We mustn't give away the secret now, must we? After all, we wouldn't want to kill the goose that lays the golden eggs." He and the others laughed uproariously.

"Mark," Stacey said a moment later, after the three men had become engaged in their own conversation. "Mark, they know who you are, don't they?"

"Yes," Marcus said.

"What did he mean about killing the goose that lays the golden eggs?"

"Ah, he was just talking. He didn't mean anything."

"No, that's not right," Stacey said. "They're getting money from you, aren't they? They are getting money to keep your secret."

Marcus sighed, and ran his hands through his hair. "Yes," he said. "Yes, they are."

"Why, that's awful! Why are you paying them?"

"You know why. If my father ever gets word of this, I'll be cut off without a cent."

"Then you should just give those men a good thrashing," Stacey said.

"Perhaps that's the way your mountain men would handle such a thing," Marcus said. "But we do it a bit differently here."

Stacey noticed for the first time that Marcus was afraid of the three men. She felt sorry for him, and she relaxed the tone of her voice and put her hand comfortingly on his. "Maybe you're right," she said softly. "After all, you have much more experience in handling these matters than I."

A man came onto the stage carrying a megaphone, and he pointed it toward the audience which had now gathered around the tables near the stage.

"Ladies and gentleman," the man said, his voice magnified but distorted by the megaphone. "The Golden Pigeon proudly presents the Gilded Lilies of the West."

The music began and a line of girls danced onto the stage. Stacey gasped. She had no idea that a woman, any woman, would appear in public dressed as these girls were. They wore what appeared to be brightly colored corsets and nothing else. Their legs were bare from their thighs down, as were their shoulders and arms. The men in the audience whistled and applauded the dancers, who in response smiled and blew kisses back to the men. Stacey was spellbound by the entire performance. When it finally ended, Marcus spoke to her.

"Well, what did you think of it?"

"I've never seen anything like it before," Stacey said. "It was . . . well, exciting, I mean to hear the people in the audience whistle and carry on so. But I don't imagine I could ever do anything like that."

"You mean dance?"

"Yes."

"No, I don't suppose you could. It takes a very special sort of person. It's too bad though, because you are a beautiful girl and you would be particularly appealing dressed as they were."

"You mean showing off my legs and arms like that? Never. I may not be proper in the sense that

Aunt Pricilla wants me to be, but I know that showing that much of your body is wrong."

"Stacey, don't abandon your honesty now. It's that refreshing streak of truth in you that I find most appealing."

"I am being honest, Mark. I don't believe I could expose my limbs like that."

"Well, maybe not," Marcus said. "Perhaps that manmade affront to nature has even reached the mountains. Someday, perhaps a hundred years from now these barriers will all be taken down, and men and women will be as free as the other creatures of nature."

"What are you talking about?"

"I'm talking about this infernal code of modesty about the human body," Marcus said. "Of all the creatures in nature, only the human being feels shame at nudity."

"And you think one day that will all change?" Stacey asked, shocked at the very idea.

"I think clothes will eventually become items which enhance the human body, rather than hide it," Marcus said.

"Enhance?"

"Show off," Marcus explained. "Show off the parts of the body that we now hide. I only regret," he added with a wistful smile, "that I shall not live long enough to see that day."

Stacey suddenly had a mental image of a dress with two round holes through which the breasts could protrude. It was a perfectly ludicrous image, and she laughed aloud at the idea.

At first Marcus was surprised by her laugh, then

70

he joined her. Finally, when their laughter had subsided, he invited her to watch him play cards.

They walked over to one of the felt-covered tables, behind which sat a dealer counting the chips out for one of the players. Marcus explained quietly to Stacey that at the tables he was known by the name of Travis. The chips were red, white and blue, and their stacks caught the artificial light vividly, contrasting sharply with the light-absorbing green felt. The dealer looked up as Marcus approached the table.

"Mr. Travis, good evening, sir, the dealer greeted him. "Will you be joining us?"

"Yes, Marcus said. He gave the dealer some money, and the man pushed several stacks of the chips over to him.

"Gentlemen, a new deck," the dealer said, opening a new box of cards. He spread them out on the table in front of the players, then flipped them over expertly. Stacey had never seen anyone who was as smooth with cards, and she was impressed.

Finally the game began. The dealer shuffled the cards and the stiff new pasteboards clicked sharply. His hands moved swiftly, folding the cards in and out, until the law of random numbers became the law of the table. He shoved the deck over toward Marcus, and Marcus cut them, then pushed them back.

"Five card stud," the dealer announced.

Marcus won one hundred dollars in the first hand, and a couple of hands later was ahead by five hundred dollars. At that point Jack Miles joined the game.

"Well," Jack said. "I see Mr. Travis is having a run of good luck."

"He seems to be, yes, sir," the dealer said easily.

"I've had some luck of my own. I wonder who is the luckiest? Perhaps we could find out, with a little showdown?" Jack suggested.

"That would deny the other players an opportunity at the game," Marcus said.

Jack looked at the table. There were three other players. "Suppose we take thirty percent from the winning hand, to be divided equally among you three?" Jack said. "What would you say to that?"

"I'd say I'm going to watch a game of showdown," one of the men laughed.

"Me too," one of the others agreed, and the third quickly assented, so that the decision was now up to Marcus.

"Very well," Marcus said. "You're on."

"How about one thousand dollars on a hand of showdown?" Jack challenged.

"One thousand dollars on one hand?" one of the three around the table said loudly, mentally computing his share of the winner's pot.

"What's that?" someone from one of the other tables asked. "One thousand dollars on one hand?" The news quickly spread from table to table and as each game ended, the other players gathered around the table to watch the card game between the man they knew as Mr. Travis, and Jack Miles.

The chips were shoved into the center of the table and the cards were dealt. When the hand was finished, Marcus won it with a pair of fours.

"A pair of fours," Jack sneered. "It wouldn't have taken much to beat that hand."

"But it was enough to beat yours," Marcus reminded him.

"Another thousand," Jack said, sliding the bet forward.

"It's your money," Marcus replied easily, pushing his own chips to the middle of the table.

That hand Marcus won with a pair of tens.

"Well, you son of a bitch," Jack swore in frustration as Marcus raked in the money.

"He may be a son of a bitch," someone from the crowd said, "but he's a card playing son of a bitch. You'd better quit, Jack, while you've still got a shirt on your back."

"And your pants," another shouted, and the crowd roared with laughter.

Jack knew that they were laughing at him, and the thought made him angrier. Finally he proposed a game of high card for twenty-five hundred dollars, all the money he had left. He slid the money toward the center of the table, and stared at Marcus. "You can't win three in a row," he said.

Marcus matched the money without a word.

"Well, I didn't think you'd have guts enough to do it," Jack snarled.

Marcus smiled. "It doesn't take guts, Jack, to play with *your* money," he said.

Again the crowd roared with laughter, and Jack's anger grew more intense. "Get on with it!" he said to the dealer.

The dealer fanned the cards out, and Marcus reached for one of them.

"Hold it!" Jack said, reaching down and grabbing Marcus by the wrist, stopping his hand just short of the card. "I'll take the one you were going to take."

Jack flipped over a king, then he grinned broadly. "Thank you, friend, for finding it for me," he said, and started to reach for the pot.

"Wait a minute," Marcus said quietly. "I haven't had my turn." He picked a card at random and turned it over slowly. It was an ace. The onlookers gasped in surprise.

Jack stared at the card for a moment, then his eyes blinked rapidly, as if he didn't believe what he was seeing. Suddenly he let out a yell and jumped up.

"He's going for a gun!" someone shouted, as the watchers started to scramble away from the table. Then the roar of a shotgun exploded from above and behind Stacey.

Jack pitched back, overturning a chair, and sprawled on the floor, his chest turning into an oozey mass of blood. Black gunsmoke drifted across the room, and the air hung heavy with its unique smell. The house guard who had done the shooting stood in his balcony vantage point from which he overlooked the game and pulled the empty casings from the still smoking chambers of his double-barrel ten-gauge shotgun.

"Are you all right, Mr. Travis?" he called.

"I'm all right," Marcus answered. He clutched his hands together to keep them from shaking, and to Stacey it looked as if he was about to faint.

"You aren't armed, are you?" the guard asked.

"No I'm not," Marcus replied.

"This man was." One of the men who had been watching the game now bent over Jack's body. He pulled out a short-barreled pistol. "I reckon you saved Mr. Travis's life," he called up to the guard.

Marcus closed his eyes and sat perfectly still as they carried Jack's body out of the room. Most of the curious left with the body, and a moment later there was no one left except Marcus, Stacey and the dealer.

"Mark, we'd better leave," Stacey said anxiously.

"What? Oh, yes, I guess so," Marcus answered vacantly. But he made no attempt to move.

"Mark, please," Stacey said again. "We'd better go."

"The young lady is quite right, Mr. Tremain," the dealer said quietly. "It wouldn't do for you to be here when the police start asking questions."

"What? You know my name?" Marcus asked.

"Of course, sir. Everyone does. But we have respected your wish for privacy. However, if the police come and start asking questions, I'm afraid. . . ." He left the statement unfinished.

"Yes, yes, you're right," Marcus said. He stood up, though not without some effort.

"Here is the cash for your chips, sir," the dealer said.

"Oh, you'd better hold out the thirty percent for the . . . ."

"I did, sir," the dealer interrupted him. "You'd best hurry. You can use the back exit."

"All right, thank you," Marcus said, putting the money in his pocket. He took Stacey by the arm. "Come on."

Stacey looked toward the front of the large room, where the staff gathered around Jack's body. "It served him right," she said.

"What?"

"That Jack. He has been cheating you all this

time, Mark. He's been telling you he would keep your secret, and he took money from you, when all along everyone knew who you were anyway."

"Yes," Marcus said. "Yes, I suppose you're right." He put his hand on his forehead. "Let's go, quickly. I'm afraid I'm going to be ill."

Chapter Nine

They left through the back door of the Golden Pigeon and the cool night air somewhat revived Marcus, though another wave of nausea overcame him just before they claimed their buggy, and he had to excuse himself and move quickly into the bushes. He returned a moment later, looking somewhat sheepish, ashen-faced, and dabbing at his lips with a handkerchief.

"Mark, would you like me to drive us home?" Stacey asked.

"No," Marcus said weakly. He folded the handkerchief and put it away gingerly. "I really should drive."

"But it would be absolutely no trouble for me to drive. And you don't look as if you are up to it."

Marcus managed a small smile. "No doubt you could handle the team much better than I could, even if I felt well. But I think that driving will help me shake the nausea and dizzyness."

"Was this the first time you've ever seen anyone shot?"

"Yes."

"Then you have absolutely nothing to be ashamed

77

of. The first time I ever saw a man gunned down, I was sick for a week."

"You mean you've seen things like this before?" Marcus asked, as if unable to believe that this beautiful and delicate looking creature beside him had ever been subjected to the sight of such violence.

"Yes," Stacey said. "My own father was murdered by a gunman."

Marcus put his hand tenderly on Stacey's shoulder. "Of course, I had forgotten that for a moment. In a way, this must have been worse for you than it was for me. Oh, Stacey, can you ever forgive me for bringing you to such a place? It must have awakened memories which are best left forgotten."

"No, I never want to forget," Stacey said. "I want to remember the man who killed my father, so that someday I will be able to stand in the crowd and watch him hang."

The intensity of Stacey's remark left Marcus speechless for a moment, and when he finally recovered he moved her gently toward the buggy. "Come on," he said. "We must leave before the law gets here."

As Marcus started the team down the back road, the effort to drive did help him to overcome his nausea, just as he hoped it would, and within a few moments, he was feeling much better.

"I see what you mean about your talent with cards," Stacey said, hoping to engage him in a conversation which would take his mind off what had just happened. "You were really good. How did you develop such a skill?"

"I can't explain it," Marcus said, warming to the subject. "But it's almost as if a mysterious heat comes off the cards when I'm near them. I *know* which cards are best. I tell you if I were to go broke tomorrow, I wouldn't starve."

"Then why do you worry so about your father cutting off your inheritance?" Stacey asked.

Marcus laughed. "I don't know. I guess it's just the natural urge to want a great sum of money. Especially if it is yours."

"But it's your father's money, isn't it? Not yours."

"You're right there," Marcus agreed. "I've always had a feeling of guilt over knowing that I will be wealthy someday as the result of my father's toil, and not my own. But the guilt has never been strong enough for me to seriously consider abandoning my inheritance."

"Oh, I don't know about that," Stacey said.

"What do you mean?"

"Maybe that's why you do the things you do. Maybe you don't have the strength to come right out and abandon your inheritance, but you secretly want your father to take it away from you."

Marcus laughed. "It is an interesting thought. Do you know what you are doing now? You are delving into my psyche."

"Into your what?"

"Into my mind, trying to explain why I do certain things. That's called psychology, from the Greek words *psyche* which means mind, and *logos* which means the study of."

Now it was Stacey's turn to laugh. "Is that something else you learned at Harvard?"

"Yes. It was quite interesting, really. A man named Wilhelm Wundt has created a whole new field with his work in psychology. It is a science now, just as astronomy is a science."

"You mean there are people who do nothing except try to figure out what other people are thinking about?" Stacey asked.

"What they are thinking and why," Marcus answered.

"What a foolish waste of time."

"On the contrary. The subject is quite fascinating, actually. And even you engage in it, though without giving it a name."

"Maybe I should go to Harvard and study this," Stacey laughed.

"Oh, ho, wouldn't I like to see that though?" Marcus said. "Unfortunately, women aren't allowed at Harvard."

"Why?" Stacey asked, bristling quickly. "Don't they think women are smart enough?"

"There are schools of thought on that subject too," Marcus said. "The male brain is somewhat larger than the female brain, therefore, most scholars believe the male is smarter than the female."

"And you?" Stacey challenged. "What do you believe?"

"No, my dear, you aren't going to get me embroiled in this discussion. I was merely giving you the benefit of my studies, not my opinion."

"But I would like to know your opinion," Stacey insisted, refusing to relinquish the subject.

"Well, I'm afraid I've seen too much of the cunning of women like Mrs. Sinclair and your Aunt Pricilla, to feel that women are of an equal intelligence. And then I meet someone like you, a woman with a keen, analytical, though unschooled, mind, and I'm ready to develop a theory which is contrary to prevailing thought and say that among women, as among men, the degree of intelligence is based upon individual development, and not predetermined by sex."

Stacey smiled. "I think you are saying you don't really believe that men are smarter than women."

"Not as a group, no, I don't think men are smarter than women," Marcus said. "Though Stacey, if you ever bring this subject up at one of your aunt's social functions, I will swear that this conversation never took place."

"Aha," Stacey said. "I thought so. It turns out that you're really no diff—"

Bang!

Stacey's sentence was interrupted by a gunshot, and the sudden appearance of two horsemen in front of the buggy. The horses reared at the loud noise, and it was all Marcus could do to bring the animals under control.

"You idiots, what are you trying to do, kill us?" Marcus shouted angrily as he fought to quiet the team.

"Now that might not be such a bad idea, since you caused my brother to be killed."

"Miles!" Marcus cried, now recognizing the two riders. One was Billy Miles, and the other was Lorin Keefer.

"You know very well that Mark had nothing to do with your brother's death," Stacey said. "He was killed by the guard, and he had it coming to him. He was going for a gun to shoot Mark."

"That was his mistake," Billy said. "He thought Tremain was enough of a man to fight his own battles, rather than have someone else do it for him. I won't make that same mistake."

"Don't be absurd," Marcus said. "I couldn't very well fight your brother; I wasn't even armed."

"Well, we're going to fix that right now," Miles said. "Lorin, do you still have that little pepperbox stuck up your sleeve?"

"Yeah, I got it, Billy. But you know that's just for emergencies."

"Well, this is an emergency. Take it out and give it to Marcus. I want him armed when I kill him."

"What?" Marcus asked, gasping in quick fear. "What are you talking about?"

"I'm going to kill you," Billy Miles said as easily as if he had just announced that he was going to brush the dust off someone's coat. "But you will be armed, so it will be a fair fight."

"Armed, with a pepperbox?" Stacey said. "That's a woman's firearm."

"Well, then it should be appropriate, don't you think?" Billy asked with a laugh. Then the smile left his face. "Give him the gun, Lorin."

For just a moment Billy took his eyes off the two and looked over toward Lorin, and Stacey, who had been waiting for her chance, took that opportunity to make her move. She grabbed the buggy whip and used it to knock the gun cleanly out of Billy Miles's hand. The buggy whip was not much more than a riding quirt so she had very little mechanical advantage with it. How she wished for one of the bullwhips that she used to drive the stage! With it she could have jerked Billy Miles out of the saddle. As it was, the gun was all she could manage.

"What the hell?" Billy shouted, watching his gun flying toward the side of the road.

"Heah, team!" Stacey shouted, popping the whip over the heads of the team. The horses leaped forward, and the buggy shot down the road, pulling away from the two startled horsemen. Unfortunately, Marcus was just as startled by Stacey's move as the two horsemen were, and he dropped the reins. Stacey made a grab for them, but watched helplessly as they fell across the dashboard and slid out of sight, trailing behind the horses.

"My god! What'll we do?" Marcus shouted.

"There's nothing we can do," Stacey shouted back, "except sit tight and hope the team can outrun them on their own."

Perhaps if Stacey had managed to get the reins she could have driven them out of there. Two perfectly matched horses, pulling a light buggy, driven by a skillful driver down a good road, would have had a chance against the horsemen who were now in hot pursuit. But, running loose as they were, there was no direction for the horses and soon the two men on horseback came even with them, grabbed the harness and pulled the team to a halt.

"Well," Billy said, when the horses were still, "you surprised me, girl. I didn't think you had that much spirit."

"Come on, Billy, let's kill them both and get out of here," Lorin said. "This whole thing is making me nervous."

"No," Billy said. "I've got a better idea."

"What?"

"Tie them both up," he said.

"You're going to shoot them while they are tied?" Lorin asked.

"No. I'm not going to kill them at all."

"What are you going to do?"

"You'll see. Just tie them up like I asked."

Marcus submitted to the indignity without protest or struggle, and a moment later he was securely bound to a nearby tree. After he was tied, Billy walked around testing this tree and that, until he looked back toward Lorin, who was holding a gun on Stacey. "Yes," Billy said. "These trees will do nicely."

"What are you talking about?" Lorin said.

"Have you ever read how the Apaches spread-eagle their victims? They stake them out in the sun."

Lorin laughed. "So what are you going to do? Stake the girl out under the moon?"

"Yeah," Billy said. "Get her over here."

"This is ridiculous," Stacey said. "What do you hope to prove by this?" Suddenly she realized what they were about to do. "No," she cried. "I'm not moving from this seat."

Billy pointed his gun toward her and cocked it. Stacey could hear the metallic click as the hammer came back and the cylinder rotated. It sounded unusually loud to her. "Oh, you'll come here willingly, or I'll shoot you and bring you over here. You see, I'm going to do what I want, whether you're dead or alive. Now which will it be?"

"For god's sake, Stacey, do what he says," Marcus suddenly pleaded.

"Mark, do you know what he wants to do?"

"Yes," Marcus said. "Do it, Stacey. He'll kill you otherwise."

"He may anyway," Stacey answered.

"This way at least, you have a chance," Billy said. "Now what will it be?"

Stacey gave a sigh of resignation, then stepped down from the buggy and walked over toward Billy, who stood smiling evilly at her in the moonlight. "Now, that's the smart thing to do," Billy said, tying a rope around one of her wrists, then another rope around her other wrist. A few moments later Stacey was lying on the ground with her arms and legs outstretched, tied to four trees which were perfectly positioned to spread-eagle the frightened young girl.

"Now, for the final touch," Billy said, removing his cravat and gagging Stacey into silence.

"What about him?" Lorin asked, pointing at Marcus.

"Let him watch," Billy said, unbuckling his pants. "He might learn something."

Stacey watched in horror as Billy dropped his pants, then got on his knees between her splayed legs. He pulled her skirt up to her waist, then jerked and tore at her undergarments, until that which he sought was exposed to him. He grabbed the bodice of her dress and jerked it down until he could see her breasts, two creamy mounds of young flesh, gleaming in the silver moonlight.

"They're a little small," Billy complained, looking at them. "I prefer larger tits on my women. But these'll do."

Then, to Stacey's horror and surprise, he leaned

over and took one of them in his mouth. My God, she thought. He's going to bite it off!

But Billy didn't bite. He began sucking on it, and he pulled the nipple in between his teeth and flicked his tongue across it.

Stacey felt a strange, tingling sensation at the action of his tongue. She had been prepared for the intense pain of being bitten. Instead, the tongue was moving back and forth with a savage tenderness which was, strangely enough, pleasurable.

But the puzzling pleasure which coursed through Stacey at the moment didn't assuage the fear which was running through her, and the fear grew more acute when she felt Billy's hands move to the soft down which did little to protect her most private part. His finger gouged into her, painfully, and a moment later she realized that his finger had been replaced by the battering ram which hung between his legs. He fell across her and plunged, and what had been painful became momentarily excruciating, as he drove himself deep into her.

Though the severity of the pain subsided, the humiliation didn't, and Stacey cried out against the gag which covered her mouth. She felt blood trickling down her legs, and she bit against the cloth in her mouth and rode with the evil thrusting until she felt him grow tense, then heard a shuddering explosion of his breath and realized with gratitude that he was finished. Slowly he lifted himself from her body.

"You want to try it?" Billy asked Lorin, as he stood up and packed his shirt tail into his trousers.

"No," Lorin said shortly. "Come on, let's get out of here before someone comes along."

"You sure you don't want to try her?"

"No. I'd rather visit a girl at the whorehouse than take any more time here. Come on, Billy, let's go," Lorin begged.

"All right," Billy said, laughing. "But you don't know what you're missing."

"What about them? What are we going to do with them?"

"Untie one of them."

Lorin started toward Stacey.

"What are you doing?" Billy asked.

"I'm going to untie the girl so she can untie Tremain."

"Hell no, don't untie her. She'll leave Tremain tied to the tree and come after us. Untie Tremain. He's too spineless to do anything."

Lorin looked over at Marcus, who hung his head in shame. "Yeah," Lorin said, smiling. "Yeah, I guess you're right. All right, Tremain, I'm going to untie you, but give us ten minutes before you untie the girl. Ten minutes, do you hear?"

"Yes," Marcus said. "I hear you."

"And you're going to do it, like a good boy?"

"Yes," Marcus said. "I'll do as you ask. Just don't kill us."

"Oh, we wouldn't dream of killing you, Marcus boy," Billy said from the saddle. "We might want to do this again sometime."

Lorin laughed as he cut the ropes which bound Marcus, and he was still laughing when they rode away.

Chapter Ten

When the ropes which bound Stacey were cut a moment later, she managed to restore some modesty to her appearance by discarding her torn undergarments and adjusting her dress to cover her breasts and thighs. Then, because the gag had made breathing difficult she just sat on the ground for several seconds, sucking in the cool, night air, thankful that she was still alive.

To his credit, Marcus had cut Stacey loose immediately rather than waiting the requisite ten minutes. He walked over to the buggy and stood contritely, while Stacey effected her repairs and regained her breath. Finally he spoke.

"Are you all right?"

"Yes," Stacey answered in a small, hurt voice.

The sound of her voice brought renewed pain to Marcus. He fought against the humiliation, the frustration, and the anger of the moment, then looked toward Stacey, with all the anguish of his soul clearly visible in his eyes.

"Stacey, can you ever find it in your heart to forgive me for this?"

Stacey was surprised by the question, and she looked at him in confusion. "Forgive . . . forgive you? Why should I have to forgive you? You didn't do this terrible thing."

"I stood by, helpless as a baby, and watched," Marcus said. "You heard what they said about my spinelessness. If I had been one of your mountain men, I could have prevented this."

"Yes," Stacey said. "If you had been a mountain man you would have done something. And gotten yourself killed for your trouble." Stacey rubbed the soreness of her wrists and ankles as she talked.

"But I should at least have tried," Marcus said. "I might have been able to do something."

"No," Stacey said. "They had the drop on us. Not even Clay Conway could have prevented it."

"Who?"

"Clay Conway," Stacey said, amazed that she had even thought of him under such circumstances.

"Is he a friend of yours?"

"Hardly," Stacey said bitterly, but not wanting to elaborate. "But he's a gunman. I just brought up his name as an example of how foolhardy it would have been to try anything." Stacey stood up and started brushing at her dress, but the dirt and grass stains were too deeply ingrained to be dusted away. "Oh, look at this dress," she cried. "It is ruined."

"Come on," Marcus said, offering her his hand. "We'll ride into town and notify the police."

"No," Stacey said, jerking her hand back. "No, we mustn't do that."

"What? Why not? Those men deserve to be punished," Marcus said. "And with both of us testifying against them in court, they'll get their punishment."

"And so will we," Stacey said.

"What do you mean?"

"Marcus, think of it," Stacey said. "For the rest of my life I will be know only as 'that woman who was raped by a road agent.' And you will always be the man who stood by helplessly and watched it happen."

"I'm willing to live with that," Marcus said.

"Well, I'm not. And I don't think you are either. Marcus, the scandal would just about ruin our families, don't you see that?"

Marcus made a fist of his hand and put it against his forehead, pressing tightly. Finally he took it away and looked at her. His anguish had grown even greater. "You mean you want them to get away with it?"

"No, I don't want them to," Stacey said. "But I don't see that we have any choice. And if you were thinking clearly, you'd agree with me."

"All right," Marcus said with a sigh. "But what do we do now?"

"We go home," Stacey said easily.

"Like this? What about your dress?"

"Yes, I'd better do something about it." She thought for a moment, then said, "I know. We'll return by the service alley which runs behind my uncle's house. I can sneak across the back lawn and in through my bedroom window to change clothes before my aunt sees me. You wait for me in the alley, then I'll sneak back and you can bring me home through the front drive as if nothing has happened."

"I don't know," Marcus hedged. "What if you get caught?"

"Do you have a better plan?"

"No," Marcus admitted.

"Then that's what we'll do."

One-half hour later Stacey was in her bedroom changing clothes. She selected a new dress to wear and laid it out on her bed, then removed her old dress, poured some water into the basin, and began to wash away some of the evidence of her ordeal.

Stacey examined her body critically in the mirror, looking for any visible sign of change. Could people tell by looking at her that she was no longer a virgin? Would her aunt or her uncle see something different about her? Stacey saw the same clear amber eyes staring back at her that had looked back from the mirror this morning. Her face was the same, the skin olive complexioned and unblemished, the body youthful and unmarked. No, there would be no way anyone could know unless she or Marcus told them.

Stacey washed up quickly, then put on the change of clothes. Once she heard her aunt's footsteps coming toward her room and feared that she was about to be caught. She held her breath and tried to think of what to say to her aunt should she come in. Fortunately, the footsteps receded down the hall and the fear of the moment passed. Stacey hurried with her dressing, then checked through the window and when she saw that it was safe, dashed back across the lawn and rejoined Marcus who waited auxiously in the buggy.

"What took you so long?" he asked nervously. "I've been concerned that someone would come along and see me just waiting here and start asking embarrassing questions."

"I had to erase all traces of what happened," Stacey said. "Was I successful?"

Marcus looked at her, now wearing a fresh, clean dress, and giving no indication whatever of the ordeal that had just transpired. He smiled, the first smile either of them had enjoyed since the terrible episode.

"I don't know how you did it so quickly," he said. "But once again, I find that you are lovely."

"Then drive around to the front of the house, and we'll return as if nothing had happened."

Marcus flipped the reins over the team and they started ahead, pulling the buggy down the alley.

"Say, wait a minute," Marcus suddenly said. "What are we going to tell your aunt when she—"

"Sees me in a different dress?" Stacey interrupted.

"Yes."

"I've already got that figured out. If you recall, she left about five minutes before we did, to attend a lecture. I'll tell her that I decided I'd rather wear this dress than the other one. She knew that I was trying to make up my mind between the two anyway."

The team turned off the road and pulled the buggy up the great, curving, white chipped gravel driveway that described a large arch from the road to the front of the Prescott home. A few seconds later they stopped by the front porch, and her uncle's groom held the team while another helped Stacey step down from the buggy. She looked up at Marcus, who still held the reins.

"Mark, won't you come in for a while?"

"No, thank you," Marcus said. "I think I'd better be getting back."

"Nonsense," Stacey said in a tone that indicated that she felt strongly that he should come in. "You come in and visit with my aunt and uncle for a short time."

"Very well," Marcus said. "If you're certain I won't be intruding."

As the two walked up the steps and across the porch, Marcus spoke to her *sotto voce*: "I don't think this is such a good idea. What if they ask me questions I can't handle?"

"If you can't handle them, I'll answer them," Stacey said, realizing at that moment that though Marcus was older and better educated, she had become the dominant personality in their relationship.

Her aunt and uncle were waiting in the parlor, and they greeted the young couple as they entered.

"Anastasia dear, did you have a nice time? Why—that isn't the dress you were wearing," her aunt said.

"You knew what a difficult time I was having making up my mind," Stacey said. "After you left I went back and changed into this dress after all."

"But dear, you mean you made Marcus wait while you changed dresses again? That wasn't very nice of you."

"I didn't mind, Mrs. Prescott," Marcus smiled. "The result was well worth the wait."

"My, how gallant of you," Pricilla said.

"Marcus, would you care for a brandy?" Tobias offered.

94

"Yes, thank you, that would be very nice," Marcus accepted, realizing that he needed a brandy tonight of all nights.

"How was the art exhibit?" Pricilla asked.

"We didn't go to the exhibit," Stacey said easily.

"What? Well, I don't understand. I thought that was where you were going."

"We changed our minds," Stacey said. "Instead, we went to see a show."

"A show? But Anastasia, that's scandalous. That simply isn't done," she said, her tone of voice clearly showing her shock. "Marcus, how could you!"

"It wasn't his fault, Aunt Pricilla," Stacey said quickly. "I teased him to do it. I've never seen one, and I so wanted to."

"Well, I had never seen one when I was your age either," Pricilla said, still shocked by the revelation. "And I only see them now if I know they are for charity or some other worthwhile cause."

"Oh, leave them alone, Pricilla," Tobias said gently. "Times have changed. The young people enjoy getting out more now than they did when we were young."

"Still, to go see a show—and unchaperoned! I'm just terribly fearful of what others might say."

"The others be damned!" Tobias said.

"Tobias, please, such language isn't called for, even under these rather trying conditions."

"What did you see?" Tobias asked easily.

"We saw a dance program," Stacey said. She looked over to Marcus and saw that he was smiling into the brandy snifter, despite himself.

"A dance?" Pricilla said. "Well, thank heaven for small favors at least. A dance is infinitely more to be preferred to a play, or, heaven help us, this new thing called a 'review' that features all sort of vulgar events. But Anastasia, dear, you are still unschooled in the social graces, so please, before you do onything else foolish, at least consult with me."

"Yes, Aunt Pricilla," Stacey answered obediently.

"And as for you, young man," Pricilla said, facing Marcus.

"Yes, ma'am?"

Pricilla smiled an ingratiating smile. After all, here was the prize catch of Denver, and he seemed to be taken with her niece, regardless of Anastasia's obvious social ineptitude. Perhaps it wouldn't do to let her anger spill over onto him.

"As for you, I am pleased at least, that you were with her. I know that regardless of her unfamiliarity with life, she is safe with you as her guardian."

A sudden cloud descended over Marcus's eyes, and he looked away with a feeling of guilt. Pricilla had no way of knowing that her words had merely sparked a memory of what Marcus considered his failure to come to Stacey's aid during the rape.

"I, uh, mean merely, that I want to thank you," Pricilla said, trying desperately to undo whatever she had done with her remark.

Stacey realized immediately what Marcus was thinking, and she walked over to him and put her hand possessively on his arm. "Aunt Pricilla, I saw the show only because I was escorted by Marcus. I had confidence that with him as my guide, there would be no talk to embarrass you."

"Very well, dear," Pricilla said. "But please, in the future, try to think of all the possible consequences before you embark on any folly."

"I will, Aunt Pricilla, I promise."

Chapter Eleven

Stacey lay, unsleeping, in her bed. The others had long since retired to their rooms, and the house was quiet. Outside her window, the wind rustled through the leaves of the trees, and a dancing aspen caught a moonbeam and scattered a splash of silver through the night.

Stacey couldn't sleep because her mind was crowded with thoughts. She recalled again the fear, the anger, the humiliation she had been put through, and she said the names of the men over and over so that she wouldn't forget them: Billy Miles and Lorin Keefer.

She intended to make the two men pay for what they had done. It was true that she stopped Marcus from going to the police to avoid a scandal. But there was another reason as well. In Stacey's thinking, whatever the police did to them, if in fact they did anything at all, would leave her feeling unfulfilled. The crime had been committed against her and she would avenge it, without help from the police.

Stacey thought back to the time she and the posse had happened upon Clay Conway and the bodies of her father and his passengers. The posse had wanted to hang Clay right there, to lynch him on the spot, but she had talked them out of it. What a mistake that had been! As a result Clay had escaped. Her father's killer was even now roaming free to rob and terrorize, and no doubt laughing at her for her foolishness in enabling him to get away.

Well, that was a mistake which wouldn't be repeated. She would plan her own revenge against the two men who had attacked her tonight. And then, when she was finished with them, she would wait for her opportunity to go after Clay Conway.

Stacey tried to console herself with these thoughts, but there was scarce comfort in them. The fact remained that she had been violated today. The most private, personal part of her body had been brutally invaded by someone who was little more than a beast. It was, she knew, the single most terrifying thought in the minds of most women. She had heard of it from the time she was a very little girl. Older women whispered about rape as a possible consequence of Indian raids, and alluded to it in stories of atrocities attributed to both sides in the Civil War, though the actual word, rape, was seldom mentioned.

Stacey didn't have to hear the word. She knew what they were talking about. All girls knew; they learned without being taught and understood without explanation. That there is such a universal fear of rape is an amazing indictment of the impact of the act. Some women, Stacey knew, swore that they would kill themselves to prevent it from occurring, and there were stories handed down, though never verified, of women under seige being given a gun with only one bullet in it, to use on themselves as a last resort. This was supposed to be considered an act of mercy by the men who gave the women the guns, and an act of honor by the women who used them.

Stacey didn't know if the stories were true or not because she had never known anyone who had actually been raped. Until now. She, Anastasia Pendarrow, had been raped. And survived. She had no intention of taking her own life because of the dishonor. In fact, though she blushed furiously with shame at the thought of it, there was even a moment when she felt an unexpected pleasure.

As that unwelcome thought entered Stacey's mind her other thoughts fled, and for a few moments, in the quiet privacy of her own bed, Stacey remembered the amazing sensations a man's tongue could evoke from the nipples of her breasts. As she thought of it she was aware of the increased sensitivity of her breasts.

Stacey tried to think of other things but the tingling sensations wouldn't go away and she felt a strange feeling spreading from her nipples, through her breasts, and through the rest of her body.

Stacey tossed and turned on the bed, fluffing her pillow into many different sizes and shapes, trying to find a position which would be comfortable, and which would allow her to abandon these thoughts, and thoughts of Clay Conway.

Clay Conway?

Why am I thinking of him? she wondered, angry with herself for allowing his name to enter into the privacy of her thoughts. But even as she scolded herself and fought against it, she was unable to keep him from becoming a very real presence. And quite unwillingly she replaced the grunting, panting body of Billy Miles with that of the hated Clay Conway.

With such a thought the rape took on a new significance. For even in its brutality it had raised the curtain on the promise of forbidden pleasures which Stacey had thus far experienced only in restless dreams. Now, with substance and subject, these dreams became even more intense.

Stacey let out a sigh of anger and sat up in her bed. She looked at the moon shadow patterns on her wall for a moment, and walked out onto the veranda outside. There was a cooling night breeze through her thin, cotton nightgrown that refreshed her fevered skin. The wind, though Stacey was scarcely aware of it, plastered the nightgown against all the curves of her lovely body. Especially prominent were her nipples which had drawn into rosebuds because of her erotic thoughts.

Stacey stepped up to the edge of the veranda and leaned on the stone fence, looking up at the stars. She located Arcturus, and stared at it for a moment, wondering just what a star was, and why it sparkled so. Maybe it was like a large diamond, just hanging in the sky, or a huge nugget of solid, sparkling gold. Though many of the other stars were like diamonds, Arcturus shone like gold.

"Stacey," a man's voice whispered. "Stacey, is that you?"

"What? Who is it?" Stacey called.

"Shhh! It's me, Marcus," he said, stepping from behind one of the shrubs near the veranda.

"Mark, what are you doing out here? Heavens, I

thought you went home hours ago. What do you want?"

"It's not what I want," Marcus said morosely, as he stepped up to the veranda, then climbed over the fence to stand beside Stacey. "It's what I don't want. I don't want to be alone."

"Why not?"

"I couldn't stand it. I couldn't face being alone and having to answer the questions I would ask myself."

"But what were you doing out there?"

"I was going to toss pebbles at your window until I got your attention," Marcus said.

Stacey looked at him. The handsome young face which had explained the stars to her was now wracked with pain and guilt. "Come on into my room," she invited. "Someone may see or hear us out here."

Stacey stepped back through the open window, and Marcus followed her, then went over to her bed. He sat on the edge and leaned his forehead into his hand, his elbow on his knee. "I'm so sorry," he said contritely.

"Mark, you keep telling me you're sorry," she scolded. "But you have nothing to be sorry for. I don't blame you for what happened. Can't you see that? You were helpless."

"But I was afraid, Stacey. I was absolutely terrified."

"Did you think I wasn't afraid?"

"You were afraid," Marcus said, "but not like I was. Even *they* noticed it. Did you hear the taunts about my spinelessness? About how a woman's gun was fitting for me?"

103

"That didn't mean anything," Stacey said. "That was just the talk of a couple of ruffians."

"No," Marcus said, "it was true." His voice broke on the last word, and Stacey noticed with amazement that he was crying. She had never seen a man cry before, and for a moment she was too stunned to say or do anything. Then, terribly moved, she instinctively sat down beside him and took him in her arms.

It was an odd feeling, this, cradling a grown man in her arms, having his body shake against hers with silent sobs and feeling the dampness of his tears. It unleashed a previously untested emotion in her, and she felt constrained to comfort him in whatever way she could. She pulled him tighter to her, and pressed her cheek against his, cushioning him with her body, rubbing the back of his neck with her hands, trying to comfort him as one would a child.

And then a new emotion emerged. The instinct to mother was overcome by an even more powerful instinct as she pulled his body to hers. Through the thin nightgown, she felt her nipples responding to his proximity, and bubbles of fire began to ascend from her loins, to explode throughout her body.

"Mark," she whispered, and she turned her head toward him, then met him in an open-mouthed kiss.

Marcus bent her back onto the bed, then gently raised her nightgown. Stacey lifted her arms and let the nightgown be taken from her so that she was totally nude, lying in the dappled silver pool of moonlight. Quickly, Marcus removed his own clothes, then stretched out on the bed beside her, so that Stacey felt the burning fever of her own flushed skin relieved by contact with his cool body.

Marcus put his hands on her, and she felt his palms tracing along the curves and resilient flesh of her body. His fingers played skillfully with her bud-hard nipples, then trailed down her smooth stomach until they touched the soft growth of pubic hair.

How different this tender supplication was, she thought, from the brutal pawing she had been subjected to by Billy Miles. Before, she had fought against it in fear and anger. Now, she welcomed Marcus, and in her mind and in her body she cried for him to go on, and on, and on. She was fully aroused as she had never been before, and she knew that only one thing could extinguish the fire that now raged within.

Why doesn't he go on? she asked herself. Perhaps he is moving with caution because he thinks I don't want to go any further.

With that thought, Stacey allowed her hand and fingers to trail lightly over his body, down and around to the one place which would let him know with no uncertainty that she was ready for him.

It was limp! The feel of it, soft, and inert, startled her, and she jerked her hand away in surprise.

"No!" Marcus said, realizing what she had done. He pulled away and lay on his stomach, with his head facing away from her.

"Marcus, what . . . what is it?" Stacey asked softly. "What's wrong?" She sat up, leaning on one arm, looking down at his nude body. Her own nudity in this pose, alternately silvered and shadowed by the night glow, was as beautiful and inspirational as a statue or painting.

"I'm impotent," Marcus said quietly.

"I don't understand. What does that mean?"

"It means that I can't make love to you."

"Why not?" Stacey asked in amazement. She had always been taught that all men were by nature fiends, barely able to check their baser instincts. Now that she offered herself to Marcus, he was turning her down.

"Is it . . . is it because of me?" she asked. "Do you not find me desirable?"

Marcus reached for her, and put a hand up to rub her cheek. "Oh, no, Stacey, it's nothing like that, believe me. It has nothing to do with you at all. In fact, I think you are the most beautiful, the most desirable woman I have ever known. So much so, that I thought perhaps this once I could . . . but, I guess it's not to be. And that makes my . . . affliction . . . all the more painful.

"What causes im . . . im . . ?"

"The word is impotence," Marcus said. He rolled over on his back and put his hands behind his head, staring up at the ceiling. "That, my love, is a question no one seems able to answer. There is very little written about it. A man who suffers such a disease isn't quick to admit it, you see. It is because of this I was so affected by the taunts and jibes of Billy Miles and Lorin Keefer."

"Don't think about the evil things they said," Stacey advised.

Marcus smiled sadly, "No, I must think of them, for in a way, my dear, we were both raped. You of your maidenhood, and I of my manhood."

"I don't understand."

"It's really quite simple. In most primitive cul-

106

tures, this," he cradled his impotent member in his hand, "is the symbol of manhood, *phallus erectus*. But I can't achieve an erection; thus, I don't qualify. There was more truth to their taunts than they or you dreamed."

Marcus sat up and began pulling his clothes back on. "I suppose you won't want to see me anymore?" he asked.

"Don't be silly," Stacey said. "Of course I want to see you again."

Marcus laughed as he dressed. It was not a mirthful laugh, but rather a defeated one, laced with irony. "Yolinda Sinclair," he said. "God, how I dislike that girl and her mother. I should let them trap me, then present her with this on our wedding night. Wouldn't that be a fine wedding gift?"

"Mark, please, don't talk like that. You mustn't blame yourself so," Stacey said.

"Right," Marcus replied. "I'll keep a stiff upper lip." He laughed, again with irony. "Hey, that's pretty good, isn't it? I mean I can at least keep a stiff upper lip, if nothing else."

Still laughing, Marcus climbed out through the window and Stacey watched him until he disappeared into the shadows of the lawn.

Then, with her body aching for fulfillment, and her heart heavy with pity over the terrible cross Marcus was forced to bear, she returned to her bed.

In her fitful, troubled sleep, the dreams of passion and pleasure returned. Though she had such dreams frequently, there was a new intensity to this one which left her weak and shaken when she awakened the next morning. The substance of the dream was so real that she thought of it for several moments before she finally realized, with shame and anger, to whom her nocturnal lusts had been directed.

She had dreamed of Clay Conway.

Chapter Twelve

The relationship between Stacey and Marcus was a bittersweet affair. They shared the most intimate secrets and knew each other's vulnerabilities, but emotionally they were at a dead end, and they knew it. Aunt Pricilla was thrilled by the fact that Marcus was a frequent visitor, and already was talking to Uncle Tobias about a possible "late summer wedding." "After all," she said, "a marriage this early simply wouldn't be proper. We must talk them into waiting for a while, for appearances' sake."

"At this point I don't think that is the question," Tobias said. "I'm not as positive as you that they want to get married. Neither of them have mentioned it."

"Of course, they want to get married, Tobias," Pricilla insisted. "Why else would the young man spend so much time here?"

"It's just possible that they are very good friends," Tobias suggested.

"Nonsense. Boys and girls can't be friends. Anastasia's friends are people like Yolinda Sinclair, Mary Beeson and Cynthia Lyons," Pricilla insisted. "Why, they are all four sitting under the large shade tree out back, this very instant. And do you know what they are talking about?"

"About boys?" Tobias asked.

"No. They are talking about the Cinderella Ball. I heard one of them mention it. Isn't it exciting? You know what that means, don't you?"

"Not really."

"Why, my dear, it means that Anastasia is about to be asked to join the Daughters of the Snow. It's the most exclusive sorority in all of Denver."

"Just because she's being asked to the Cinderella Ball doesn't mean she's going to get into that sorority. One member can blackball you, can't she?"

"Well, yes," Pricilla agreed. "One vote can prevent her from becoming a member of the society. But it can't prevent her from attending the ball. But why would you suggest such a thing? Who would blackball Anastasia?"

Tobias laughed. "Pricilla, for someone who sticks her nose into everything, you certainly don't see much, do you?"

"Whatever do you mean?"

"If Stacey tries to join the Daughters of the Snow she'll be blackballed by Yolinda Sinclair."

"That just goes to show you how much you know," Pricilla said haughtily, "for it was none other than Yolinda who extended the invitation to attend the ball in the first place."

It was indeed Yolinda who extended the invitation. But at this moment, under the shade tree of the back lawn, it was Mary Beeson who was pleading the case of the Ball to Stacey.

"Oh, please do come, Stacey. It's simply loads of fun," Mary begged.

110

"Yes, and it's for charity you know," Cynthia put in. "Why, daddy said that last year we raised enough money to feed all the poor people of the city for six months."

"And of course, the Cinderella Ball is the biggest social event of the year," Yolinda put in. "There are girls in this town who would do anything for an invitation. You are quite lucky, you know, to be invited to attend in your very first season."

"But you said it was being held in a poorhouse," Stacey said. "Doesn't that make you feel strange? Holding a fancy dress ball in a poorhouse?"

A maid brought the girls lemonade and a platter of cookies, and Yolinda helped herself before she answered.

"No," she said. "It doesn't make me feel strange at all. Why should it?"

"Because," Stacey said, "it would be as if we were lording it over the poor people. They don't participate, do they?"

"Participate?" Yolinda replied, gasping at the thought. "You mean," she shivered, "ugh, dancing with us, or eating with us, or something like that? I should say not!"

"But, isn't this a little like going to their house and then not letting them in?"

"It isn't their house," Yolinda said. "The poorhouse belongs to the city. They are just unfortunate enough to have to live there. Besides, why should they be offended? After all, we are doing it for them."

"Please, Stacey, you're getting it all wrong," Cynthia explained. "After all, this is a good thing we're doing."

"All right, tell me exactly what the Cinderella Ball is," Stacey said.

"Well," Mary started to explain, excitement spilling over as she talked, "once a year, the Daughters of the Snow sponsors a dance. The purpose of the dance is to raise money to buy food for the poor."

"How do you raise the money?"

"Oh, that part is the most fun," Cynthia said. "And risqué."

"Risqué?"

"Absolutely," Yolinda said, smugly. "I daresay if anyone other than the Daughters of the Snow did it, it would be a scandal. We can get away with it because we are who we are."

"And it goes for charity, don't forget that," Mary put in.

"Bah, charity has nothing to do with it, my dear," Yolinda said. "It is a matter of social position. If one of the other tacky little sororities in town tried something like this, no matter how much money they raised, they would be ostracized by everyone of importance in the city."

"Well, what is the scandalous way of raising money?" Stacey asked.

"We have an auction," Mary said.

"An auction? What do you sell?"

"Our clothes," Cynthia replied, her eyes twinkling in amusement.

"Let me explain," Mary said quickly, when she saw the look of surprise on Stacey's face. "You see, we get all dressed up in the most divine, elegant gowns you can imagine."

"You should see them," Cynthia said. "Oh, last

year there were some of the most beautiful gowns I have ever seen."

"The men who come to the ball come in masquerade," Mary explained. "They don't remove their masks for the whole evening."

"And it is they who do the bidding," Cynthia put in.

"The men buy the clothes?"

"Yes," Mary said. "In turn, we model our gowns, and the men begin bidding. The highest bidder wins a dance with the girl who is wearing the gown he bought."

"And what happens to the gown?"

"Oh, we remove the gown and it, along with the money paid for it, is given to the poor people," Cynthia said.

"You take off your clothes?" Stacey gasped.

"Yes," Cynthia said.

"But perhaps we'd better explain," Mary put in. "We go into a dressing room and remove the gown and put on old clothes from a barrel there. You have to look through the barrel to find something to wear."

"It's the same barrel that the poor people get their clothes from," Cynthia explained.

"This way, we are showing the poor people that we know what it's like to be poor," Yolinda said. "For after we've changed, we look as bad as the poor wretches who are sitting along the side, watching us."

"And that's why it's called a Cinderella Ball," Cynthia explained. "Because at the stroke of midnight, we lose our elegant gowns and are dressed in rags."

113

"You will come, won't you?" Mary pleaded.

"If it's for charity, I don't see how I can say no," Stacey said. "Though I must say, there's something about it that bothers me."

"What? What could it possibly be?" Cynthia said.

"Perhaps Stacey can't force herself into old clothes," Yolinda suggested. She put her hand on Stacey's and smiled, too sweetly. "Heaven knows, I can almost feel my flesh crawl just imagining the bugs that might be found in that collection of old rags. But I just think of what good we are doing for those miserable wretches, and I force myself to go on. If you can't do that, though, believe me, dear, we will all understand."

Stacey sighed. It wasn't that at all. What's more she believed that Yolinda knew that wasn't what was bothering her. But there was no way she could withdraw now without that appearing to be the reason. She returned Yolinda's smile. "You're right, I mustn't lose sight of the fact that it is for charity. I'll go."

"Oh, wonderful!" Mary said. She hugged Stacey in delight.

Of the three girls who were her companions, Stacey genuinely liked Mary. She was a relatively plain girl who had the good fortune to be born to wealthy parents. She had a good heart, and when she smiled at Stacey, it was always a genuine smile of friendship.

Cynthia was too easily influenced by Yolinda, though taken alone she would have been all right. She wasn't mean, like Yolinda, but she didn't have the strength to go against her or to stand on her own.

114

As for Yolinda, to anyone sophisticated enough to recognize the signs, she had announced herself from the outset as being Stacey's enemy. Though Yolinda was quite pretty in her own right, Stacey was the prettiest of the girls. Stacey was also more vibrant, and Yolinda had immediately perceived her as a potential rival for Marcus. Therefore, Yolinda had been calculating in all her relations with Stacey.

Stacey wanted to laugh at Yolinda's efforts to snare Marcus. And she might have laughed, had the truth not been such a bitter pill, not only for her, but for Marcus. Especially for Marcus, for now Stacey knew that the seeming indifference in his face was not indifference at all, but devastating pain because of his tragic secret.

"What are you going to wear, Yolinda?" Cynthia now asked.

"I haven't decided yet," she answered. "After all, remember that we will have to sell the dresses afterward. I certainly wouldn't want to wear something that I really loved."

"No, I can see that would be too great a sacrifice for you," Stacey said.

"I'm going to wear a Beau Bandito hat," Mary said.

"Oh, don't tell me you had one made!" Cynthia exclaimed excitedly.

"Yes," Mary said. "I talked to Madame Gasneau about it, told her exactly what I wanted, and she made one for me."

"Describe it," Cynthia begged.

"It's purple felt, and it has a simply divine pink feather sweeping out from one side."

"What is a Beau Bandito hat?" Stacey asked.

"It's not a what, silly, it's a who," Mary said.

"You mean you've never heard of Beau Bandito?" Yolinda asked, with an air of superiority.

"I'm afraid not."

"He's the most dashing thing since Robin Hood," Mary said. "He robs from the rich and gives to the poor."

"And whenever he robs a stage, he always gives presents to the women."

"And he kisses the prettiest one," Yolinda added.

Cynthia clasped her hands and assumed a look of pure rapture. "Oh, wouldn't it be heaven to be on a stage that he robbed? He's so handsome . . . and if he kissed you, he would tell you that he thought you were the most beautiful girl of all."

"I'd have to make certain I was on the stage with no other women," Mary said, teasing herself harshly. The other girls laughed.

"Nonsense," Yolinda said. "You aren't that bad. Besides, some men like plain girls."

The statement had a telling effect, as Stacey could see in Mary's eyes. But Mary recovered quickly, and only the most discerning would know that she had been hurt by the remark.

"Does this Robin Hood of the West have a name?" Stacey asked.

"Yes," Cynthia said. "His name is Clay Conway."

"Clay Conway!" Stacey cried. "You can't mean that you are all mooning over that—that murderer?"

"Oh, he doesn't kill anyone," Mary said quickly. "He just robs the stages, and then he takes only the Wells Fargo money. He never disturbs the passengers."

"Oooooh," Stacey said, seething with anger. "I can't believe that he has become such a hero!"

"You act as if you know him," Yolinda said.

"I do know him," Stacey said.

"Oh, what is he like?" Mary asked. "Is he as handsome as they say?"

"Handsome?" Stacey replied. "He is a murderer. How can a murderer be handsome?"

"But they say he shoots only in self-defense."

"He murdered my father and all my father's passengers."

"Oh, Stacey, I'm so sorry!" Mary cried. "I . . . I didn't know he was that sort of man. I won't wear the hat."

"Of course you'll wear the hat," Stacey said. "The hat doesn't mean anything. In fact, I'm quite sure he doesn't wear such a hat. At least he didn't when I knew him. I think all this other business is made up too, just like the notion of his being a hero."

"You mean he doesn't kiss the women?" Cynthia asked, disappointment coloring her voice.

"No," Stacey said, remembering the morning in the barn. "That, he probably does do."

"Stacey! Has he ever kissed you?" Mary asked, perceiving Stacey's meaning.

"I . . . I prefer not to say," Stacey replied, her face flaming in memory.

"Oh, how exciting! I'll bet he has!" Cynthia said.

"Well, from what I understand, you're but one of many," Yolinda said. "So I can understand why you'd prefer to keep it a secret."

Tobias came around the house then. "Ladies," he called. "Your carriage has arrived."

"Oh, my goodness, I had no idea it was so late,"

Yolinda said, rising. "Come, girls, we must be going."

"Stacey, you will go to the ball?" Mary asked again.

"Yes, I'll go," Stacey said.

"Oh, wonderful. It will be such fun, you'll see. And even more fun with you there."

Stacey walked with the girls to the circular drive where the carriage waited for them, its liveried driver sitting quietly on the seat. There were more goodbyes, then the girls climbed aboard and the carriage rolled away.

"So," Tobias said, after the carriage vanished around the bend. "You're to go to the Cinderella Ball."

"Yes," Stacey said. "I couldn't see any way to refuse it."

"Refuse it?" Tobias repeated, and laughed. "Honey, your aunt has been worrying herself sick for the last week, wondering if you would be invited. It's by invitation only, you know, and only the most important young ladies are asked. By being invited, you are certain to please Prissy."

Stacey laughed at her uncle's reference to her aunt by the nickname she had given her. "Yes, Uncle Toby," she said. "Aunt Prissy will be pleased."

"And you'll meet some more handsome young men there as well," Tobias said. "So you should have a good time."

"Will you be going?"

"Now that you've been invited, I suppose I will," Tobias said. "Members of the young ladies' families are of course included in the invitation."

"Then if you are there, I won't have eyes for any

of the young men. You are the most handsome man in Denver, why should I look elsewhere?"

"Stacey," Tobias laughed, "has anyone ever told you that you are an outrageous flirt?"

Chapter Thirteen

Clay walked over to the rock overhang and looked down into the valley forty-five hundred feet below. There, just coming off the valley floor and starting up the winding mountain road, was the stage. From this distance it was so tiny that it looked like a toy stage and team he had once seen in a store window.

Clay was waiting for the stage at the turn-out just below the crest. It would be a long, exhausting climb for the team and Clay knew that the driver would halt the horses at the turn-out to let the animals rest, to check the brakes before the descent down the other side, and to allow the passengers time to "stretch their legs," a gentle euphemism for walking into the woods to relieve themselves.

It was because they would be stopping that Clay chose this place to wait. It made robbing the stage much easier. That way there would be little chance for the necessity of gunplay, and less chance of anyone getting hurt. And, so far, Clay had harmed no one.

Clay knew that he had at least an hour to wait for the stage so he took some jerky from his saddlebag, unhooked the canteen, and walked over to sit against a tree, eat his lunch and read the Denver paper he had found that morning. The paper was only a week old, and he read it with great interest.

There was a story about President Garfield, who had been in office less than two months and was already embroiled in a bitter battle with Congress over the appointment of Blaine as Secretary of State. Another article discussed the decline of illiteracy. The paper boasted that in 1880 only seventeen percent of the nation was illiterate.

Then Clay saw a story which both surprised and amazed him. It was entitled "An interesting experience while riding as a stage passenger, and encountering Beau Bandito, or; held up at gun-point by the robber, Clay Conway."

Beau Bandito? Where did he ever dream up such a name, Clay thought as he began to read.

He came upon us with both guns blazing, and the reins of the horse held in his teeth. "Stand and deliver!" he shouted, in a voice that was both heroic and frightening.

Clay had to laugh at that. How could he even talk with the reins in his teeth, much less sound off in a voice that was both heroic and frightening? And he wondered if any robber had ever said, "Stand and deliver."

"It is Beau Bandito!" the driver shouted to us in the passenger compartment. His voice was laced with fear and respect, for Beau Bandito, whose real name is Clay Conway, is known throughout the West as the deadliest shot alive. It has been reliably reported that Clay Conway can shoot the leg off a fly at fifty paces.

The coach was stopped and the passengers were asked to disembark. I must confess to doing so with the greatest trepidation, though the ladies of the stage were strangely devoid of fear. Rather, they seemed taken by the handsome young man who sat astride the horse, holding the brace of pistols leveled at us, looking at us with eyes keen and calculating. He was wearing a hat with a sweeping feather, and he smiled at the ladies, setting their hearts aflutter.

"Ladies, I beg you forgive this intrusion," the bandit said, "but I intend to relieve Wells Fargo of its money, and as it is being transported on this vehicle, there was no other way than to stop the stage. You will forgive me, I trust."

With that statement, the bandit produced small gifts for the ladies: a cameo brooch for the oldest, a golden locket for the youngest, and earrings for a beautiful young lady of eighteen or so. Beau Bandito placed the earrings on the lady himself, planting a kiss upon her lips as he did so. The others gasped in surprise, and the lady in question blushed a brilliant shade of red, but said nothing. Clay Conway laughed, then took the money from the messenger guard, climbed back onto his horse, and firing both guns into the air, rode away, shouting at the top of his voice, "Beau Bandito strikes again!"

Clay laughed out loud, and wondered how anyone could write such a thing. He had never heard the term Beau Bandito, much less used it. And as for kissing one of the lady passengers . . . well, he had seen a few he would enjoy kissing, true enough. But he had certainly never done so!

There was, however, an element of truth to the article. Clay did give trinkets to the ladies, bits of glitter he'd buy from itinerant drummers. It had started as an accident, when he had given the bouquet of flowers to a young woman during his first robbery. Afterwards he reasoned that if he could keep the ladies from being too frightened, the men would be less likely to do anything rash. And the less likely they were to try something, the fewer chances of anyone getting hurt.

Clay read a while longer, then walked over to check on the approach of the stage. He guessed that it would reach its stop within another ten minutes or so. There was nothing left to read in the paper, except the page labeled *Of Special Interest to the Ladies*, so Clay turned to that page and began reading.

Plans Set for Gala Cinderella Ball

The Daughters of the Snow announced plans this week for their annual Cinderella Ball. The event is a charitable, as well as a social, occasion, and is held in the Denver Poorhouse. All funds raised by the event go to feed the poor in the city of Denver.

The ladies at the Ball all wear elegant gowns, which, at the stroke of midnight, are auctioned off to the gentlemen. The identity of the gentleman making the purchase is never known, as they are required to wear masks, and must remain disguised throughout the entire evening.

The gentleman who purchases the gown gets the privilege of a dance with the young lady, but not until the young lady has retired to the dressing room, removed her frock and emerged dressed in clothes from the "rag barrel" which serves the poor. It is from this midnight metamorphosis that the affair receives its name.

One of the honored guests at this year's event is a candidate for membership in the Daughters of the Snow. The young lady so honored is, Anastasia Pendarrow, recently arrived in this city to take up residence with her uncle and aunt, Mr. and Mrs. Tobias Prescott.

So, Clay thought, that's where she is. Clay considered the article, then heard the pop of the driver's whip and realized with a start that the stage was nearly upon him. He walked over to his horse, patted it gently, then swung into the saddle. "Are you ready, boy?" he asked. "Here it comes."

Clay rode into the trees and waited there for the stage to reach the turn-out. It arrived a moment later, the horses snorting tiredly, straining into the harness.

"Whoa, hold it up there, team," the driver shouted, pulling on the reins. The stage rumbled to a stop. "Folks," the driver called down. "We gotta let these here animals get their wind back before we start down the other side. They's a real purty view from up here, so why'n't you take a break and stretch your legs a mite?"

Four people left the stage, two men and two women. One man was obviously a farmer, and as far as Clay could tell unarmed. The other was small and mousey-looking, the type usually found keeping books in dry goods stores. Of the two women, one was an attractive female of forty or so, and the other a beautiful young girl of around eighteen. Clay imagined that the older woman was the younger one's mother, as they looked somewhat alike, and stayed together as they moved away from the stage. There was obviously no danger from any of the passengers.

Clay turned his attention to the driver and guard. The driver was not wearing a sidearm, and was near the lead horses, adjusting a loose harness. The shotgun guard had leaned his gun against the front wheel and took several steps away from it to stretch, to start the circulation back into his legs. This was the perfect opportunity for Clay to make his presence known.

"Good afternoon, ladies and gentlemen," he said, riding into the clearing. He tipped his hat, but as yet, showed no weapon.

"What the—? Who are you?" the messenger demanded. His hand started toward the shotgun.

"Don't do that," Clay said crisply.

"What?"

"Don't reach for that scatter gun," Clay said. "I would hate to have to shoot you."

"What are you talkin' about, mister? You don't even have a gun in your hand."

Clay flipped his jacket to one side, and the messenger could see the black handle of his pistol, sticking up from his holster. "No, but I have one right here," Clay said easily.

"Don't try it, Morgan; do you know who this here is?" the driver said quietly. "It's Clay Conway."

"Oh, my God, he's gonna kill us all!" the meek-looking man said.

"I've no intention of killing anyone," Clay said, "if you follow my instructions."

"What do you want?" the older woman asked.

Clay recalled the line in the article, the line he was supposed to have spoken, and he smiled. "Ladies, I beg you to forgive this intrusion, but I intend to relieve Wells Fargo of their money."

"We ain't carryin' much money," the driver said. "Probably no more'n fifty dollars."

"I'm not greedy," Clay said, still smiling. "Would you get the money for me?"

"I've got some money," the store clerk said, shaking in fear. "I'll give it to you if you spare us."

"Keep your money," Clay said. "I told you, I don't want to hurt any of you."

The driver climbed onto the coach and reached under the seat. He hesitated for a moment, then looked at Clay. A sixth sense, sometimes developed by creatures on the run, told Clay that the driver was thinking of reaching for a gun.

"Driver," Clay said coolly. "You may have less than a second to live."

The driver picked up the pouch and held it and his hands in the air.

"That's better," Clay said. "Now take the money out and hand it to the pretty young lady there."

The driver removed an envelope, and the girl

walked over to receive it. While she was doing that, Clay said, "Messenger, would you be so kind as to break open that scatter gun and throw the shells on the ground?"

The messenger did as he was told. Clay reached into his saddlebag and took out a pearl pin and a golden locket. He swung down out of the saddle and walked over to the older lady.

"Ma'am," he said politely. "The pearl in this pin brings out the beauty of your eyes. I hope you'll wear it and think of me." He pinned the pearl onto the lady's bodice, and she blinked her eyes and smiled in embarrassment and pleasure.

"And you, Miss," he said, looking toward the younger woman who still held the envelope in her hand. "Would you please bring the money to me?"

The girl did as instructed. Clay slid the envelope into his pocket, then held up a golden locket, and hooked it around her neck. Again, inspired by the newspaper article, he leaned toward her and kissed her, very lightly, on the lips. He was smiling as he pulled away from her, while she remained immobilized by pleasurable shock.

"Thank you, ladies and gentlemen, for your courtesy." Clay climbed back onto his horse and tipped his hat. "Oh, there's a paper under the tree over there, not more'n a week old. You might enjoy reading it. Goodbye, now." He turned and started away at a gallop. Then, with laughter bubbling out of him, he shouted into the wind, "Beau Bandito strikes again!"

Chapter Fourteen

Marcus Tremain was the most sought-after bachelor in Denver. He was the wealthiest young man, to be sure, but there were other things about him which appealed to the women. He was handsome in a clean, drawing-room sort of way, and though he didn't have the looks of a rugged outdoorsman, he had penetrating eyes that belonged in a bedroom and an aura of intense maleness that women sensed immediately.

"When he looks at you, it's as if he sees you without your clothes," Mary once whispered to Cynthia.

Marcus Tremain did nothing to discourage such talk. He had laughed at Tobias's reference to the bawdy house at the dinner party which introduced Stacey to society, and he didn't deny the persistent rumors that he was a frequent visitor to such establishments. His entire conversation with Stacey about the natural state of nudity during the show at the Golden Pigeon was but one more aspect of the sham with which he surrounded his life. Marcus had constructed this subterfuge in order to protect the secret of his impotence, a condition that filled him with despair, and had once nearly driven him to suicide.

Marcus was in love with Stacey, and that was a secret he guarded as carefully as the secret of his impotence. He kept his love locked away in the deepest, innermost compartment of his heart, lest Stacey see it and discover his true feelings. For he knew that if she found out, he would lose that intimacy they now shared.

Stacey had come to depend more and more upon Marcus. She didn't realize that in so doing she was causing him pain. She considered Marcus her friend, and with the sexual intrigue usually present in the relationships between most men and women absent here, she felt a complete freedom with him.

Stacey's father used to tell her that she could do anything she put her mind to. Such a philosophy had always served her well, and was once again being put to the test as she set about capturing Denver society.

It wasn't that Stacey had suddenly become socially conscious, as much as it was her natural instinct to accept a challenge. And Yolinda had clearly though indirectly issued the challenge. She had told Stacey, in effect, that Denver society was her own private preserve, and Stacey had better stay clear. Stacey had no intention of heeding Yolinda's unspoken warning.

Stacey also possessed a natural *joie de vivre* and this, too, propelled her. Escorted by Marcus, Stacey began to enjoy all the offerings of the city and she was seen often at plays, operas, and parties. Marcus made a good escort for her, because with him along she was able to flirt outrageously with all the eligible young bachelors, then retreat, coyly, back to

the protective arm of her escort, flashing a teasing smile toward her latest victim. It was in this way that she brought much pain to Marcus, though if she had known that, she would have stopped immediately. That is, she would not have halted her flirtatious behavior, but she would stop using Marcus. He realized this, and it was for this reason he didn't tell her how he felt about her. He would rather be used than ignored. His relationship with Stacey was purely emotional. It was, he realized, the most intimate relationship he could ever have with a woman.

For her part, Stacey was directed in her attitude toward men by the three great experiences of her life. She had been used and hurt by Clay Conway, brutalized by Billy Miles, and disappointed by Marcus Tremain. Men had become objects she could toy with, but never again would she expose her feelings for them.

"I swear, that Tommy Kyle is the silliest thing," Stacey said, returning to Marcus's side as they stood in the lobby between acts of the opera. Marcus handed her a light drink.

"And why is he so silly?" Marcus asked, his voice carefully controlled to show no emotion.

"He just announced to the entire crowd that he intends to buy my gown at the Cinderella Ball. Why, all the men are supposed to be masked. If he makes such a big show of it now, everyone will know who he is."

"He can make as big a show as he wishes," Marcus said, "but I intend to buy your gown."

"No, you mustn't," Stacey said.

"And why not, may I ask?"

"Marcus, I want you to buy Mary's gown."

"Mary's gown?" Marcus asked, his eyes reflecting the question. "Why?"

"I heard that last year she was the last one to sell her gown, and she sold it for the least amount of money. I want you to bid on her gown first, and Marcus, pay a lot of money for it. Promise me?"

Marcus smiled, and took Stacey's hand in his. "My dear, sometimes when I see you at these functions," he gestured with the hand which held his drink, "I'm afraid you might be succumbing to the social disease of snobbery. But then you surprise me pleasantly with something like your concern for Mary. Don't ever lose your naturalness, my love. And I promise you that I will buy Mary's dress."

"Oh, thank you," Stacey said, kissing him spontaneously on the cheek. Even as she was kissing him, she heard the mumble of disapproval from some of those standing nearest them, and when she looked at them pointedly, the women looked away. The men, however, returned her look with appreciative stares of their own.

"Act two in five minutes," one of the ushers called, and the crowd began moving back into the theater.

Marcus looked over the crowd and saw Tommy Kyle making moon eyes at Stacey, who by now had completely forgotten about him. When Kyle saw Marcus looking in his direction, he began an intent study of the playbill, trying to hide his interest in Stacey. Marcus laughed to himself. He knew Tommy Kyle was nothing but a minor diversion for Stacey and took some measure of satisfaction in knowing that Kyle, who thought he was cutting in on Marcus, was accomplishing nothing. The relationship he had with Stacey, at least helped to assuage feelings of jealously.

The ensuing days passed in a succession of morning rides, afternoon teas, and evening dinners. Among the socially active people of Denver, it seemed, the entire summer was one party after another, and Stacey commented on that to Uncle Tobias one afternoon as they sat in the drawing room.

"Perhaps that is because it is so cold in the winter that people feel they must crowd all their activities into the summer," Tobias answered. "Lucky for you, I suppose, that you arrived here when everything was going on. Are you enjoying yourself?"

"Oh, yes, very much!"

"You are spending a lot of time with Marcus Tremain."

"Marcus is my very good friend," Stacey said. "In fact, you might say he is my best friend."

"Friends? Nothing more?"

"Nothing more."

"Your aunt will be disappointed to hear that. She is already hearing the wedding bells ring."

"And you?" Stacey asked. "Are you disappointed?"

"No," Tobias said. "I'm not disappointed." He smiled. "I'll be honest with you, Stacey, girl, I can't see any of these men interesting you. They are all so . . . so . . . well, dammit, I can't think of a word to explain them, but they just don't seem to me to be man enough for you."

Now it was Stacey's turn to laugh. "I'm glad you

said that, Uncle Toby. I've noticed the same thing. And it's not just Marcus; it's everyone I've met. I don't think you could get an honest day's labor out of the lot of them."

"That's the truth," Tobias agreed. "Well, as much as I like Marcus, I have to admit that he's no different from any of the others."

"You aren't like that, Uncle Toby," Stacey said.

"No," Tobias answered, "I'm not. But my background is different. I wasn't born to this kind of life. I had to chop my way here with a double-bitted axe. I've earned everything I have by the sweat of my brow."

"Aunt Prissy doesn't appreciate that, does she?"

"What do you mean?"

"Oh, I've mentioned once or twice what a remarkable thing you've accomplished, to work your way from poverty to being one of the wealthiest men in Denver. I should think Aunt Prissy would be very proud of that, but whenever I try to talk about it, she always changes the subject."

"Your Aunt Prissy has the strange idea that new money is worth less than old money. Of course the idea isn't original with her; there are others who feel the same way and they let me know in ways that aren't too subtle. But I've got news for you, girl. New money spends as well as old and it certainly opened a lot of doors for your aunt."

"You know, Uncle Toby, blood should tell and I should side with Aunt Prissy. But, for some reason, I feel so much closer to you."

It was an honest statement, and it called for a spontaneous display of affection. Tobias held his arms open, and Stacey went to him, allowing him to squeeze her in a bear hug. She felt the muscles under his shirt, still hard despite his years, and she instinctively sensed a great virility about him. Perhaps it was that—the virility he possessed—which was missing in all the young men of her acquaintance, which caused her to lean into him, pressing her body full length against his. His strong arms about her sent an unexpected chill through her body, and she reveled in it.

Then, amazingly, she thought she felt a bulge in her uncle's pants pressing against her. Instinctively she moved into it. Then with a little gasp of exasperation, her uncle suddenly broke off the embrace and twisted away.

"Uncle Toby, is something wrong?" Stacey asked.

"No," he answered too quickly. Stacey didn't press the issue. "I . . . uh . . . have some things to do," he added, "and you'll be wanting to get ready for the Cinderella Ball tonight, so I'd better not bother you."

"Uncle Toby, you're never a bother," Stacey said earnestly.

Tobias turned to look at Stacey, and there was an expression on his face that was difficult for Stacey to comprehend. It was almost an expression of pain.

"Stacey, girl, you're young and innocent, and you don't always know what you are doing. You need to be more careful or there are some who would take advantage of you."

Now Stacey knew what he was talking about and she smiled. She was just learning to use the wiles at her disposal, and she found a great delight in seeing the effect she had on men. And even Tobias,

135

whom Stacey considered as sophisticated as anyone she had met in Denver, was not immune. It was an exhilarating experience, made even more exciting by the fact that he was her uncle.

"Why, Uncle Toby, I certainly have no need to fear *you*."

"No, of course not," Tobias said, smothering a cough. "Nevertheless, it is something you need to watch out for. If you'll excuse me now, I think I'll go get a drink."

Stacey watched Tobias pass through the door, then went to her own room and lay across the bed. Her body was fully flushed with what she knew was desire. Why, that would be incest! But no, she reasoned, he was not her uncle by blood, only by marriage.

"Oh, what is wrong with me?" she asked herself aloud. She couldn't really be thinking about having sex with Uncle Toby—it was out of the question. And yet here she was doing just that very thing.

Though Stacey had never heard the term sexual frustration, she was certainly suffering from it. First, there had been the brief but disturbing incident with Clay Conway. Then, she had been ready to give herself to Marcus, only to be disappointed in him too. Now, still unfulfilled, she found her nerves raw with unrequited desire. It was only natural that a handsome, virile man who showed an interest in her would have an effect on her. Even if that man happened to be Uncle Toby, the end result would be the same—there would still be a quickening of desire. And that desire would bring on an even greater frustration, for Stacey's mind would never let her do what her body longed for;

certainly not with her uncle. She sighed, then slowly undressed to bathe and dress for the ball. Stacey had never seen a bathroom before coming to her Aunt Pricilla's house, and now, having experienced the luxury of warm, relaxing baths, the bathroom had become her favorite room in the entire house.

Chapter Fifteen

To those few people who didn't know what was happening, the proceedings at the Denver Poorhouse were indeed strange. Rich music from a full orchestra spilled out onto the street where elegant carriages arrived in a steady stream to disgorge their occupants. There were beautiful young ladies in every carriage, girls who floated up the front steps wearing butterfly-bright dresses and golden ear bobs that sparkled and flashed beneath the black, brown, or yellow curls hanging saucily from their heads. There were young men as well, gaudily constumed and masked, and laughing self-consciously as they made sport of each other's apparel. And there were the poor, in whose name this was being done. They gathered in little groups against the walls of the room to watch the party, and their stoic faces betrayed nothing of what was going on in their minds. They were kept out of the proceedings by the presence of guards, off-duty policemen hired for the occasion.

Stacey, with her aunt and uncle, arrived just ahead of Mary Beeson and her mother and father. When she saw Stacey, Mary asked her parents' permission to go inside with her.

"Oh, Stacey, what a gorgeous gown!" Mary enthused as the two girls walked up the poorhouse steps together.

"Thank you, Mary, though mine isn't nearly as pretty as yours. You are absolutely beautiful in yellow."

"Oh," Mary said, beaming at the compliment, "do you really think so?"

"I know so," Stacey said.

"I agree," Tobias said, joining them. "If married men could bid on the gowns, I do believe I would put my own bid in on that one."

"Oh, Mr. Prescott, you're too kind," Mary said, her eyes sparkling.

The six of them climbed the steps, all but Stacey oblivious to the stares of the more curious of the poor who had gathered on the front porch to watch the arrivals. The ball, which was being held in the dining room, glowed brightly with the light from several gas-pole lanterns which had been brought in, and from borrowed candelabra, which decorated the long buffet. The table was laden with hams, chicken, fruits, breads and pastries. A neatly lettered sign explained that leftover food would be donated to the Poorhouse.

The party was already ebbing and flowing as parties do, and groups formed, merged for an instant, then exploded with bursts of laughter. From the ceiling in the middle of the room a large mirrored ball was suspended. It picked up the candleglow and the light from the gleaming gas lanterns and threw it back in pinpoints of golden light, making star patterns on the walls and on the sea of faces below it.

Stacey wrote many names, all pseudonyms, on her dance card, as one masked admirer after another approached to claim her for a dance. She strove to identify them, through their voices or some other characteristic, flirting outrageously with each. Then, as she stood on the sideline enjoying the spectacle, under the watchful eye of her aunt, another of the costumed, masked men approached her.

"I hope your dance card isn't filled yet," he said. He was wearing a white silk shirt, a long flowing white cape, a white mask and a white cavalier's hat.

"No, it isn't, I still have. . . ." Stacey stopped and stared at the man, smiling at him. "Do I know you?"

"Of course," the man replied easily.

"No," Stacey replied, "but, there is something about you, something familiar."

"It's the mask," the man said. "It makes us all look alike, though I must say that is an advantage for some of us."

"I feel you are being modest, sir," Stacey said with a laugh. "Very well, what name shall I use for you?" she asked, holding her pencil poised over her dance card.

"How about the White Knight?"

"The White Knight," Stacey said, writing the name on her card. "I'm glad you didn't say Beau Bandito."

"Beau Bandito? Who is that?"

"It is no one I care to dance with, I assure you." Stacey said resolutely. "He's a thief and murderer who has managed, somehow, to capture the imagination of all the girls here. And many of the men too, from the number of them who are calling themselves Beau Bandito tonight. You mean you haven't heard of him?"

"I'm afraid not," the man said. "I've been east for months."

Stacey wrote his name in two more slots. "Then I shall give you my remaining dances," she said, "for it will be a relief to spend time with someone who doesn't think Clay Conway is a hero."

"Clay Conway? I thought you said Beau Bandito."

"They are one and the same," Stacey said. "Clay Conway, the killer, is Beau Bandito, the 'Robin Hood of the West,'" she added, grimacing at the words Robin Hood.

"Tell me," the stranger said, "if the others find this Clay Conway such a romantic figure, why are you different?"

"I've had the misfortune to meet him," Stacey said. "He murdered my father."

"I'm very sorry to hear about your father," the man said. "Was Conway found guilty of the crime?"

"He was never tried," Stacey said. "He got away from the posse before they could bring him in."

"Then you aren't certain that he murdered your father, are you?"

"Yes, of course I'm certain," Stacey said. "There was a witness who saw everything."

"I see," the stranger said. "What does Clay Conway say?"

"He says he is innocent, of course. What would you expect him to say?"

"Then you have his word against the word of the

witness," the stranger said. "I suppose it is a question of whom you believe."

Stacey laughed, a short, bitter laugh. "There is no question. The witness is a respectable lawyer. Clay Conway has become Beau Bandito, the outlaw."

"Perhaps he had no choice," the stranger said.

"I've heard enough of Beau Bandito!" Stacey exclaimed. "The only reason I put your name on my card was to avoid talking about him—remember?"

"Ah, yes, my apologies, Miss Pendarrow." The man gave a short bow and touched the brim of his hat.

There was a drum roll and the orchestra leader turned toward the milling guests. "Ladies and gentlemen, this is our first dance of the evening. Those of you gentlemen who were lucky enough to write your names on these lovely ladies' dance cards, may claim your first partners now."

The first name on Stacey's card was Arcturus. There had been no question as to his identity, and Stacey smiled broadly as he approached her for the dance. Marcus wore formal clothes instead of a costume, and only a half mask covered his eyes but did little to conceal his identity. It was, he had told Stacey, his form of protest at the foolishness of having the men in costume.

"Remember," she whispered in his ear, "you are to bid on Mary's dress."

"I remember," he said. "And I see you remembered your astronomy lesson, otherwise you would never have recognized my cunning disguise."

"Arcturus is my favorite star, after all."

"Then I shall give it to you. The star Arcturus is yours."

143

"You are giving it to me? How can you do that?"

"Easily. No one is going to take it away, are they?"

"I guess not," Stacey said. "And I accept your gracious gift."

The dance was a waltz, and they didn't speak until it was almost over. Stacey looked at Marcus, and could read in his face the suffering he was enduring.

"Oh, Marcus," she said softly, her eyes moistening. "Oh, Marcus, if only . . . ."

"No," Marcus said abruptly. "Please, Stacey. Tonight, if just for this night, let's pretend we are like the rest of the guests. Let's not think of my problem."

"Of course," Stacey said. "And we *are* having a marvelous time."

The orchestra held the last chord for a beat longer, and the couples separated and drifted to the sidelines, as the men searched for their new dance partners. The gaiety continued.

Stacey didn't recognize her partner for the second dance; her Uncle Tobias had the third; and she didn't recognize her partner for the fourth dance, though she thought it might be Tommy Kyle. After the intermission there were three others she wasn't sure she recognized, and then the stranger who had signed her card as the White Knight stood before her to claim his dance.

"Are you having a good time?" Stacey asked.

"Now I am, yes," the man said.

"Whom have you danced with?"

"No one."

"Oh? You mean all the other cards were full?"

144

"I mean I didn't ask anyone else," the stranger said. "I came here to dance with you."

"But you have only three dances with me," Stacey said. "Surely there's no fun for you in that."

"I take my pleasure where I can find it," the man said.

He was a polished dancer, and Stacey enjoyed herself with him. When the music stopped, and he brought her to her chair, she found she was looking forward to the next dance with him. Her amber eyes skimmed across the ballroom floor while she was dancing with her next partner. Finally she saw him, leaning against the wall near the end of the buffet. He was watching her, and when their eyes met, he gave a slight wave. Stacey, embarrassed that he had caught her looking for him, blushed and quickly looked away. Finally it was time for his second dance with her.

"I'm glad you were looking for me," the stranger said.

"I wasn't looking for you," Stacey replied. "I was merely glancing around the room to see who was dancing with whom."

"Nevertheless, I'm glad," the man said. They didn't speak for the rest of that dance; they just glided to the music, lost in their own thoughts.

"Who was the fellow you were dancing with?" Marcus asked conversationally as he claimed Stacey for his next dance.

"I don't know," she said. "I haven't been able to figure it out. He gave his name as the White Knight."

Marcus chuckled. "I think a dance like this brings out the little boy in every man. They can

145

dress up in costumes and take on elaborate names. It's really very amusing. The White Knight, you say? I wonder who he is."

"I don't think he is anyone you know," Stacey said.

"Oh? What makes you say that?"

What *did* make her say that? Stacey wondered. Then, with a start, she realized why. Because the stranger had something neither Marcus nor his friends possessed. The stranger, like her uncle, had a great animal magnetism which even the costume could not disguise.

The stranger had his last dance with her before the bidding began. As that dance concluded and just before the stranger took his leave, he whispered, "I shall have the next dance with you as well."

"Perhaps you will," Stacey said. "Though others have told me the same thing. We shall just have to wait and see, won't we?"

There was a loud drum roll, then a buzz of excitement, and finally a hush, as the grand event of the evening began.

"Ladies and gentlemen," a distinguished looking, unmasked man said. "It is my pleasure to present Congressman Jordan Jaynes, who will conduct the auction."

There was a round of applause, and Congressman Jaynes, who was also without a mask, held his hands out to the audience, thanking them.

"This is indeed an honor and a pleasure," he said. "And I am tempted to take this opportunity to make a speech."

146

There was a barely perceptible groan from the crowd.

"But I won't," he added, laughing. "Instead, I'll get right to the bidding."

This time the applause was spontaneous and loud, and everyone waited to see who would go first. Yolinda Sinclair had claimed the honor for the last two years, but most of the guests were saying that Stacey Pendarrow would receive that distinction this year.

"Now, who will open the bidding?" Congressman Jaynes asked.

"I will bid two hundred dollars for Miss Mary Beeson," a voice said.

A gasp of surprise rolled through the room. One hundred dollars was the most that had ever been bid, and for such a bid to be made for Mary Beeson was more than a surprise—it was a shock. When the guests recognized Marcus Tremain as the bidder, they were even more shocked.

"Did you say two hundred dollars, sir?" Congressman Jaynes asked, in a voice strained with incredulity.

"I did say that, sir," Marcus said again. "And that bid is for Miss Mary Beeson."

"Do I hear any other bids?" Congressman Jaynes asked.

There were no other bids, and Marcus Tremain paid two hundred dollars to the Congressman, while Mary hurried happily off to change into the old clothes.

Stacey was the next girl bid for, and the stranger with the white cape and white hat, true to his word, and as Stacey had hoped, won the bid with one hundred and seventy-five dollars.

The high bids seemed to establish a precedent because Yolinda, who was next, went for the same price, and the girl who followed Yolinda brought over a hundred dollars.

By the time Stacey returned to the floor, dressed in pants and a shirt she had found in the barrel, and infinitely more comfortable in that attire than she had been in her gown, the last of the girls had been auctioned off, and those bids which normally would have been around fifteen or twenty dollars were between fifty and seventy-five dollars. All around her, she could hear the enthusiastic response over the amount of money that had been raised.

"So," Stacey said, as the stranger approached her. "You've come to claim your final dance."

"Yes." He looked at Stacey. "I must say, you look at home in those clothes."

"I should," Stacey said. "This is the type of clothes I wore all my life."

"I know. The last time I saw you, you were dressed that way."

"What?" Stacey gasped. "Who . . . who are you?" A sick feeling began creeping into her stomach as she suddenly realized who the stranger was.

The stranger removed his mask, and Stacey found herself staring into the cool blue eyes of Clay Conway.

"Stacey, I swear to you, I didn't kill your father," Clay said. "You must believe that."

"You . . . you dare to come here?" Stacey asked in a small voice.

Clay stepped up to her and put his arms around her. He kissed her deeply, and for just a second, Stacey remembered the fevered kiss in the barn in the early morning rain. Her head spun with dizzying excitement; then she realized where she was and who was kissing her.

The kiss didn't go unnoticed by the others, and the laughter and the conversation fell into shocked silence as everyone stared at the scene unfolding before them. Finally, Stacey put both her hands on his shoulders, and managed to push him away from her.

"Murderer!" she shouted. "How dare you come here? How dare you kiss me! Listen to me, everyone, do you know who this is? This is Clay Conway, the murderer! Somebody shoot him! Please, anybody, if you have a gun, shoot this murderer for the mad dog he is!"

"Stacey, please!" Clay said, holding his hand toward her. "I didn't do what you think I did. I'm innocent!"

"Of course you are," Stacey said sarcastically. "And you haven't been robbing stagecoaches either."

"I don't deny that, Stacey. But I'm innocent of any wrongdoing toward your father."

"Shoot him!" Stacey shouted. "There's a reward out for him. Shoot him, and give the money to charity!"

Seemingly from nowhere, a gun appeared in Clay's hand. The women screamed, and the men began backing away, so that as Clay eased out of the room, a path opened up for him.

"I hope none of you are foolish enough to take

149

the lady up on her suggestion," he said. "She is upset."

"Upset?" Stacey shouted. "I am furious! You killed my father, Clay Conway, and I want to see you dead!"

Stacey ran to one of the police officers who had been hired to guard the proceedings. The officer was terrified at the possibility that Clay would recognize him as a policeman and shoot him. Before he could react, Stacey grabbed his gun.

"Stacey, you put that down," Clay said, holding his hand out toward her. "You could hurt someone."

"Hurt someone? I want to kill you!" she shouted. She held the gun up with both hands and pulled the trigger. There was a deafening roar and the heavy bullet crashed through a window just behind Clay.

Clay threw her a kiss, laughed, turned and dashed through the front door, just as Stacey fired a second time. By the time the smoke of her two shots had rolled away, Clay was gone, dashing down the street on the horse he had tied to a nearby tree. Stacey dropped the gun, then hung her head and wept. She knew that she had made a scene and that everyone was looking at her. But she wasn't crying about that. She was crying because she had tried to shoot Clay Conway, and she had missed.

Chapter Sixteen

Obviously such a dramatic and sensational ending to the Cinderella Ball wouldn't go unnoticed, and many newspapers carried the story. Tobias, with a few well-placed dollars, managed to get the editorial tone of the stories slanted favorably toward Stacey. One reporter called her a "heroine, and true daughter of the West, who exhibited enough courage and quick wit to attempt the capture of Clay Conway, one of the most dangerous outlaws in the country."

Stacey may have been a heroine to the average person, but to the young ladies who were influenced by Yolinda Sinclair, she had committed the social blunder of the season. Mary Beeson remained loyal, of course, as did Marcus Tremain. But the expected invitation to join the Daughters of the Snow never materialized, though Pricilla haunted the mailbox and hounded the servants to make sure that the note hadn't merely been misplaced.

When it became obvious that Stacey was not going to be invited to join the sorority Pricilla retired to her room and refused to be seen in public for almost three weeks. She was trying to steel herself, she said, to withstand the barrage of pity her friends were going to heap on her for having the unfortunate luck to have a niece who was the talk of every barroom and saloon in Denver.

Tobias, on the other hand, seemed to take pride in Stacey's action, and didn't mind talking about it at all. He admired her spunk, and told everyone that she was "cut from good timber" and that more women should be like her.

Marcus too, seemed to appreciate Stacey more, so that if her social standing with the young ladies of Denver was strained, her relationship with Marcus was not, and they continued to be seen togather. Marcus even joked, in his self-deprecating way, that he wasn't frightened to go anywhere, as long as he had her to protect him.

Finally, Pricilla hit upon what she hoped would be the solution to the problem. Stacey's eighteenth birthday was approaching, and Pricilla decided to give her a birthday party which would magically restore the young lady to the good graces of the "better people." She set about making plans for the gala event. Naturally, every member of the Daughters of the Snow was invited, each by a hand-delivered, engraved invitation. It was, Pricilla hoped, a bold stroke, whereby one greatly successful party would propel her niece back into the thick of things.

Stacey would as soon not have had the party, but Pricilla became obsessed with it, and spent all her waking hours making plans. The party was to be arranged by a caterer from San Francisco who had once organized a party for visiting royalty, and he and his staff would arrive by train the day before the big event.

Finally the day itself arrived, and Pricilla knocked on Stacey's door at the crack of dawn, imploring her to "get up and get busy. Nothing must go wrong today, do you hear me? Nothing!"

"I promise, Aunt Pricilla, I won't even be armed tonight," Stacey replied.

"I do *not* think that funny, young lady!" Pricilla shrilled. "Now hurry, we have work to do."

Pricilla made Stacey work all day, polishing silverware which had already been polished, selecting perfect tapers for the candlelabra, and going over the menu with the caterers. Finally, late in the afternoon, a delivery carriage arrived from Madame Gagneau's, the most exclusive dress shop in the city. The delivery man held three boxes, each containing a dress.

"Aunt Pricilla, what is this?" Stacey asked, looking at her aunt.

"I brought those three dresses on approval," Pricilla said, smiling. "I'm going to let you choose the one you wish to wear tonight."

"Why, thank you, Aunt Priss . . . Pricilla," Stacey said. She laid the three boxes on the drawing room sofa but didn't open them. "Which one do *you* think I should wear?"

"I leave that choice up to you, my dear," Pricilla said. "It is my hope that you select wisely, for this may be your last chance."

"I'll take them to my room," Stacey said, "and make the selection after my bath."

"Remember, dear, choose wisely," Pricilla cautioned again.

*　*　*

Later that evening, Stacey stepped from the tub, pink and glowing, her skin softened by scented bath oils. She walked back to her bedroom wrapped only in a large towel. As she hurried down the hall a scent of lilacs lingered on the air.

Once inside her room she unwrapped the towel and draped it across the chair, then walked nude toward her bed. She caught her reflection in the mirror and stopped for a moment to appraise it.

So, she thought, this is the body of a woman. It's funny, but it looks exactly like the body I had yesterday when I was a seventeen-year-old girl.

She laughed and took a silken robe from a hook, then wrapped it about her, restoring some modesty to the scene.

Stacey had put the three dresses out on her bed, and now she looked at them. One was white and demure; another, blue and elegant; and a third, red and daring. She studied them closely, her finger pressed to her cheek and her amber eyes taking in each detail.

There was a knock at the door.

"Come in," Stacey called.

The door opened and Tobias came in. His silver hair shone luxuriously in the soft light of the gas chandelier.

"Oh, Uncle Toby," Stacey said in surprise. "I thought it was Aunt Prissy again."

"Prissy," Tobias said, using the nickname with a smile, "is still seeing to the preparations for the party."

"Has she done anything else for the last week?" Stacey answered.

"Are you disappointed that it's only me?" Tobias asked.

"Disappointed? No, of course not," Stacey said. "Perhaps you can help me with a difficult problem."

Tobias smiled. "Now, what problem could be difficult for any girl on her eighteenth birthday?"

"This," Stacey said, pointing to the bed and to the three dresses. "I can't make up my mind which one I want to wear."

"Well, now, that *is* difficult," Tobias agreed with a smile.

Stacey leaned over to pick one up, and as she did so, the neck of her robe fell forward slightly, affording Tobias a short, pirated glance at her breasts, two delightfully curved mounds of flesh tipped by tightly drawn nipples. For Tobias the impact was the same as if he had suddenly jumped from a great height and he gasped quickly to recapture his breath.

Stacey heard him gasp, and realized at once what had happened. A quick heat flared inside her, flashing through her body like summer lightening. She felt the same sensation she had felt on the day of the Cinderella Ball when Tobias had hugged her and she had sensed that his interest in her wasn't only that of a loving uncle. There was an unbridled excitement in the prospect of facing a situation pregnant with peril, yet knowing that she was in complete control.

And Stacey was in control. She had practiced this game many times now, with many of Marcus's friends. She knew what it was like to cause a man's blood to run hot, to lead him a merry chase, and then in the very teeth of danger to step cleanly away. Of course, before she had Marcus as a shield. Now, she had no one, but she wasn't afraid. It was doubly exciting to her, not only for the risk it represented, but also because it released passions and desires in her own body which, though she had yet to satisfy them, were none the less pleasurable in the exquisite tortue of self-denial.

Stacey picked up the white dress and held it against her. "Aunt Prissy would no doubt prefer this dress," she said. "It proclaims purity," she added. She picked up the blue dress. "Or this one, reeking with regality. But you, Uncle, would much prefer *this* dress, I'm certain. It's scarlet and scandalous."

Tobias laughed. "And you, my dear—are you scarlet and scandalous?"

"Very scarlet, and very scandalous," Stacey replied, smiling slyly. She began untying the belt which held her robe together. She timed the action perfectly, so that she stepped behind a dressing screen just at the instant her modesty would have been compromised. She passed the robe across the screen, handing it to Tobias, and at the same time displaying bare shoulders.

"Perhaps you would hand me the dress *you* prefer," she said, looking over the top of the screen. "After all, I can't come from behind the screen now until I'm dressed."

Tobias walked over to the bed and looked at the three dresses. With but a second's hesitation, he pointed at the red one, hearing Stacey chuckle as he did so.

156

"Why, Uncle, I knew you wouldn't disappoint me," Stacey said.

Tobias looked back toward the screen, then saw something Stacey hadn't realized. He discovered that Stacey's nude form was completely visible in the mirror behind her. He stared pointedly at the reflected beauty.

Stacey saw her uncle's look, then gasped as she realized she had miscalculated. At that moment her control of the situation slipped away with dizzying suddenness. She tried to make a grab for the robe Tobias had cast aside, but as she did so, she accidently upset the screen, so that now she stood, fully nude, before her uncle's burning gaze.

"Please," she said in a small voice, "look away."

Tobias was upon her within three quick steps. He stood before her, looking at her through lust-inflamed eyes. He was so close now that Stacey could feel his breath on her face and smell the tangy aroma of the brandy he had drunk earlier.

"Uncle Toby . . . Tobias, please, I must get dressed now," Stacey said in a soft, frightened voice.

"I'm sorry, Stacey," Tobias said, "but it isn't that simple."

Stacey made an ineffectual effort to cover herself with her arms, but Tobias pushed them away, then put his hands on her flesh and pulled her against him. Stacey jumped involuntarily, shocked at the unplanned turn of events.

"No," she said. "I didn't mean it to go this far, I only wanted to. . . ." but her entreaty was interrupted by his kiss.

Stacey pushed against him, trying to work free

from his grasp. But her uncle was too strong for her, and her struggles were in vain. She was aware of Tobias's hands kneading and squeezing her derrière. Excitement and wantonness began racing through her body, overcoming even the fear and guilt she felt. Tobias's mouth pressed more tightly against hers, bringing a slight though pleasant pain, and she opened her mouth to his.

With a hunger and brazenness that surprised her, she allowed her hands to stop fighting, and began to explore the body pressed against her. With a dizzying sense of excitement she felt the hardened bulge in front of his trousers.

"A happy birthday kiss, I presume?" Aunt Pricilla's icy voice said, cutting through the room with the sharpness of a dagger.

Chapter Seventeen

"I shall shut the door now, Tobias," Pricilla said quietly. "When you have finished your business with this woman, please pay her as you would any other whore, and send her on her way. I will arrange for train tickets and transportation to the railroad station. She can be on her way tonight."

"Pricilla, I . . . ." Tobias started, but Pricilla closed the door on his statement, and Stacey could hear her heels click as she walked quickly down the hall toward her own room. "Oh, my God," Tobias said, pressing his fist into his forehead. "Oh, my God, what have I done?"

Tobias, the strong, virile man of action, the man who had indulged Stacey's spoofs of her "Aunt Prissy's" prissiness, was now ashen-faced and weak. He walked away from Stacey, keeping his eyes averted to avoid looking at her nudity, then picked up her robe from the floor. He tossed it back to her.

"Put this on," he commanded, still not looking at her.

Aunt Pricilla had a right to be upset, and Stacey felt guilty over having hurt her mother's sister. After all, despite the teasing and the sharp words which had passed between them in the past, Pricilla had only been doing what she thought was right for Stacey. Stacey could easily understand her aunt's actions. But she was clearly surprised by her uncle's reaction.

"Uncle Tobias," Stacey said as she restored her modesty by tying the robe tightly around her. "You love Aunt Pricilla, don't you? You really love her."

"Yes," Tobias said. "Why is that so surprising?"

"It's just that I thought . . . I mean, you are so different . . . it never occured to me that you could actually love her."

"I love her more than life itself," Tobias said. "She is the personification of all womanhood to me. She represents all I have ever worked for."

"But you . . . the way you act sometimes . . ."

"My act is all a sham, Stacey," Tobias said. "I am afraid to let her know how much I really do love her, for fear I will frighten her with the responsibility of it. But what's the use of talking about it now? I've ruined everything. I've hurt her more than she'll ever be able to bear. And with her own niece."

Tobias walked over to Stacey's bed and sat down, resting his forehead on his fist and his elbows on his knees. He was the picture of remorse, anguish, and he was unable, or unwilling to talk to Stacey any further. Finally she realized that there was only one thing she could do, so she took a deep breath and left her room to do it.

Stacey knocked on Pricilla's bedroom door but there was no answer. She knocked again, and called out, but still no one answered. She pushed it, found that it was open, and stepped inside.

Pricilla was sitting at her dresser holding a handkerchief to her eyes. When she saw Stacey she turned away from her.

"What is it?" she asked in a choked voice. "What do you want now?"

"Aunt Pricilla, I'm sorry," Stacey said.

"You're sorry?" Pricilla answered. "You come in here and tell me you are sorry, and that's going to make everything better, as if you had merely spilled a glass of milk at the table?"

"No," Stacey said. "I know it won't make everything better. But I wanted to say it anyway."

"Well, you've said it. Now, if you don't mind, I'd like to be alone."

"Aunt Pricilla, wait," Stacey said. "I want to talk to you."

"There is nothing to say," Pricilla said. "What I saw seemed perfectly clear to me. Tobias and you were . . . were about to . . . ."

"No," Stacey said, "not Tobias."

"What do you mean, not Tobias? I saw him kissing you with my own eyes. And you were totally naked!"

"But he wasn't," Stacey said easily. "Or didn't you notice?"

"Notice what? What are you talking about?"

"Aunt Pricilla, didn't you notice that Uncle Tobias was fully clothed?"

"So what if he was? You certainly weren't."

"That's just the point," Stacey said. "Don't you see, Aunt Pricilla? I tricked Uncle Tobias—he was totally innocent of any wrongdoing. It was all my fault."

"I don't believe you," Pricilla said, and turned away.

Stacey sighed. "It's true. He knocked on the door to see if I was ready. I asked him in to help me choose a dress, and while he was looking at the dress I took off my robe. When he turned around I kissed him, and that's when you walked in."

Pricilla turned back to look at Stacey. There was a flicker of hope that what the girl said was true, for that would mean that she had not been betrayed by Tobias. But there was also hurt that Stacey could do such a thing to her. Finally she put her confusion into words.

"But why, Anastasia?" Pricilla asked. "Assuming that what you say is true . . . why would you do such a thing? *How* could you do such a thing?"

"I don't really know," Stacey said. "I guess I was just playing a game."

"A game? You call that playing a game!" Pricilla gasped.

"I can't explain," Stacey said. "It's just that I wanted to see if I could . . . well, make him want me."

"Of course you could," Pricilla said. "Child, don't you realized how dangerous that is? Any nude woman can make any man want her. It is in the nature of things. God gave men this . . . this terrible affliction, and it takes all their will power to keep it under control. To think that you would come along and do something like this on purpose! It is unspeakable!"

With a sad smile, Stacey thought of Marcus Tremain, and the tragi-comic aspects of such reasoning, but she said nothing. Instead, she nodded in agreement, for it strengthened her argument now to have her aunt believe such a thing.

"Then you can see that it wasn't Uncle Tobias's fault," Stacey said. "In fact, he is so upset over what you saw, and what you must be thinking, that I can't even talk to him. He loves you, Aunt Pricilla. He loves you more than you will ever know."

Pricilla dabbed her eyes with a handkerchief. Finally, she put her hand out and squeezed Stacey's hand quickly, then let go.

"It took a lot of courage for you to tell me this, child," she said, "and I respect you for that. But I don't know if I can forgive you . . . Perhaps in time I can. I know I can never forget it, though. And that will always be between us."

"I'll leave tonight," Stacey offered.

"No, I withdraw what I said when I was in your room. You are welcome to stay here. I'll not mention this incident again."

"Aunt Pricilla, I'm eighteen now. The court decree stipulated that I had to have a guardian only until I reached my eighteenth birthday. I think it would be best for all of us if I left."

"But where will you go? What will you do?"

"I'll go back to MacAllister," Stacey said. "I have a lot of friends there. I can get a job. I'll get by nicely."

"But what about the party tonight? The guests will be here any minute!"

"Make an excuse—tell them I'm ill—anything—and have the party anyway. After all, it *is* my birthday."

"I . . . I don't know," Pricilla said.

"Aunt Pricilla, it's the only way," Stacey insisted. "As long as I'm here, you will be reminded of this night. The wound will never heal."

163

"Very well," Pricilla sighed. "Perhaps you're right. I'll not stand in your way."

"Thank you," Stacey said. She turned to leave, then stopped in the doorway and looked back at her aunt. She felt a wave of remorse overtake her as she saw her aunt wiping at the tears she had caused.

"Goodbye, Aunt Priscilla," she said softly. "I hope someday soon you will forgive me."

Stacey hurried down the hall to return to her room before Pricilla could respond. When she stepped inside the door she saw that Tobias was still there, sitting on the edge of her bed.

"Where did you go?" Tobias asked.

"I went to speak with Aunt Pricilla," Stacey said. "I told her it was all my fault. I told her I tricked you."

"What? Stacey, that isn't true," Tobias protested. "I was as much at fault as you were. More so really, for you were only playing a game and I called your hand."

"It doesn't matter," Stacey said. "The thing is, Aunt Pricilla now believes that it was my fault."

"Well, I'll set her straight at once," Tobias said, rising and starting for the door.

"Toby, no, wait!" Stacey called. Somehow, calling him "Uncle" seemed inappropriate now. "Why would you do anything so foolish?"

"Because it isn't right for her to place all the blame on you."

"Listen to me," Stacey explained. "I am leaving here tonight. You are going to remain behind. Who better to accept the blame than someone who won't be around?"

Tobias hesitated at the door, and it was apparent to Stacey that he, too, had seen the obvious.

"What did she say?" Tobias asked finally.

"She offered to let me stay here."

"Good. Then you will stay here, and soon everything will be back to normal."

"No," Stacey said. "As long as I'm here, things will never be normal. You do love her, don't you, Toby? You weren't just telling me that?"

"Yes, I do love her."

"Then don't lose this chance to make things up to her. Believe me, my leaving is no sacrifice. I didn't want to come here in the first place, if you remember."

"I remember," Tobias said. "Where will you go?"

"Back to MacAllister."

"Do you have any plans?"

"Yes," Stacey said. "But I didn't tell Aunt Pricilla what my plans were."

"What are they?"

"I'm going to work for Wells Fargo," Stacey said. "My father worked for them for years, and was killed while driving one of their stages. They owe me that much."

"Well, if that's what you want, girl, I wish you luck," Tobias said. He reached into his back pocket and brought out his billfold. "This was to be your birthday present," he said. "I thought you would be using it on frivolous things. Now I guess it is going to take on more importance for you."

"What is it?"

"It's five hundred dollars, Stacey," Tobias said. "From your *aunt*. . . ." Tobias set the words off in view of what had just happened, "and me."

"Oh, Uncle Tobias, thank you," Stacey said, putting the "uncle" back before his name. She took the money. "This will keep me going for months. It's just what I need until I can get on with Wells Fargo."

"Stacey, child, can you ever forgive me?" Tobias asked.

"Forgive you? Forgive you for what?"

Tobias smiled. "For allowing you to take the brunt of this."

Stacey returned his smile. "Toby, there may have been more truth in my confession to Aunt Pricilla than even you realize."

Chapter Eighteen

The Wells Fargo stage that made the run from Medford to MacAllister was right on time as it left the rest stop at the top of Eagle Mountain. MacAllister, the coach's destination, was located in a valley at the base of Eagle Mountain. There was only one road leading into the town, and it came over the mountain through Eagle Pass, six thousand feet above sea level and three thousand feet above the town. Thus it was said by the stage drivers that they didn't drive into MacAllister, they descended into it. The illusion was further heightened by the fact that MacAllister became visible as soon as the stage crested the pass, and remained visible, like a toy village in a toy valley, as the stage wound its way down from the clouds which clung to the top of the mountain.

Stacey was a passenger in the coach, and as she rode she peered through the window at the tiny town below, wondering how she could ever have thought it big or exciting. The entire town could be placed into three blocks of Denver's business district.

As she thought of Denver she looked down at her hands, folded in her lap, and felt her cheeks flush in shame over the hurt she had caused her aunt. Neither Pricilla nor Tobias had come to the depot to see her off and for that she was grateful. It was difficult enough with Marcus, who came to the station with her despite her protests.

Stacey didn't lie to Marcus and was gratified to discover that Marcus made no judgment of her actions. In fact, Marcus tried to accept the blame, claiming that his "peculiar affliction" had driven Stacey into the arms of her uncle. Stacey dismissed the idea as ridiculous, and spent the time waiting for the train trying to talk Marcus out of his depression. Then, when she finally boarded the train and settled into a seat, she discovered what a relief it was to be alone at last. It seemed to her that for the past several hours she had borne the weight of Pricilla's hurt, Toby's remorse and Marcus's despair. And Stacey, who had a heavy emotional investment in the problems of all three, had no one to shed a tear for her.

The train ride to Medford had given Stacey enough time to sort things out in her own mind, and now, riding the stage from Medford to MacAllister, she was ready to pick up the reins of a new life.

Stacey glanced back inside at her fellow passengers. Sitting next to her was a woman perhaps five years older than she, travelling with her six-year-old son. The woman was pretty and friendly, but quiet, and Stacey was grateful for that as she was not in a talkative mood. The boy was very active, as all six-year-old boys are on long trips, and continually changed seats from one side of the coach to the other. Directly across from Stacey sat a fat, red-

168

faced man who held a handkerchief with which he constantly wiped at the sweat which dampened his forehead. He wore a suit and vest, and carried a watch in his vest pocket secured by a gold chain. He took the watch out several times, opened it, then snapped the case shut, as if calling attention to his fine timepiece.

He had just finished checking the watch for perhaps the fifth time, when he cleared his throat.

"We're right on schedule, I see," he said.

No one answered his comment.

"You see that little town down there, lady?" he asked, pointing through the window at MacAllister.

His question was directed to Stacey, and she had no choice but to answer him. She tried to discourage him by using a one word answer."Yes."

"It's called MacAllister," the man, who was a travelling salesman, or "drummer," said. "It's about the widest open, wildest town I've ever seen."

No answer.

"And believe me," the drummer went on, undiscouraged, "I've seen a few wild towns in my days. Fact is, I've tamed a few, back in the days when I was a lawman."

"You were a lawman?" the wide-eyed boy asked.

"That I was, lad," the drummer answered, appreciative that someone, even a child, had shown an interest. "And I know wild towns when I see 'em. Why this town here is so bad that a single lady— you are a single lady, aren't you, ma'am?" he asked Stacey, then went on without waiting for an answer, "—a single lady can't even go out for dinner unescorted, without runnin' the chance of getting molested. That bein' the case, ma'am, I'd be glad to take you to dinner tonight."

"Thank you for your concern, sir," Stacey replied coolly, "but I would prefer to dine alone."

"Have it your way," the drummer said, wiping the sweat from his forehead. "Far be it from me to try 'n influence you in any way. But I was talkin' to Clay about it just the other day. Clay, that is, Clay Conway, you've heard of him, haven't you, ma'am? He's called Beau Bandito by some."

"Yes, I've heard of him."

"Clay Conway is one of my best friends. Anyway, he told me that one of these days he wanted me and him to get together and clean out some of the riff-raff in MacAllister that's botherin' the ladies now."

"You said you was a lawman," the boy said. "Why didn't you arrest Clay Conway when you saw him?"

"Because, I told you, he is my friend. And I'm not a lawman anymore."

"Clay Conway is the fastest man with a gun that ever lived," the boy suggested knowingly. "That's why you didn't arrest him."

"That's almost the truth, son," the drummer said. He leaned back and hooked his thumbs into his vest. "But the fact is, I gave him his first shootin' lesson. I've often wondered since then if I did the right thing, seein' as what Clay has become."

"You mean you taught Clay Conway how to shoot?" the boy asked excitedly.

"That I did." the drummer said. He glanced toward Stacey to see how she took this bit of news but she was once again looking out the window, seemingly paying no attention to the drummer's braggadocio.

"Boy! If you taught him how to shoot, you must be even faster!"

The drummer chuckled. "I wouldn't say I was faster," he said. "Clay caught on real good. In some ways I'd say he's as good as, or maybe even faster, than me. I'd hate to see what would happen if we ever had to face one another down."

"Oh, wow! Would I like to see that!" the boy exclaimed.

"Richard, that's quite enough now," his mother said, addressing him sharply. "Leave the man alone."

"Oh, Ma, I want to hear all about it," Richard protested.

"It's all right, ma'am," the drummer said, beaming under the boy's admiration. "I don't mind telling him the story."

"I'm sure you don't," the boy's mother said.

Stacey swallowed a laugh by forcing a cough.

"The truth is, son, before I was a lawman, why I'm 'shamed to say I followed a life of crime. I was a gunfighter, but I give that up. You see, that's no life for a man, and I don't want you studyin' on goin' into it. I'm in an honest line of work now. I sell pots and pans. It's a lot more rewardin' than killin'."

"How many men did you kill?" Richard asked.

"I guess eight or nine," the drummer said. He flipped his jacket back and patted the handle of his gun. "I used to have the handle notched, but it just invited the young gunfighters who were trying to make a name for themselves to try me out, so I took that handle off and put a new one on."

"What about Clay Conway? How many men has he killed?"

"Probably ten or eleven by now," the drummer said. "Though I can tell you that every one of 'em needed killing. Clay's not the sort to kill for the fun of it."

Stacey bit her lip to keep from speaking out at that last statement. It was obvious to her that the drummer was spreading tall tales, and equally as obvious that no one but the boy believed him, so she had no intention of dignifying it by discussing Clay Conway with him.

"I wish Clay Conway would hold up this stagecoach," the boy said. "I'd like to see that."

"Oh, I don't think he would do that," the drummer replied. "If he saw me he'd have to back off."

"Why?" the boy asked.

"Because I'd have to protect this stage, and you and the two ladies. That means Clay Conway and I would have to go up against each other. It would be friend against friend. And I don't know who would win. No, sir, I don't think there is any danger of Clay Conway hitting this stage."

As the drummer spoke the last word a shot rang out and there was a sharp exclamation of pain from the driver. The driver shouted at the team, and the stage came to a halt. "Don't spook the team, mister!" the driver said in a pained voice. "I've got women 'n kids inside, 'n I'm hit bad. I couldn't stop a runaway."

"Maybe you people inside better come on out here then," a gruff voice said.

"It's a holdup!" the boy exclaimed excitedly, and he opened the door and jumped out before his mother could grab him.

"Richard, come back here!" she called sharply, following him outside.

Stacey and the drummer followed them outside, and Stacey saw the bandit. He was wearing a long, flowing cape of the type Clay had worn on the night he crashed the Cinderella Ball, and a hat with a big feather. His head was covered with a flour sack so that his features weren't visible. Stacey looked up at the driver and saw that he was holding his chest. Bright red blood was spilling across his fingers.

"You'd better watch out," Richard told the bandit. "You know who this man is?" He pointed to the drummer.

"Richard, that's quite enough!" his mother said.

"Yes," the drummer hissed to the boy. "Don't say anything else."

"Well now, is everyone out?"

"Yes," Stacey said quietly.

"Hey, ain't you the pretty one, though?" the bandit said to Stacey.

"Allow me to introduce myself, ladies. I am the Beau Bandito."

"Then you must know who this man is," Richard said again.

"Why do you keep sayin' that, son? Who the hell is he?"

"He's the man who taught you how to shoot," Richard shouted. The drummer eased his way around behind Stacey and the boy's mother.

"Taught me how to shoot, huh?" the bandit said,

laughing. He holstered his pistol. "Well, then why don't you get out from behind those women's skirts and see if I learned my lesson well?"

The drummer didn't move.

"Come on," Richard urged. "Show him. You can beat him."

"How about it, teacher?" the bandit taunted, opening and closing his fingers just over the handle of his gun. "You wanna give me a test?"

"No, no!" the drummer shouted, ducking behind the two women. His voice climbed to a falsetto in his fear.

The bandit laughed again, a heavy, mocking laugh. "Don't worry. I'm not gonna kill you. I only kill men. You and the other ladies, I'll give presents to." The bandit reached into his saddlebag and took out three lockets. He tossed them casually toward the group of passengers, then laughed. "Here. Here are three presents for you three ladies."

The lockets lay on the ground.

"Pick 'em up, drummer," the bandit ordered.

The drummer recovered the lockets, gave one each to the two women, and slipped the third into his vest pocket.

"That's better. Now climb up on the driver's seat and get the money pouch and hand it over to me."

The drummer climbed up to get the pouch as directed, then he handed it over to the bandit, and the bandit hooked it on the pommel of his saddle. He slapped his legs against his mount and started off at a gallop. "Beau Bandito strikes again!" he called out.

As soon as the bandit was gone, Stacey climbed onto the driver's seat to look at the driver. His face was white and his lips were purple, and he was gasping for breath.

"I'm hit bad," the driver said. "I dassn't try and drive us into MacAllister. If I pass out, the stage could go over the side. Everyone would be killed," he gasped.

"My God," the drummer said. "What are we going to do?"

"We've got to get him inside," Stacey said. "Help me get him down."

"But who's going to drive us into town?" the drummer asked again. "We can't stay out here forever."

"I'll drive us into town," Stacey said easily.

"What? *You* are going to drive this stage? You heard what the driver said. If we go over the side, we'll all be killed."

"Then I'll try not to go over the side," Stacey said. "Now help me get the driver down."

Stacey, the boy's mother and the drummer managed to get the driver down from the seat and lay him across the coach seat.

"Dan, it's me," Stacey said to the driver. "Stacey Pendarrow."

"Stacey?" the driver said, coughing up specks of blood. "I didn't recognize you when you boarded the stage, girl. You've changed."

"I may look different," Stacey said, "but I'm as good a driver as I always was. I'll take us into town."

"Watch old Ben," the driver warned. "He tries to have his way, and you've got to hold him back going down the grade here."

"Which one is Ben?"

"He's the lead horse on the left," the driver said. He started coughing again.

Stacey looked at the other woman. "Stop the bleeding in his chest," she ordered. "And do what you can to make him comfortable."

"All right," the woman said. "Are you really going to drive this coach?" she asked anxiously.

"I thought I might give it a try," Stacey said.

"I'm not so sure it's a good idea," the drummer announced. "Maybe I'd better try!"

Stacey looked at the driver. "You make the decision, Dan," she said. "Which one of us would you rather have drive?"

"There's no decision to make," Dan said. "You drive." He coughed again from the exertion of talking.

"I'm not riding with any woman driver," the drummer said.

"Suit yourself," Stacey replied as she started up to the driver's seat. "Wait around out here if you want. I'll send someone back for you."

The drummer thought for a second, then crawled inside. "All right," he said. "I'll come along. But only because you may need some help."

"Let us hope not," the boy's mother said.

"You didn't even try to draw on him," the boy suddenly accused. He had been staring at the drummer the whole time, and was obviously hurt to see his idol's image shatter so abruptly.

"What could I do?" the drummer replied. "He had the drop on me."

"He put his gun away," the boy protested. "He gave you a chance to go for it.

"It's an old trick," the drummer said. "He had

someone hiding in the trees who had the drop on me. The moment I went for my gun, his confederate would have shot me down."

"I didn't see anyone in the trees," the boy challenged.

"That doesn't mean a thing," the drummer said. "I know Clay Conway."

"Here, team," Stacey called out, popping the whip over the team. The stage jerked forward, and the driver groaned as the woman tried to ease his pain.

When the stage rolled into MacAllister an hour later, it created quite a stir. It was unusual enough to see that the regular driver wasn't handling the team. It was more unusual to see the driver replaced by a woman, especially one as lovely and as elegantly dressed as Stacey. But the biggest surprise of all was that she demonstrated as much skill as anyone who had ever negotiated the streets with an eight-horse hitch. By the time Stacey pulled the team to a halt in front of the Wells Fargo office, there were thirty or forty people running alongside to see what had happened.

"We've been robbed!" the drummer shouted, hopping out immediately to try to assume some authority.

"Who did it?" someone in the crowd asked.

"Why, who do you think it was?" the drummer answered. "It was none other than Clay Conway himself. He was wearing a flour sack over his head, but I could see those eyes, and I recognized him all right. I've seen him enough times to know."

"Okay, boys," the sheriff said. "Get saddled up. It looks like Conway pulled off another one."

"It wasn't Clay Conway," Stacey said as she climbed down from the driver's seat.

At the sound of her voice, everyone stopped talking.

"Hello, Stacey," the sheriff said. "I saw that was you bringing in the stage. I thought you were in Denver."

"I've come back," Stacey said simply. "Sheriff, I don't know who the robber was, but I know who it wasn't. It wasn't Clay Conway."

"What do you mean, it wasn't Clay Conway?" the drummer asked. "Little lady, you was probably too upset to be thinkin' right. If you wasn't, you would'a known it was Clay Conway, by the fact that he give you that trinket like he gives all the ladies."

"Oh," Stacey said coolly. "You mean like the one he gave you?" She reached into the drummer's vest pocket and pulled out the locket the bandit had given him. When the laughter died down the sheriff asked, "Stacey, why do you say it wasn't Clay Conway?"

"Because I know Clay Conway. The man who robbed us was bigger, and had a different voice."

"Well, I know Clay Conway too," the drummer said. "And I'm sayin' it was him what robbed us."

"I'm inclined to believe the girl," the sheriff said, dismissing the drummer's remarks.

"Why would you take her word over mine?" the drummer asked. "Surely, sir, I'm a reputable source?"

"You didn't really know Clay Conway," the boy Richard accused the drummer. "You was just tellin' me a story."

"Even the kid knows when you're tellin' a tall tale, mister," someone in the crowd said.

The drummer looked at the boy, then squared his hat defiantly on his head. "Have my luggage brought to the hotel," he ordered the station agent, and walked away, followed by the laughter of the crowd.

"Miss Pendarrow, I don't know if you remember me, I'm Howard Mason," a tall, thin man said, stepping forward from the crowd. "I'm the chief agent for Wells Fargo here in MacAllister, and I want you to know how much we appreciate this. If there is ever anything I can do for you, please let me know."

"Perhaps there will be something, Mr. Mason," Stacey said. "I'd like to talk to you tomorrow if I can."

"Certainly," Mason answered. "Anytime, anytime. Right now if you'd like."

"No, now I want a hotel room, a bath and a meal, in that order," Stacey said.

"Miss Pendarrow, may I take the liberty of reserving a table at seven o'clock? I hope you will be my guest for supper," a new voice broke in.

Stacey looked toward the speaker and saw the admiring eyes of Bramwell Caulder.

"Yes," she heard herself answering. "I accept your offer, Mr. Caulder."

Chapter Nineteen

When Stacey came down to dinner that evening, Bramwell Caulder was standing by an elegantly laid table in the hotel dining room, waiting to greet her. Stacey's brief sojourn in Denver had taught her how to enhance her natural beauty and she made a breathtaking appearance in a gown of golden satin, the skirt of which billowed out in layers like the petals of a yellow rose.

"You are lovelier than I ever imagined, my dear," Caulder said, holding a chair for her. "I do hope you've been able to put the unpleasantness of this afternoon behind you."

"I was relieved to hear that Dan would survive," Stacey said as she sat down. "And I feel much better after my bath."

Bramwell looked at her closely, his eyes reflecting his appreciative appraisal of her.

"I must say, Stacey, that Denver did well by you. Never have I seen such a fantastic blossoming of natural beauty into elegant loveliness. Did you enjoy your stay there?"

"Yes," Stacey said, realizing even as she said it that she had indeed enjoyed the excitement of the social whirl. "But I am more than happy to return to Oregon. I missed my mountains."

"What are you going to do now?" Bramwell asked.

"Mr. Mason asked me to stop by and see him. I'm going to tomorrow, and I'm going to ask him for a job. I am badly in need of one."

"Well, I might be able to find something for you," Bramwell said. "What sort of job do you want?"

"I want to drive a stagecoach," Stacey said.

Bramwell laughed.

"Why do you think that's so funny?" Stacey flared. "You saw me bring that stage in today. I had to bring it down the side of the mountain—that's as dangerous a pass as anywhere on the line. But I didn't have any trouble with it."

"You're right," Bramwell said. "I had no right to laugh at you. But Stacey, look at you now. You look as if you should be the hostess of a gubernatorial reception, and you're talking about driving a stage. The idea is a difficult one to adjust to."

"I can't help it," Stacey said. "Bram, it's what I want to do more than anything else in the world. Surely Mr. Mason wouldn't deny me that chance? Not after what happened to my father . . . not after what I did for them today?"

"I like it when you call me Bram," Bramwell said. He leaned back in his chair and studied Stacey for a moment. "I'll tell you what I'll do, Stacey," he went on. "I'll make you my *cause célèbre*. I'll plead your case for you, if necessary, all the way to the Wells Fargo front office. Now how will that be?"

"Would you really do that for me?"

"Absolutely," Bramwell said. "If that's what you want, that's what I'll do."

"Oh, Bram, do that and I'll forever be in your debt," Stacey cried.

"And that's all I want," Bramwell replied.

Bramwell had ordered the dinner in advance, and they dined sumptuously on roast squab, wild rice, peach flambé and chilled champagne. After the meal, Bramwell, after asking her permission, lit a cheroot and waved the used dishes away. "Have you a place to stay?" he asked.

"I've taken a room here in the hotel," Stacey replied. "It will be fine for the time being."

"A single room? Oh, no, that will never do," Bramwell said. "I have a suite of rooms right here which I keep for clients and associates who come to MacAllister. They aren't being used at the moment, so allow me to place them at your disposal."

"Oh, no, I couldn't do that," Stacey said. "That wouldn't be proper."

Bramwell laughed. "My dear, why is it that I feel that word is artificial, applied to you?"

"Are you suggesting that I'm not proper?" Stacey asked sharply.

"Yes, but not in the sense you are taking it. I'm saying that someone like you can rise above social propriety. You aren't bound by rules, Stacey; you're as free as you want to be. Your wanting to drive a stage proves that. Believe me, I meant it as a compliment."

"Very well," Stacey said. She smiled, softening her stance. "I suppose I'm a bit gun shy on the subject, after Denver. There, no one can be himself."

"Then I take it that all of Denver wasn't enjoyable?"

"There were a few uncomfortable moments," she conceded, without elaborating.

"Well, what about my offer, Stacey? I don't live here in the hotel, if that would make you feel better. I have an apartment behind my law office."

"Sure," Stacey said. "Why not? That sounds more comfortable than a single room, and right now, I'm interested in something comfortable. In fact, I may just sleep all through tomorrow, I'm that tired."

"Forgive me, Stacey, of course you are," Bramwell said. "I won't detain you unnecessarily." He took a key from his pocket and held it out for her to see. "It's suite 206, second floor, all the way to the rear of the building. This is the only key I have, so you needn't worry about privacy. I'll have your things moved from your room to the suite now, and then take my leave."

Bramwell signaled a waiter, handed him the key and charged him with the instructions. "Now, my dear," he said as the waiter hurried off to see to the matter, "we will just about have time for a nightcap."

"You're too kind, Bram," Stacey said. "I don't know how I will ever be able to repay you."

"I'll find a way," Bramwell smiled. "Ah, this is an excellent sherry." He held the glass toward Stacey. "Enjoy it."

Bramwell Caulder's suite consisted of a bedroom, a sitting room, and to Stacey's pleasant surprise, a bathroom. Earlier, she had bathed in the public bathroom, at the end of the hall, and though the door had been locked, she had watched the door-knob intently the whole time, lest someone try to enter and disturb her privacy.

The bed was large and inviting, the cover was already turned down, and the pillows were fluffed. A kerosene lantern burned low on the bedside table, awaiting only the twist of the wick key to flood the room with bright, golden light.

Stacey left the lamp low, preferring to undress in the semi-darkness, and finally, as she slipped in between the cool sheets, she turned the key to snuff the flame entirely. Sleep was upon her in a matter of minutes.

She had no idea how long she had been asleep when something awakened her. She sat up abruptly, senses attuned to whatever had disturbed her. Then she heard it, a faint sound at the window. Curious now, she struck a match to light the lamp. The wick flamed up, illuminating the room, and she swung her feet over the edge of the bed and walked toward the window, dressed only in her white silk nightgown, a birthday gift from Marcus.

It was typical of Stacey that she would go toward the sound, rather than away from it, for Stacey was a girl of immense courage and unbridled curiosity. Thus it was that the prncipal question in her mind was more of who was at her window, than why.

"Who are you, and what do you want?" Stacey asked, standing just inside the window.

"Stacey, it's me," a voice said. "I want to talk to you."

"Who? Who is it?"

The window shutters were pushed inward, and a

man swung from the ledge outside through the open window. There, standing in the soft light of the lantern, was Clay Conway.

"You!" Stacey gasped. "What are you doing here in the middle of the night?"

"Do you suggest I come to see you in the middle of the day?" Clay answered. "I'm a wanted man, Stacey."

"I certainly do not suggest that, sir. I suggest that you don't come to see me at all! How dare you, after what you have done?"

"That's just it, Stacey," Clay said. "I didn't do what you think I did."

"You're lying!" Stacey said. She saw a water pitcher on the dresser, and she grabbed it and raised it high, preparatory to smashing it down over Clay's head. Clay managed to catch her arm just in time, and he gently removed the pitcher and set it down.

"Stacey, you are going to listen to me!" he demanded.

"I am not!" she said. "You get out of here right now, or I'll scream!"

Stacey opened her mouth to scream, and Clay put his hand over it.

"Promise me you won't scream," Clay said.

Stacey shook her head in the negative.

"Very well, I shall keep my hand here."

Stacey bit him, so Clay pulled off the silken scarf which he wore around his neck, and quickly, despite Stacey's struggles, fashioned a gag. He pushed her over to the bed, then down onto it. He sat on the bed and held her arms pinioned to the sheets.

"I said you are going to listen to me, Stacey, and

I meant it," Clay said again. Finally, Stacey stopped struggling, and looked at him with angry, amber eyes.

"That's better," Clay said. "Now, first, I want to thank you for coming to my defense today. If you hadn't spoken up, there would have been one more robbery attributed to me."

Clay saw the questioning look in Stacey's eyes, and he laughed. "I know, you want to know how I found out. Well, I have ways. But this is an example of what I'm talking about, Stacey. Everything is blamed on me. If I did as much as people said I did, I'd have to have wings to fly from place to place. I'll admit that I've robbed a few stages, but that's because I have no alternative now. I'm a wanted man. I can't show my face anywhere without someone wanting to shoot me. And that includes you."

Stacey lay on the bed, looking up at him. She tried to say something and it came out mumbled.

"I'll take your gag off, if you won't scream," Clay said. He reached down and removed the gag.

"Yes," Stacey said, after gasping for breath for a moment. "I did try to shoot you, and I will shoot you the first chance I get."

"Stacey, all I ask is that you give me a chance to tell my side of the story."

"All right," Stacey said. "Let's hear your side of the story. If you didn't kill my father, who did kill him?"

"I don't know," Clay said.

"You don't know? How can you come in here and beg me to hear your side of the story when you

187

don't have a story? What do you mean you don't know? You were there, weren't you?"

"Yes, I was there," Clay said. "But I don't remember a thing about it. One moment your father and I were talking, and the next I was waking up in an abandoned stage. Someone must have hit me from behind, then robbed and killed your father and the passengers while I was unconscious."

"Then why weren't you killed as well?"

"For a very good reason. Whoever did it wanted the blame to pass to me. And I must say that their plan has worked well, for now everyone, including you, believes that I did it. As if I could do such a thing."

"But . . . but it had to be you," she said, her voice now showing the first hint of indecision.

"No, Stacey, it wasn't me," Clay said. He had noticed the slight change of tone in her voice, and it gave him hope. He relaxed his grip on her shoulders, and sat up, looking into her eyes. "Stacey, you do believe me, don't you?"

"I . . . I don't know what I believe," Stacey said. "Bram swears that he saw you do it. Why would he swear such a thing if it wasn't true?"

"There can be two answers to that," Clay said. "He either saw someone else and mistook him for me, because by then I was unconscious and out of the way—or he himself did it."

"No," Stacey said, "that I don't believe. Bramwell Caulder couldn't have done such a thing. He's too much of a gentleman."

"Stacey, didn't you learn in Denver that everyone with a cultured manner is not necessarily a gentleman?"

"I don't know," Stacey said. She suddenly started struggling again. "Go away, Clay Conway. Go away and leave me alone. I don't want to listen to you anymore."

Clay again grabbed her arms to subdue her struggles. "I'll leave," he said, "but not until I have done this."

Clay leaned down and kissed her with hot, hungry lips. The impact of the kiss took Stacey's breath away. Twice before she had been kissed by this man, and each kiss had burned into her soul with the heat of a branding iron. Her head started spinning, and then she felt his tongue, first brushing across her lips and then forcing her lips open and thrusting inside.

The sensations so overwhelmed Stacey that for the moment she forgot her struggle, and Clay quickly took advantage of it to pull the silk gown up and over her head, exposing her body to his view. His hands moved gently across her smooth golden skin, spreading fire wherever they went, and though now Stacey had renewed her struggle, it was a struggle against her own feelings as much as against Clay.

Stacey couldn't account for what she was feeling. It was a sexual response, but that in itself wasn't new to her. She had been shown a hint of what it could be like during the brutal rape by Billy Miles, her response to Marcus had been eager, though futile, and even Tobias had aroused her. But this was much more intense than anything she had ever felt. There was as much difference between what she was experiencing now, and what she had felt be-

189

fore, as there was between a gentle spring rain and a violent thunderstorm.

"Stacey, I've nearly driven myself mad over you," Clay said. "Don't you realize that?" His hand finally reached between her legs. The heat and dampness of her desire showed him in no uncertain terms that she reciprocated his passion.

"No, I won't let you do this," Stacey cried though her body trembled with fire under his touch. She was flooded by such feelings that the very passage of time seemed unreal to her, and she watched him adjust his clothes, aware of his action, but surprised nonetheless when a moment later he thrust himself into her.

Stacey gasped, and raked his bare back with her fingernails—whether in a burst of passion or a last effort to fight against him, she couldn't be sure. Clay responded to the raking as if it were a passionate embrace, and Stacey couldn't be sure it wasn't. He moved his mouth over hers, stifling her cries with smothering kisses and a darting tongue which moved in and out of her mouth in perfect rhythm with the rest of his invading body. Then, with all pretense gone, Stacey gave herself up to him.

Lightning struck Stacey: once, twice, three times, as for the first time in her life she knew the searing heat of total fulfillment. She felt the breath leave her body and she was lifted to the stars, there to become a blazing comet, exploding in golden ecstasy, that went on and on and on.

Then, all at once it was over for Clay. His body went rigid. A groan escaped from his lips, and as convulsions of pleasure racked his body, Stacey could feel them enter her own. His manhood strained inside her and then slowly slackened. But when he rolled off her, she could still feel the pleasure of him with her. He lay on one side breathing heavily for a few moments. Finally, he spoke.

"Now you have to believe me," he said.

And as he spoke, cold realization came over Stacey. She had just made love with the man she believed killed her father. His words had not convinced her, but her body had betrayed her.

"And why must I believe you, sir?" she asked coldly. "You have just shown me how well you regard decency, by raping me."

"Rape?" Clay asked, sitting up and looking at her with surprise on his face. "Stacey, surely you can't call what we just shared rape?"

"I do call it that, sir," Stacey said. "And unless you are now prepared to bind and gag me again, I suggest that you leave immediately. Please, leave me alone now."

Clay readjusted his clothing quickly, and started toward the window. He looked over at Stacey who was lying in the rumpled bed in the golden bubble of light from the lantern, dabbing now at tears with the same scarf he had used to gag her.

"Stacey, I'm sorry you considered this an act of rape. Believe me, that was not what I intended. That was not what I intended to do at all."

"And what, Mr. Conway, did you intend it to be?" she asked, trying hard to keep her voice calm.

"As I love you, Stacey, I intended it to be an act of love," Clay said softly. He blew her a kiss, then slipped through the window and out into the dark night.

Chapter Twenty

Stacey awakened slowly the next morning, then stretched luxuriously. Never, it seemed, had sleep been so delicious, or a bed more comfortable. Her entire body seemed to tingle with contentment and relaxation, and the soreness of muscles which had been dormant in Denver, only to be reawakened by yesterday's exercise, was in itself a pleasant feeling.

And there was something else, something which almost approached euphoria. It was the still-lingering afterglow of the total fulfillment she had realized in Clay's loving embrace, the night before.

"No!" she suddenly shouted, realizing what she was doing. She was basking in the afterglow, deriving pleasure from thinking of Clay Conway. But she couldn't be doing that—she shouldn't be thinking such thoughts about the man who killed her father! Anyway, it wasn't her fault, she rationalized. Clay Conway clearly had raped her. She did not invite him here; he entered her room by stealth, and then he took her by force.

Stacey held that thought securely in her mind, allowing it to grow larger and larger. When a small voice of truth tried to make itself heard inside her head, she pushed it aside, along with any lingering feelings of pleasure, so that by the time she got out of bed, the dominating impression of Clay Conway was one of a man who was both murderer and rapist. Reason and truth were smothered by rationalizing and guilt, and her resolve to seek revenge from Clay Conway was greatly intensified. That he had declared his love for her was all but forgotten.

When Stacey walked into the dining room for breakfast she saw Bramwell Caulder sitting at the same table they had dined at last night. He was reading a newspaper and sipping a cup of coffee.

"Miss Pendarrow?" a waiter asked, approaching her. "Mr. Caulder's compliments, ma'am, and he asks if you would join him for breakfast?"

"Very well," Stacey said. "Thank you."

Bramwell stood as Stacey approached the table, then held her chair as she was seated. "Did you have a pleasant night?" he asked.

For an instant, Stacey considered telling him what had happened, but quickly decided that it would only re-open the hurt in her own heart, and would arouse too many questions from Bramwell Caulder.

"I had a most pleasant night, thank you. The bed is very comfortable."

"Keep the suite for as long as you wish," Bramwell offered. The waiter brought breakfast at that moment. "I took the liberty of ordering for you; I hope you don't mind."

"No, not at all," Stacey replied.

"I've done something else for you too."

"What?"

"I spoke with Howard Mason this morning. He's going to give you a job with Wells Fargo."

194

"Oh, Bram," Stacey cried excitedly. "Oh, thank you, very much. This is more than I hoped for!"

"Now, wait a minute, wait a minute," Bramwell said, holding his hands out toward her as if to dam up some of her enthusiasm. "Wait until you hear all of it."

"All of it? What else is there? I'm going to drive for Wells Fargo!"

"That's just it," Bramwell said. "You aren't going to drive."

"I'm not? What am I going to do?"

"You're going to be the station agent, here in MacAllister."

"Why can't I drive?" Stacey asked hotly. "Dan was badly hurt. Surely they need to replace him?"

"Charles Gideon is going to replace Dan. He's had his application for driver in for a long time. You are going to replace Gideon as the station agent."

"I see," Stacey said, dejectedly. "Well, my name has gone on the driver waiting list though, hasn't it?"

"Well, uh, Mason is a little difficult about that," Bramwell said. "But not to worry. I told you I would pursue this matter further, and I shall. I won't stop my efforts, Stacey, until you are a driver. Believe me."

"I believe you, Bram, and I thank you for it," Stacey said. "Actually, I'm a little surprised that Mason even agreed to allow me to be the station agent. That too is supposed to be a man's domain."

"I had to talk a lot to get that job for you," Bramwell said. "But, under threat of a lawsuit, he finally agreed."

"But why MacAllister? I know that Eddie Clark would like to come back to MacAllister from Sky Meadow, so that his daughter Melissa can go to school. And, to be honest, I'd rather go back to Sky Meadow than stay here."

"He chose MacAllister, because as chief agent for the entire Wells Fargo district, he is stationed in MacAllister. And he feels that he can keep an eye on you."

"I see," Stacey said, disappointment coloring her voice. "In other words, he intends to run MacAllister himself, and I'm just his assistant."

"That could be his idea," Bramwell admitted. "I know that he had not intended to run the operation by himself. I doubt that his plans have changed that much, just because you are going to be there."

"What did he say? How did he take the idea of my working here?"

"As I say, I had to practically force him into it. I think he finally went along with it because he feels you will become disenchanted and quit after a short time. That, I believe, is his ace in the hole."

"He will never get a chance to play that ace," Stacey said determinedly, "for I have no intention of quitting that job. In fact, I intend to go over there immediately after breakfast."

Bramwell Caulder smiled, a slow, crooked smile. His eyes were flashing brown and insolent, and Stacey tried to identify the look on his face. He was not as jaded in appearance as Marcus, though he had the same "bedroom look," as Mary had called it, about him. Also, he was more rugged-looking than Marcus, but lacked the easy confidence and fluid grace of Clay Conway. Like Clay Conway, however, a sense of danger seemed to flow through him, and Stacey was always cognizant of that danger when she was with him.

"I told him that there was no doubt you would see it through," Bramwell said.

"I will quit that job only when I leave to drive a stage."

"And I will persist in my efforts to get you that opportunity," Bramwell said. "Now, enough business talk, let's talk of something else."

"What, for example?"

"Well, for example, I would like to see more of you."

Stacey laughed. "Mr. Caulder, you've seen me practically every moment since I returned. Dinner last evening, breakfast this morning. . . ."

"And dinner this evening, I hope," Bramwell interrupted. "And I liked it decidedly better when you called me Bram. Besides, if you have dinner with me this evening, I shall throw in a bonus."

"What?"

Bramwell slid the newspaper across the table, and pointed to an article. "A theater stock company is coming to town. I thought that after dinner you might enjoy seeing the play."

"Oh, it's the Augustine Daly Troupe," Stacey said, reading the article.

"You've heard of them?"

"Yes, they were in Denver and Mrs. Tremain hired them for a private performance. They are very good. They will be doing *Taming of the Shrew*, I hope? Miss Rehan was especially good as Katherine."

"I believe that is the play they are doing, yes. Then you will come?"

"Oh, yes, I wouldn't miss it for anything," Stacey said.

"Wonderful," Bramwell replied. "Tickets, I understand, are going to be in short supply, so I'll make arrangements the first thing after breakfast."

"Thank you, Bram. That's very considerate of you," Stacey said.

"Now, let's have breakfast before it gets cold," Bramwell suggested.

Forty-five minutes after breakfast, Stacey Pendarrow stood in the front room of the Wells Fargo office, waiting patiently for Howard Mason to conclude his business with a customer. As she waited, she examined a showbill which advertised the visiting troupe, and looked forward to the evening's entertainment. Stacey had accepted Bramwell's invitation without a second thought because she very much wanted to see the play, but she realized that such a thing would have been unheard of just six months ago. He wouldn't have asked her, and she wouldn't have accepted.

The customer finally left and Stacey looked at Mason. He was tall and thin, with sunken cheeks and piercing black eyes. He always wore a black suit and her first impression of him had been that he was either a preacher or an undertaker. Mason tried to smile at Stacey, but on a face long accustomed to grimness the smile barely came off. Stacey, however, gave him the benefit of the doubt and returned his effort with a flashing smile of her own.

"I am really looking forward to working with you, Mr. Mason. My father always spoke of your dedication and sincerity."

That wasn't quite true, but it wasn't quite a lie. Seth Pendarrow had said many a time that Howard Mason was a man so involved with petty detail that he nearly lost sight of the big things.

"Well, I—I thank you," Howard replied. "Uh, won't you come into my office, Miss Pendarrow? We can discuss the arrangements there."

Mason's office was dominated by a large desk and a huge, dark green safe. The logo "Wells Fargo" was printed across the front of the safe in letters of gold, but the letter "g" was missing and could be read only because it was a lighter and cleaner shade of green than the rest of the door.

On the wall there was a calendar which showed the month and year, July, 1881, and a clock which was adjusted to the correct time daily by a telegraph signal from the Wells Fargo office in San Francisco. It was the yardstick by which all the drivers adjusted their own watches, for the four standard time zones which the railroads wanted had not yet been established. There were, in fact, one hundred different railroad times in 1881, and as Wells Fargo had to coordinate much of its activity with the railroad, it was imperative that all Wells Fargo offices had a common time zone in which to convert to the various railroad time charts and tables.

Stacey knew about the clock, from her father, who, after a run, would adjust the clock at Sky Meadow to the current driver's watch. Adjusting the clock had been one of Stacey's first regular jobs as a small girl, and it was in that way that she had learned to tell time.

"Have a seat," Mason offered. "I want to be honest with you, Miss Pendarrow. While I owe you a great debt of gratitude, I was persuaded to hire you against my better judgement. Let there be no misunderstanding as to my feelings on this matter."

"I appreciate your honesty, Mr. Mason," Stacey replied, coolly. "And I will tell you that I am accepting this job only as an interim position. It is my intention to become a driver."

"That, Miss Pendarrow, you will never do," Howard said. "However, if you apply yourself diligently, it is possible that you will put to rest my fears over hiring you as an assistant agent."

"Assistant agent?"

"Yes, here in MacAllister."

"I was under the impression I was to be the agent."

Howard removed a pair of wire rim glasses from his pocket, and polished them pointedly, before he slipped them on, pulling the hooks carefully over each ear.

"I will act both as chief agent for the district, and station agent for this station," he explained. "You will function as my assistant."

Stacey sighed. "Very well. I know that even if I had been given the title you would not have given me the responsibility. And I don't want the title if I don't do the work."

"Yes. Well, I see that we understand each other," Howard said. "Now, Miss Pendarrow, when would you like to start?"

"I'll start today," Stacey said. "Right now, if you wish."

"Excellent." Howard took down the timetable and shipping charge chart. "Do you know what this is?"

"Yes. I used to accept shipments and issue tickets at Sky Meadow. I know how to use that."

"Good. We have a customer out there right now, I see," Howard said, looking up as the front door opened. "Why don't you take care of him?"

Stacey took the well-worn copy of the timetable and the shipping charge book with her, and prepared to greet her first customer in her new career.

Chapter Twenty-one

There was a side of Stacey's personality that contradicted the high-spirited girl who wanted to be a stagecoach driver. It was a side that not only recognized that she was a woman, but embraced it with joy, and took pride in being beautiful as well. Thus, on those occasions when she really wanted to present the kind of appearance lauded by her Aunt Pricilla, that of a cultured and refined lady, she could do so, and with great aplomb.

As Stacey told Caulder, she had already seen the Augustine Daly Troupe's performance of *The Taming of the Shrew* when she was in Denver. Afterward, she met Miss Ada Rehan, the leading lady. Miss Rehan had been exceptionally charming, and Stacey had suggested to Aunt Pricilla that they invite her to dinner, but Pricilla said that "theatre people" were not the sort one associated with socially, save for the occasional charitable functions of the type sponsored by Mrs. Tremain.

Stacey, however, had defied her aunt, and urged Marcus to invite Miss Rehan and several others of the company to dinner in the Marshall House. Tonight would be the first time Stacey had seen Miss Rehan since that evening.

The play was being given in the Opera House, a building which had never seen an opera, but functioned well for dances, lectures, concerts, town meetings, and occasionally a play. Tonight's performance would be by far the most skilled and professional performance ever given in the MacAllister Opera House, and as Stacey and Bramwell walked from the hotel to the theatre, they saw that crowds were already overflowing onto the boarded sidewalk in front of the building. There was a commotion at the ticket window as people fought for tickets, and offered ridiculous prices for the few remaining. Stacey was glad that Bramwell had had the foresight to purchase their tickets that morning.

Inside the theatre, the atmosphere was much rowdier than it had been at any of the events Marcus had taken Stacey to in Denver, and for the first time in her life, Stacey felt more sophisticated than those who surrounded her, instead of less, as had so often been the case in Denver. The curtain parted, and a man stepped through. Stacey recognized Arnold Peavley, the mayor of MacAllister, who announced the evening's bill, along with mention of the fact that he, as mayor, had arranged to bring the show to town. Finally, Peavley left the stage, the curtain opened, applause swelled and died, and the play began.

Ada Rehan dominated the stage with her presence. She had a radiant beauty which, from behind the footlights, was eminently more powerful than it was in person. Her figure was superb, and her hair shone as if it had captured moonbeams. Though the play was perhaps a bit deep for the unsophisticated appetites of the Westerners, Ada Rehan managed to carry it off with such skill and finesse that as the curtain was lowered for the final time, the audience still responded with thunderous applause.

"Did you enjoy it?" Bramwell asked.

"Yes, very much," Stacey said. "And you? What did you think of the play?"

Bramwell lit a cigar before he answered. "I enjoyed Miss Rehan's performance before," he said. "It's a pity we couldn't have seen her in some other role."

"But Bram, Katherine *is* her role! She's become world famous playing that part."

"Ah, yes, I'd forgotten that you acquired culture while you were in Denver," Bramwell teased.

"And you? Aren't you cultured? Aren't you a gentleman?"

"Not all gentlemen are cultured," Bramwell said.

The statement hit Stacey with the impact of a slap in the face. What was it Clay had said last night? Not everyone with a cultured manner is necessarily a gentleman. The similarity of the statements took her breath away.

"Stacey, what is it?" Bramwell asked, noticing her reaction.

"Nothing," Stacey said quickly. "It was just a thought, that's all."

As they returned to the lobby of the hotel, the clerk nodded at Bramwell, and Bramwell returned a slight wave, then looked at Stacey. "I've taken the liberty of having a bottle of chilled champagne delivered to your suite. I hope you will be gracious enough to share it with me?"

"You mean entertain you in my room?" Stacey

asked, her voice displaying surprise that he would suggest such a thing.

"My dear, I have already mentioned that you are above social propriety. The very fact that we are being seen together and you are staying in a suite known to belong to me has already started talk. If I visited you in that room, there would be no greater comment than there is already."

Bramwell had taken Stacey's hand in his as he talked to her, and she had turned to face him. She could feel a disturbing attraction to this man and she knew that if she let herself, she could be stirred by him. Did she want to? Well, why not? she thought. She had reacted to Clay who, despite her aversion to him, seemed capable of eliciting the wildest response from her with a touch, or a look. Perhaps a small, controlled diversion with Bramwell Caulder would smooth over those strange, tumultuous feelings that Clay aroused.

"You may come to my room, Mr. Caulder," she said quietly.

As Bramwell had promised, there was a green bottle of champagne protruding from a silver bucket in which ice had been packed. Two champagne glasses sat on the table next to the bucket, and a white card leaned against a bouquet of bright yellow roses. The only writing on the card was the engraved name of Bramwell Caulder.

"Oh, Bram, how beautiful!" Stacey said. She pulled one of the roses from the vase to smell it. "They don't smell as nice as the red ones, but they're more beautiful. Thank you; that was so thoughtful."

The champagne cork popped, and Bramwell

poured two glasses of the sparkling liquid. He held one out to Stacey.

"Look at the bubbles," Stacey said. "They look like stars. There, that one looks like Arcturus."

"Arcturus?"

"My star," Stacey said, smiling. "Did you know that stars have names?"

"Yes, I think I read that someplace. I didn't know you were interested in their names, though. Where did you learn about that?"

"From a friend in Denver," Stacey said.

"Not a man friend, I hope," Bramwell said.

"Yes, as a matter of fact, it was a man friend," Stacey said. "Why? What difference does that make?"

"I think I might be jealous," Bramwell said. "In fact, I'm jealous of any man who looks at you."

"Why are you jealous?"

Bramwell ran the back of his hand gently across her cheek, then into her raven-black hair. "Because I think you are the most beautiful woman I have ever seen," he said. "And I don't want to share you with anyone."

"Oh? And when did you become so possessive?"

"I think I have always been, from the first time I saw you, back at the Sky Meadow way station," Bramwell said. "I remember that rainy morning— you were cooking breakfast for the passengers. I was in the other room, but I wasn't asleep. I saw you and Clay Conway, and I heard him ask you out. I think I was jealous of him even then, and I didn't even know your name."

"Clay Conway," Stacey said, spitting his name out in disgust. "I hate him."

"Oh, forgive me, Stacey, that was unthinking of me," Bramwell said. "Of course you wouldn't want to recall that day."

"There you are wrong," Stacey said. "I do want to recall it. Until my father's murderer pays for his crime, I never want to forget it. Bram, tell me—did you actually see Clay Conway kill my father? You're quite sure it was Clay? Could you have mistaken someone else for Clay in all the confusion?"

"There was no mistake," Bramwell said firmly.

"Tell me what happened."

"Stacey, are you sure you want to go on with this?"

"Yes," Stacey said determinedly.

Bramwell sighed. "Very well, I'll tell you what I remember. There were, as you recall, six of us in the coach. Two women and four men, counting myself. Your father stopped the coach when we reached the top of Radcliffe Pass, and told us we could get out for a few minutes while the animals caught their breath."

"Radcliffe Pass is not that difficult a climb," Stacey said. "Why did he stop there? He didn't usually stop there."

"I don't know," Bramwell said. "Perhaps Clay forced him to stop there. Anyway, I walked away from the rest of them over into the rocks away from the road. I won't be indelicate enough to go into the reason why I had to get away from the stage, but it was while I was there that I heard the first shot. I started back on the run, but stopped behind a large rock outcropping when I got to the edge of the road, shocked by what I was seeing."

"What was happening?" Stacey asked.

"Your father was already slumped across the driver's seat and the passengers were standing outside. Clay Conway was holding a gun on them."

"Oh, why didn't you shoot him them?"

"Believe me, I've wished a hundred times since then that I could have. But you see, I was unarmed—as was everyone except Clay Conway himself. The lieutenant's wife, you remember the pretty young lady? She cried out, 'What are you doing? You're supposed to be protecting us!'"

"And what did Clay say?"

"He laughed at her. 'Don't worry, Miss where you're going you won't need protection,' he said. And with that, he shot her, then each of the others in turn."

"Oh, how awful," Stacey cried, turning away.

"I think he forgot all about me, because he put his gun away and climbed back onto the seat above the money box. I sneaked up behind him, hit him over the head, then ran back to the way station. I was half out of my mind or I would have taken one of the stage horses. I'm afraid, though, that all I could think of was getting out of there and going for help."

"So, there's no way you could have been mistaken, is there?" Stacey asked. "It was Clay Conway."

"It was Clay Conway," Bramwell said. "Why are you doubting it?"

"Because it seems so different from his later jobs," Stacey said, not mentioning the two times she had spoken with Conway and heard his protestations of innocence. "He's practically a hero now, did you know that? He's written about in newspapers and dime novels and I heard he's even being portrayed on the stage in St. Louis. He leaves trinkets for the women, robs only the Wells Fargo Company, and never shoots anyone. They are calling him the Robin Hood of the West."

"How can you say he never shot anyone when he shot Dan just yesterday?"

"I told you, that wasn't Clay Conway."

"But how can you be sure?" Bramwell asked. "Everyone says the bandit wore a mask, and admitted being Clay Conway."

"That's just it, isn't it?" Stacey said. "If he admitted being Clay Conway, why would he wear a mask?"

"I suppose you're right," Bramwell said slowly. "Anyway, it doesn't mean anything that he hasn't shot anyone for a while. He's living the life of an outlaw now, Stacey. Outlaws have no friends, nowhere to turn, and no place to run. His only chance is to have a slight edge, and he has created this image of himself as the people's hero in order to give him that edge. For the time being it serves his purpose to be known as the Robin Hood of the West. But believe me, girl, if it became necessary, he would kill again."

"Yes," Stacey said, "I'm afraid you're right."

Stacey felt dejected, though she shouldn't have, for she had known all along that Clay did indeed kill her father. But he had been so insistent that somewhere, in the back of her mind, a tiny spark of hope had flared—a hope that by some miracle it hadn't been Clay. Now, though, there seemed to be no doubt.

"There now," Bramwell said. "I should have

known better than to speak of all this. You're quite upset by it."

Upset? Stacey thought. Yes, she was upset, but not for the reason Bramwell supposed. Stacey was upset for allowing that spark of hope to develop in the first place; and she was angry with herself for harboring any feelings for Clay Conway. Her best bet now, she reasoned, would be to extinguish that spark of interest in him. But how to do that? She looked at Bramwell, then suddenly smiled broadly, invitingly at him. After all, forest fires were fought by starting backfires, weren't they? Why not start a little backfire of her own?

"I would like some more champagne, please," she said, holding her glass toward Bramwell.

"Now, that's more like it," Bramwell said, returning her smile and filling her glass.

Their conversation drifted on, covering the play, the people they had seen there, dinner, and her stay in Denver. It moved far away from the disquieting aspect of her father's death, and then when the time seemed appropriate Stacey held her head at an angle that was just right for inviting a kiss.

Bramwell realized it immediately, and he kissed her full on the mouth. His lips were warm, and his breath tasted of champagne. Stacey surrendered to the kiss with a sigh, returning it with the ardor she had learned was at her command, surprising Bramwell by its intensity.

Gently, and without further conversation, Bramwell began undressing Stacey. It was as obvious to Stacey that Bramwell had undressed women before, as it was now to Bramwell that this was not

211

going to be the first time for the alluring creature with him.

A moment later, and a nude Stacey was stretched out on her bed. Bramwell leaned over to kiss her breasts, and the touch of his tongue to her nipples sent shudders of pleasure rippling through her.

Bramwell stood up, then undressed quickly, looking down at her body as he did so. This was a first for Stacey. With the rapist, her dress had been torn to allow the foul deed. With Marcus, Tobias, and Clay, there had been no time for languid appreciation of her beauty. But now, she felt Bramwell's slow, hot gaze taking full measure of her, and this, too, she found pleasurable.

When Bramwell got into bed with her he began to caress her; skilled, tender supplications with fingers and tongue explored her body with the easy confidence and expertise of one who has worshipped at the altar of love many times before. Soon those bubbling passions which lay always just beneath the surface in Stacey spilled over until she was hungrily, boldly returning his caresses.

Bramwell entered her with gentleness. With a short cry of pleasure, she rose to meet him, and put away all the comparisons she had made between Bramwell Caulder and Clay Conway. But even with the heat of the backfire burning brightly within, a sudden, vivid memory of last night returned, and she could see, through the flames of this union, the golden blaze of the comet which had streaked through her body at that supreme moment with Clay Conway.

212

Chapter Twenty-two

The sound of a shot rolled down the mountainside, picked up resonance, then echoed back from the neighboring mountains. A young man holding a smoking pistol turned and looked at his audience of three with a smile on his face. He had just broken a tossed whiskey bottle with his marksmanship.

"I'd like to see Beau Bandito do that," he said, twisting his mouth on the words Beau Bandito.

The young man was about twenty, dressed in denim jeans and a white, collarless, stained shirt. His chin bristled with irregular patches of beard and his eyes were like those of a hawk: small, dark, beady, and piercing. He called himself the Texas Kid though, in fact, he had never been to Texas.

"Tex, why do you worry so much about Clay Conway?" The man who asked was well dressed, well groomed, and handsome in a dark and sultry way. He was known to the others as Barney.

"I don't worry about him," Tex said. "He should worry about me. If I ever get a chance to come face to face with him, I'll kill him."

"What?" one of the other two men asked. "And kill the goose that lays the golden eggs?" The man who spoke called himself Brewster. His companion

213

was Athens, though those weren't their real names. Brewster and Athens had only recently joined the group, and the clothes they wore, though now dirty and worn, reflected the style of a city and better times.

"Brewster's right," Barney said. "We've got to keep Conway around and keep him active just a little longer."

"Why?" Tex asked.

"If I explained, you wouldn't understand."

"Try me."

"All right. Soon a railroad is going to be built from Medford to MacAllister."

"What does that have to do with keeping Conway alive?"

"Railroads need money to operate," Barney said. "I have it on pretty good authority that within the next few weeks over a hundred thousand dollars is going to be transferred to the MacAllister Bank."

"And we're going to take that money," Tex said. "Sure, I can follow that. But what does that have to do with Clay Conway?"

"It's simple," Barney said patiently. "Right now every Wells Fargo job is blamed on Conway. That job will be blamed on him as well if we keep him around. And as long as they are looking for him, they won't be looking for us."

"Yeah, I can see that," Tex said.

"Good, I'm glad I can count on your cooperation."

"What about the girl?" Tex asked.

"What girl?" Barney asked.

"You know what girl—the one who knew I wasn't Clay Conway when I held up the stage."

"Nothing about her. Why do you ask?"

"I mean, I should kill her, shouldn't I?"

"No, I think not."

"You sure? It won't be no trouble now. I could handle it all right."

"Yes, I realize that," Barney said. "You don't seem to have trouble killing women, do you? I had to do it once, and it wasn't easy."

"Now me, I like it," Tex said. "Fact is, killin' a woman always gives me a hard-on."

"You're crazy," Brewster said.

Tex's face flamed in anger. His hand hovered meanacingly over his gun belt. "Yeah? Well, didn't you tell me a story about rapin' a woman once?"

"That's not killin' her," Brewster said.

"They's some women would rather get killed than raped," Tex said.

"Maybe it depends on who's doin' the rapin'," Brewster said. "In your case, I guess maybe you're right. A girl would rather be killed than be with you."

Before Brewster could finish his statement, Tex had his gun out with the barrel resting on Brewster's upper lip, just below his nose. "Well now," he said slowly cocking the gun. The cylinder turned with a metallic click. "We'll just have to see how purty the girls think you are without your nose."

Athens raised his arm and a small pistol popped into his hand from its concealed position up his sleeve. He put the small gun to Tex's temple.

"Now put your gun away, Tex," Athens said quietly.

Tex laughed. "Haw! Whatta you think you're goin' to do to me with that little pepperbox?"

"Put a little bullet in your little brain," Athens answered.

Tex held his pistol on Brewster for a moment longer. "I could kill him before you pulled that trigger," he warned Athens.

"I don't care all that much about him anyway," Athens said. "But if you drop that hammer on him, I'm goin' to kill you."

"Back off, both of you," Barney said. "If we are going to be successful, we need everyone."

Tex waited a moment longer, then he eased the hammer down on his gun. "Sure," he said, smiling. "I didn't mean nothin' by it anyway."

"You men are going to have to get along with each other," Barney said, "and stay sober! Tex, you've been drinking, haven't you?"

"Hell yes, I been drinkin'," Tex said. "How do you think I got that empty bottle to shoot at?"

"I've warned you about it. Brewster, where did the bottle come from?"

"I don't know, Barney," Brewster replied, relief evident in his face, now that the gun was no longer under his nose. "He got it somewhere."

"Tex, when you get drunk, you get mean," Barney went on. "One of these days you're going to kill one of us."

Tex smiled. "It seems to me that that's your problem."

"And yours," Barney said. This time Barney smiled. "You see, we have an insurance arrangement."

"Insurance? What do you mean?"

"If you kill one of us, those of us who survive will kill you."

"Yeah? What if it's a fair fight?"

"That doesn't matter," Barney said. "It doesn't even matter if it's an accident. If one of us die, then you die."

"Ain't it sweet that you love one another so? Is that love like the Bible says? Or is it somethin' else?" Tex laughed shrilly.

"I told you," Barney said easily. "It's strictly an insurance policy. So my advice to you is to lay off the booze."

"I gotta drink, or go crazy," Tex protested. "There ain't nothin' else to do around here."

"I've got something for you to do," Barney said.

"That's more like it," Tex replied, grinning broadly.

"Yeah," Brewster said. "I'm getting a little bored myself."

"What is it?" Athens asked.

"You're going to hit the MacAllister stage tonight. It's carrying five thousand dollars."

"Five thousand? Hey, that's pretty good," Brewster said. "How do we do it?"

"You two will stay back in the trees, just to cover Tex in case something goes wrong." Barney said. "Tex, you're going to play the role of Beau Bandito again, so wear your outfit."

"Right," Tex answered.

"And I've got a special instruction for you on this job."

"What?"

"I want you to kill the driver."

"You mean the shotgun messenger, don't you?"

"No, I mean the driver. You can shoot the messenger if you have to. But the driver must be killed."

"Why?"

"What difference does it make to you?" Barney asked. "You've killed before."

"Yeah, but I agree with Tex," Brewster put in. "Why do you want the driver killed?"

"It has to do with setting up Wells Fargo for the hundred thousand," Barney replied. "Believe me, I wouldn't do it if I didn't think it was necessary."

"Barney, I don't think we should do that," Brewster protested. "I mean, the driver won't have a chance."

"Don't worry about it," Tex said. "It don't bother me none at all. Fact is, ever' one I kill it's like doin' it without them havin' a chance. There cain't nobody beat me anyhow."

"Clay Conway perhaps?" Brewster suggested.

Tex laughed, a short, bitter laugh. "I could take Conway as easy as I could take either of you. Or, all three of you," he said, taking in Barney as well.

"I should'a pulled the trigger earlier," Athens said.

"Maybe you should'a," Tex said, "'cause it was the last chance you're ever goin' to get."

There was a sudden thump as Barney, who had moved behind Tex, brought the butt of his pistol down on Tex's head. Tex fell to the ground like a poleaxed ox.

"I should have realized he'd been drinking too much when I first arrived," he said. "I thought you men were going to keep him away from whiskey."

"He had a bottle hidden somewhere," Brewster apologized. "He came out here to drink it, and was already drunk before we realized what he was doing."

"Listen, I don't know about you two," Athens said. "But I'm scared of this man and I'd just as soon kill him right now."

"We can't," Barney replied. "He's the only one who can make people believe he's Clay Conway. We need someone who is as fast with a gun as Conway is."

"Is he that fast?" Athens asked.

"Who knows?" Barney asked. "But for one third of one hundred thousand dollars, it's worth keeping him around a while longer."

"One third?" Brewster questioned. "But there are four of us."

Barney smiled broadly. "No, Brewster, there are only three of us," he said, pointing with long, almost delicate fingers to Brewster and Athens. "Young Tex will remain alive only as long as he is useful to us. After he has served his purpose I shall arrange his demise, along with that of the real Clay Conway."

Brewster and Athens laughed.

"That sounds good," Brewster agreed.

"What about him now?" Athens asked, pointing to the still figure stretched out on the ground.

"Start feeding him coffee when he comes to," Barney ordered. "And keep him away from whiskey. You've got to get him ready for tonight, and keep him ready for any other jobs that come up."

"Right," Brewster replied.

"In fact," Barney said, "the only reason I brought you two into this deal in the first place was to ride herd on this idiot. Now if you don't think you can do it, let me know and I'll get someone else."

"Don't worry about it any more," Brewster said. "You can count on us from now on."

"Good," Barney said. He started back toward his horse. "I've got business in Winchester. I'll check with you later."

Brewster and Athens watched Barney ride away. Athens spoke first. "I don't know, Billy, I'm beginning to think that we should never have left Denver."

"Did you want to stay around there with a reward on your head?"

"No. Christ, why'd you have to go and rape that girl for? Weren't whores good enough for you?"

"I was upset because of my brother gettin' hisself killed. Besides, who would'a ever thought that cowardly son-of-a-bitch she was with would have enough nerve to put up a reward for us?"

"It's like I told you," Athens sighed. "If you got enough money, you don't need any courage. You can always buy it."

Chapter Twenty-three

The stage was due in at six o'clock in the evening. There were times when it had been late by as much as three hours, but now it was nearly midnight, and the coach had not yet arrived in MacAllister.

Howard Mason, secretly called "Rabbit" by Stacey because of the way his nose seemed to twitch when he was worried or disturbed about something, looked up at the wall clock for perhaps the hundredth time. His nose twitched, and he removed his glasses and polished them, then carefully replaced them, putting the hooks over the ears one at a time, and looked again at the clock.

"It could be that Mr. Gideon decided to go back to Sky Meadow," Stacey suggested.

"Why would he do that?"

"That's a dangerous pass for an inexperienced driver. If for some reason he didn't get away from Sky Meadow until nearly nightfall, he may have had second thoughts about trying to drive that road in the dark."

"Would you have turned back?" Mason asked.

"No, I would have brought it on through."

"Then I'm sure Gideon will bring it through."

"Not necessarily," Stacey said. "You see, I'm a much better driver than Gideon, and Gideon knows it."

"Mr. Gideon is a qualified driver, Miss Pendarrow. Wells Fargo does not entrust the lives of its passengers, or the safety of its consignments, to inexperienced and unqualified drivers."

"I mean to take nothing away from Gideon," Stacey said. "There are many drivers who wouldn't want to run that pass at night."

Mason's nose twitched and he looked at the clock again. It was only one minute later than the last time he looked, and the hands registered seven minutes before midnight.

Suddenly there was a loud banging at the front door. It startled Stacey and Mason, and they jumped. The banging continued.

"Well," Mason finally said, "see who's at the door."

When Stacey opened the door she saw a big, bearded man standing there, dressed in homespun.

"This here the stagecoach station?" he asked.

"Yes," Stacey said. "Who are you?"

"Name's Aaron Wiese. I got a fella from the stage out in my wagon."

"What fellow?" Mason asked.

"I got 'im 'bout six, maybe seven hours ago," the man said. "Found 'im on my place. He's hurt pretty bad. He's the onliest one of the whole bunch left alive though."

"What? What are you talking about?" Mason asked.

"I'm talkin' about a stage wreck, mister," the man said. "Right before sundown the stage come rollin' and tumblin' down the mountainside, landin' right on my spread. Me 'n the missus went runnin' out there, and I never seen such likes in my life. It was the awfulest thing you ever seed. The stage warn't no more'n kindlin' wood. There was three people, two of 'em dead, and this here'n, who's more dead than alive. Even all the horses was killed."

"My God!" Mason exclaimed.

"I put the other two in my ice house, and hitched up my wagon to bring this fella into town. It took me 'till now to get here, 'cause I come around river road."

"The river road? That took you miles out of the way," Stacey said. "As badly as you say this man is hurt, you should have got him here right away."

"Miss, I told you how that stage looked," the man said. "They warn't no way I was gonna try 'n come over that pass tonight."

"Stacey, go get the doctor," Mason ordered, starting toward the wagon.

"Don't need to do that," the man said. "I dropped my missus off at his office on the way here. I 'spect the doctor'll be here in a moment, now."

Stacey followed Mason and the bearded man out the door and over to the wagon which stood where the stage would be standing, had it arrived. There was a man lying in the back, covered by blankets.

"I made him as comfortable as I could," the bearded man said.

"Who is he?" Mason asked.

"My name is Roy Wagner," the man said. "I was a passenger on the stage." His voice was muffled and laced with pain.

"What happened, Mr. Wagner? How did the stage go over the side?"

"I'm not sure," Wagner said. "After the robbery, the shotgun guard tried to bring us in. He took us over the edge, I guess."

"Robbery? What robbery?"

"It was Clay Conway," the passenger said. "It had to be. He was greased lightning with a gun. There couldn't nobody be that fast except Conway. He shot the driver."

"He . . . he *shot* the driver?" Stacey repeated.

"Yes, ma'am," Wagner said. "And there weren't no reason for it. He just drew 'n shot 'im in cold blood."

"What about the other passengers?" Mason asked. "Could any of them still be alive anywhere?"

"No," Wagner said. "There weren't but two passengers on the stage, and the other one is back on Mr. Wiese's farm."

"I thought Wiese said he found two dead passengers."

"No, sir," Wiese put in quickly. "I said I found three people, two of 'em dead."

"One of 'em was the shotgun guard," Wagner explained. "The other was my business partner, Mr. Matthew Harmon."

"That means Gideon's still out there," Stacey said.

"There were no women or children on board?" Mason asked.

"No," Wagner answered, coughing. "When's the doctor going to get here? My leg's starting to hurt somethin' awful."

"Here he comes now," Stacey said, as she looked

down the street. The doctor was running, as were fifteen or twenty other people, drawn to the scene by morbid curiosity, and the sheriff, brought by duty.

"How bad is he hurt, Doc?" the sheriff asked as the doctor finished examining Wagner.

"I have no way of telling how badly he's busted up inside," the doctor said. "But his leg is broken in two places. He'll never walk normally again."

"Damn that Clay Conway!" the sheriff said, slamming his fist into his hand. "Is there no limit to what he'll do?"

"Sheriff, would you ride back up to the pass and see if you can find Charles Gideon?" Stacey asked. "There's a chance he might still be alive and I'd hate to think of him spending the night out on the road, injured."

"Yes, yes, of course, Stacey," the sheriff said. "Would anyone volunteer to go with me?" he asked.

"I'll go with you, Sheriff," a voice called from the drakness, and Stacey recognized it as Bramwell Caulder's.

"Thanks, Bramwell. Where's your horse?"

"He's at the stable."

"Mine too. Come along, we'll get goin'."

"I'll be right with you, Sheriff," Bramwell said. "Stacey, are you all right?"

"Yes, I'm fine," Stacey said. "When did you get back from Winchester?"

"I didn't get back until late tonight," Bramwell said. "I stopped by the hotel but you weren't in."

"I've been down here, waiting for the stage . . . what time did you make the pass?"

"About an hour after sundown," Bramwell said.

"Bram, you may have passed right by poor Gideon, wounded on the side of the road," Stacey said.

"If I did, I didn't see anything, Stacey," Bramwell said. "I'm sorry, but I saw nothing at all out of the ordinary."

"Poor Mr. Gideon," Stacey said. "I hope there's a chance that he is still alive."

"God, Stacey, that could have been you," Bramwell suddenly said. "Listen, I'm not sure you should drive."

"I'm going through with it," Stacey said. "Besides, if it had been me, whoever held up the stage might not have shot me."

"Because you are a woman?" Bramwell said. "I wouldn't count on that. It looks like Clay Conway is beginning to get desperate."

"If that *was* Conway," Stacey said.

"What do you mean, if that was Conway? Of course it was," Bramwell said. "You heard what the passenger said."

"The passengers were also convinced that the man who robbed our stage was Clay Conway," Stacey said. "But I know that it wasn't. And that robber shot our driver, just as this robber shot Charles Gideon. It could be that they were the same person."

"You got a point there, Stacey," the sheriff said. "Come on, Bramwell, time's wasting. If there's any chance the driver is still alive, we need to get on up there as soon as we can."

"All right, Sheriff," Bramwell said, starting toward the stable with the sheriff. He looked back over his shoulder. "I'll see you tomorrow, Stacey," he called out.

The doctor had the passenger taken back to his office, where a small treatment room and bed was set up. Most of the curious followed the wagon as it pulled Wagner to the doctor's office at the opposite end of the street, and Mason and Stacey watched the crowd move down the street, then went back inside.

"There's enough coffee left for one more cup, Mr. Mason," Stacey said, as she closed the door behind her. "Would you like it?"

Mason sat in the chair behind his desk and took his glasses off. He pinched the bridge of his twitching nose, and squinted his eyes. "Yes, Miss Pendarrow. That would be nice, thank you."

Stacey poured the cup, then set it on the desk in front of him. "Mr. Mason, what are you going to do about the stage run tomorrow morning?"

"I'm going to cancel it, I suppose," he said. "There's nothing I can do."

"Why cancel it? We've three spare stages here, and an extra team. Besides, the people are depending on us to keep the route open."

"You don't understand," Mason said. "I'm not cancelling because I want to. I'm cancelling because I have to. I don't have anyone to drive."

"I'll drive," Stacey said.

"No."

"Mr. Mason, you know I'm a capable driver. You need a driver. Why are you so dead set against my taking the job?"

"Because," Mason said, "it simply isn't done."

"You mean it's never been done before. That doesn't mean it can't be done. Is there anything in the Wells Fargo regulations which specify that the driver must be a man?"

"What? Uh, I'm sure there must be," Mason said.

"No," Stacey replied. "There's nothing at all that say's a woman can't be a driver."

She opened the top left drawer of his desk to pull out a blue-bound book. "Listen," she said, reading from the book. " 'District agents shall have the authority to hire drivers as needed. Drivers must be capable, sober, honest, and able to get along with passengers, in order to represent Wells Fargo interests in the best possible manner.' " She closed the book triumphantly. "See," she said, "it doesn't say that I have to be a man, only that I be capable, sober, honest, and able to get along with passengers. I meet all those qualifications, Mr. Mason."

"I don't know," Mason hedged. "That's assuming a lot, on my own responsibility."

"Responsibility," Stacey said. "*There's* a good word to look at." She flipped through the pages of the book, and again read. " 'It is the responsibility of all regional, district, and station agents to move the passengers, specie, mail, and freight in as expeditious a manner as possible. When in doubt as to procedure the agent shall keep in mind that this is the priority responsibility for which he is charged.' " Again, Stacey slammed the book shut. "I think that's pretty clear, isn't it? According to that directive you would be derelict in your duty to cancel tomorrow's run."

Mason sighed, and once again pinched the bridge of his nose. Finally, he spoke. "Very well, Miss Pendarrow. You will take the morning stage run."

"Thank you!" Stacey shouted enthusiastically. "Oh, Mr. Mason, you won't be sorry, I promise you that! Thank you very much!"

In her exuberance Stacey kissed Mason soundly, right on the end of his twitching nose, and he almost smiled.

Chapter Twenty-four

The stage out of MacAllister was due to leave at six o'clock the next morning but Stacey was down at the stable by a little before five, in the pre-dawn gloom. The stable hand had just begun to round up the horses which would make up the team and Stacey went to each animal, patted its face and spoke soothingly to it.

"Give each of them an extra ration of oats," she told the ancient stable hand. Known only as Jack, the man seldom left the stable, even sleeping and taking his meals there. It was said that Jack knew every horse within a fifty-mile radius but few humans, though he himself was well known. Stacey liked him, despite his reputation for crustiness.

"Wells Fargo don't pay for no extra, Miss Pendarrow," Jack said.

"I shall pay for the extra," Stacey said.

"No need. I already put an extra ration in," Jack said gruffly. "You got any preference on how you want 'em teamed?"

"The two grays will be the lead-team," she said. "Then the chestnuts, then the other four by size, I guess. I've never driven this team, so I don't know how they like to work."

"You sure you can handle this?" Jack asked, throwing part of the harness over his shoulder.

Stacey smiled. "Jack, are you going to be like all the others? Of course I can handle it. I've been handling the ribbons since I was twelve years old."

"Yeah, but you always had your pa with you. Now you're goin' out on your own."

"Trust me," Stacey said. "I'll be back after you've got them hitched up. I'm going for breakfast now."

The staff and clientele of the hotel dining room had grown used to seeing Stacey take breakfast in the dresses she wore for work in the Wells Fargo office. When she entered the dining room dressed in pants and a shirt, there was a buzz of surprise and wonder.

"Miss Pendarrow?" the waiter asked, coming over to her table. "Forgive me for my boldness, but why are you dressed in such a manner?"

"Because I'm driving the stage to Sky Meadow," Stacey answered with a broad smile.

"Excuse me, miss," a well-dressed gentleman at a nearby table interrupted. "Did I understand you to say *you* were driving the stage to Sky Meadow?"

"Yes," Stacey said.

"Oh."

"Are you going to be one of my passengers?"

"I . . . I don't know," the man said. "I may be detained on some additional business."

"Nonsense, Phil," Bramwell said, coming into the dining room at that moment. "Your business is concluded and you know it. You can leave on the morning stage."

"Are you sure?" Phil asked. "I mean. . . ."

Bramwell laughed. "Come out with it, man. Are you nervous about riding with a girl?"

"I suppose so, yes. That stage has to go over Eagle Mountain. I've seen the road there. The slightest wrong move and we could be over the edge."

"Precisely why you have no worry with this driver," Bramwell said. "Trust me, Phil, she's the best driver on the line. She would have to be better than most or, since she's a woman, they would never let her drive. Surely you can see that."

Phil laughed nervously and laid some coins beside his plate to pay for his breakfast. "All right, Bramwell, you've convinced me," he said. "Young lady, I hope he knows what he's talking about."

"I'll be especially careful for you," Stacey said. "We leave promptly at six, so don't be late."

"I'll be there . . . I guess," Phil said.

Laughing, Stacey and Bramwell watched the nervous passenger leave the dining room.

"Well," Bramwell said. "It appears that have accomplished your objective.

"Yes," Stacey said. Her face clouded over. "Though I had no desire to be promoted over Charles Gideon's body. Did you and the sheriff find him all right?"

"Yes," Bramwell said. "He was lying right in the middle of the road, dead of a gunshot wound."

"Poor Mr. Gideon," Stacey said.

"Stacey, please be very careful," Bramwell cautioned. "This fellow Conway is obviously a desperate man who will stop at nothing."

"If it was Conway."

"How can you possibly doubt it?"

"Bram, there's something you don't know. Something I haven't told you," Stacey stated.

"Oh? What?"

"It's about Clay Conway. He's come to see me, Bram. He's come to see me twice."

"What? You can't mean that!"

"Yes. He visited me once while I was still in Denver, and then. . . ."

"Then?"

"The first night I was here he sneaked into my bedroom in the middle of the night."

"I see," Bramwell said coldly. "I didn't realize that you were keeping company with the notorious Mr. Conway. I imagine my attentions toward you must have paled in comparison to the illustrious romancing of Beau Bandito."

"No, Bram, you don't see at all," Stacey said. "I didn't ask him to come. I didn't welcome his visits. He just showed up."

"For what reason?"

"To protest his innocence," Stacey said. "He insists that he didn't kill my father."

"So that's why you questioned me the other night," Bramwell said. "You had been listening to Clay Conway."

"Yes," Stacey said.

"I see. And how does Clay Conway explain the fact that I saw him?"

"He says you were either mistaken, or . . . ."

"Or?"

"Or lying to cover up the fact that you did it yourself."

"And you, Stacey? What do you believe?"

"Oh, Bram, I'm so confused. I don't know what to believe."

"Stacey," Bramwell said calmly. He made a tent with his long, almost delicate fingers. "There is no room for confusion in this question. You either believe me, or you don't believe me. And if you don't believe me, then you must believe that I killed your father and those passengers. Now, do you honestly think I could have done that and have the nerve to pay you court?"

"No," Stacey said. "No, I would find that very hard to believe."

"Then there is no confusion," Bramwell concluded, with the logic of a lawyer summing up his case.

"But I have just as much difficulty believing that about Clay Conway," Stacey said quietly.

Bramwell sighed, then stood up. He looked at her with an expression on his face which at first looked like anger, but which Stacey understood to be hurt. Finally, he turned to go.

"I've got to get over to my office," Bramwell said quietly. "And you have to take the stage out. Perhaps I should give you time to consider what we have discussed here. But remember this, Stacey. Clay Conway is a known killer. And the issue is very clear. You either believe me or you believe that criminal. There can be nothing in between."

"Bram, I'm sorry," Stacey said. "Of course I don't believe you killed my father."

Bramwell smiled, the same slow, hot smile Stacey had seen many times before. "I'm glad you see it that way," he said. "Now, Godspeed, and I'll see you tonight."

When Stacey climbed onto the driver's seat of the stage at one minute before six o'clock there was only one passenger ready to board. It was the man she had met at breakfast, called Phil.

"Are you going to go with me?" Stacey asked. "Or are you going to wait until the two o'clock stage like the others?"

Phil was not a particularly attractive man, but he had a pleasant face and a winning demeanor about him. He smiled at Stacey.

"Miss Pendarrow, I'm a traveling salesman, and I reckon I've ridden over every stage route in the Northwest. As a matter of the law of averages some of those drivers had to be poor risks, but I said nothing about it because they were men. If Wells Fargo says you can handle this rig then who am I to argue just because you are a woman? I know I sure as hell couldn't handle it just because I'm a man. Excuse my language, ma'am; I meant no offense."

"No offense taken," Stacey replied, returning Phil's broad smile with one of her own. "Now climb in and make yourself comfortable because I'm about to give you the smoothest ride you've ever had."

The arrival and departure of any stage was enough of an event to bring several people to the Wells Fargo office. The fact that the stage was being driven by a woman, and a very beautiful woman at that, was enough to bring out more than the usual number of curious onlookers, despite the early hour.

"Phil, any last words?" someone from the crowd yelled, and his call was greeted with laughter.

"Goodbye, fellas," Phil replied, waving through the open window of the stage. "I'll see you on my next trip."

"That is, assumin' you survive *this* trip," the wag called again, and again there was laughter.

"It could be worse, Tom," Phil replied.

"Oh? How could it be worse?" the jokester shouted back.

"You could be drivin' this thing," Phil said.

This time everyone laughed. Then Stacey called to the team and snapped the whip over their heads. The horses swung the stage around and began trotting briskly down the main street of the town, headed for the road which would take them over Eagle Mountain. Most western stages were pulled by four- or six-horse teams. The MacAllister – Sky Meadow – Winchester run was always pulled by an eight-horse hitch because of the elevation of the mountain pass and the steepness of the grade. Therefore, the entrance or exit of one of these stages was a scene of majestic grandeur. It was a thrilling sight which never failed to halt pedestrians and riders alike, and as she drove the team along the main street, on parade as it were, Stacey felt excitement tingling through her.

Later, as the town of MacAllister dropped off behind and below her, Stacey found time to think about things. These moments of introspection had been rare lately. As a young girl at Sky Meadow she had often spent the lonely hours in meditative contemplation. The excitement of the social whirl in Denver had preempted that exercise, and her work as an assistant agent with the MacAllister Office had precluded the opportunity to engage in much serious thinking. Now, however, with a four-hour run to Sky Meadow, she would once again have time to consider events, and put them in their proper perspective.

There had been many things happening in her life in the past months which had not been given their full measure of contemplation. Now, as if filing papers in the Wells Fargo office, Stacey began considering those events one at a time, formulating her attitude toward them.

The first and most significant event had been her father's untimely death. Seth Pendarrow had been more than a father to her. He had been a friend and a teacher and the long, quiet hours with him at Sky Meadow had been happy ones. From Seth she learned to tend animals, love nature, and drive teams. And it had been Seth who augmented her casual education by applying for correspondence courses and insisting that she study them. She loved her father and missed him very much.

And that brought her to the next event. Had she allowed her grief over her father's death to color her judgement with regard to Clay Conway? Bramwell Caulder insisted that Clay was guilty, but Clay was just as insistent that he wasn't. That meant that it was Bramwell's word against Clay's. Why, then, was she so ready to believe Bramwell? And if she didn't believe Bramwell, did that mean that he was guilty and not Clay? No. That was more than she was willing to accept. Despite Bramwell's insistence that Clay did it, Stacey was willing to give him the benefit of the doubt and believe that Bramwell had made an error in his identification through an honest mistake, not through evil intent. That is, of course, assuming that Clay was, as he claimed, innocent.

Just why, she asked herself, was she willing to even consider the possibility of Clay's innocence? Was it because she had never given him a chance in her own mind? Or was it because she had allowed him to make love to her?

No, that was wrong; she had been raped by him, she reminded herself. But no. . . . in this innermost part of her mind, she had always been honest with herself, and she was going to be honest now. Clay did not rape her, he made love to her. Considering his innocence was as normal as considering Bramwell Caulder innocent, because she had allowed Bramwell, too, to make love to her. She would have to face it: Bramwell might be guilty of the deed.

Stacey felt a quick chill pass through her. She had not really considered *that* possibility before.

Why not? she asked herself. Was she so ready to believe Clay guilty and Bramwell innocent that she didn't look for any suggestion to the contrary? There were questions that had never been given substance in her mind, but had hung shrouded in the mists of confusion. For example, Bramwell Caulder had told her on that fateful day that the ten thousand dollars had been taken. *How had he known the exact amount of money?* Such shipments were generally kept secret and he could not have known the exact amount, unless there was some reason for it. *Why was he even riding the stage that day?* Bramwell Caulder was an excellent horseman who made frequent trips to Winchester, but, as far as Stacey knew, he had never used the stage before or since. Why was that day an exception? *And how could he have avoided seeing Charles Gideon's body last night?* It was found lying in the middle of the road, there had been a bright moon, and he had supposedly passed through there after the robbery and accident.

But how could he be the guilty one? He was tender and caring and loving. Clay Conway had lifted her to the stars with his lovemaking but Bramwell Caulder was also an accomplished lover whose skilled fingers were able to play upon the strings of her sexual needs the way a master violinist played upon his instrument.

Now it was time to consider something which had become a dominant factor in her personality. Stacey had made a discovery which was both frightening and thrilling. It was as if a two-headed monster resided within her being, seeking to devour itself. There was a disquieting battle of emotions as she wanted to give in to the pleasure of the flesh, while reason and decency told her she should subdue such behavior.

It all had started this spring and summer, beginning with the morning she had awakened from a sleep-induced episode of masturbation, through the frightening sensations she felt during the brutal rape by Billy Miles, to the frustrating experience with Marcus, followed by the shameful scene with Uncle Toby—and now the relationship with Bramwell Caulder.

Wait a minute, wait a minute! the listening voice within her called. What about Clay Conway? Nowhere in this lurid recital of sexual experiences was Clay Conway mentioned. Why not?

Why not indeed? Stacey wondered. And then an unwanted answer suggested itself. Could it be that these other experiences were examples of the uncontrollable lusts which lived within her body, while the relationship with Clay was the response to a higher emotion, an emotion like love?

Stacey had no answer for that question though she was honest from the depths of her soul. But since it was raised it was one worth considering and as frightening as the prospect was, it was something which couldn't be avoided.

Chapter Twenty-five

The rims of the stage wheels were covered with steel bands, and they rolled over the hard dirt road with a quiet, crunching sound. As the wheels whirled around, dirt adhered to the rims for about half a revolution, then was thrown back in little rooster tails to be carried off by the whispering breeze. The sun was still early-morning low over the mountains, and way down in the valley a morning mist wrapped itself around the Ponderosa pines, clinging to the branches in flowing tendrils of lace as delicate as the finest bridal veil.

Stacey rode high on the driver's seat, looking out over the broad backs of the eight horses, loving this scene that represented at last the fruition of all her hopes and ambitions. She was driving a stage! She was back where she belonged. How could the sterile society of Denver parties, balls, and afternoon teas ever hope to compete with this? This was the purpose for which she was born, and never had she felt such elation!

She was about an hour out of MacAllister, though that community could still be seen as a cluster of tiny white buildings on the valley floor far below them, when Clay Conway suddenly dropped down from a rock outcropping, landed lightly on top of the stage, then slipped down onto the seat beside her.

"Oh!" Stacey gasped, startled by his sudden appearance. She began to halt the team.

"No," Clay said, "keep it moving."

"What are you doing here?" Stacey asked angrily. "And why should I keep the stage going, just because you ordered me to?"

"Your first responsibility is to the safety of your passenger," Clay said easily. "If you stop now he might try to do something foolish. I wouldn't want him to get hurt."

"I see," Stacey said. "And did you come to rob me?" she wanted to know, asking the question in a taunting, mocking voice.

"No," Clay said easily. "I have enough to last me for a while."

"I dare say that you do," Stacey said. "The five thousand dollars you got last night should have fattened your coffers quite adequately."

"Five thou . . . What are you talking about?"

"I suppose you're going to deny having robbed the stage last night, and killing the driver?"

"Of course I'm going to deny it," Clay said. "I've been away—I just returned this morning. I saw the stage approaching, and I saw you driving it. I knew nothing about the stage robbery last night."

"Then it goes without saying that you also know nothing about the wreck," Stacey said. Still, the tone of her voice was taunting, disbelieving.

"What wreck?"

"After the driver was killed, the shotgun messenger tried to bring the stage in. He went over the edge of the road and was killed, along with one of the passengers."

"God, no, I didn't know that," Clay said. "You said one of the passengers. Then there were survivors?"

"One," Stacey said. "He says you were the robber."

"He's mistaken," Clay said. "I told you, I was in Portland. Anyway, even if I had been here, that's not my style. I don't kill people."

"Tell that to my father," Stacey said.

Clay sighed. "Stacey, as God is my witness, I had nothing to do with that except in my dereliction of duty. I was charged with the safety of your father and the passengers and there I admit that I failed. But that is my only guilt. Since then I have robbed a few stages, yes, but I have never hurt anyone, and I've kept a very close accounting of the money I've taken. So far it's been $831.76. That's certainly less than the five thousand dollars you said I took last night. I swear to you I didn't rob that stage."

"Maybe you didn't," Stacey admitted.

Clay looked at her with surprise on his face. "You mean you believe me? You're willing to believe that I didn't rob that stage?"

"I didn't say I believe you for certain," Stacey replied. "I just said maybe. I know for a fact that you didn't rob the stage I was on, yet if I hadn't been there you would have been blamed for it."

"Then couldn't you believe that I am also innocent of any wrongdoing in your father's death?"

"I don't know. . . ."

"I was framed for that, Stacey. Just as I'm being

framed for so many other Wells Fargo robberies."

"Who is framing you?" Stacey asked. "And why?"

"The why is easy," Clay replied. "So far, whoever it is has gotten ten thousand dollars from your father's stage, five thousand last night, and if the papers are to be believed, a total of at least another five thousand from the other stages. That's twenty thousand dollars, and that's enough of a reason for anyone to want to frame someone else."

"All right, that's the why. Now who?" Stacey asked. "Who do you think is doing all this?"

"The who is just as easy for me," Clay said. "But *you* are going to have a difficult time with it."

"Clay, you aren't going to tell me it's Bramwell Caulder, are you? Because I just don't believe that."

"I'm sorry, Stacey," Clay said, "but that is exactly what I am going to tell you."

"Don't forget," Stacey reminded him, "I was on one of the stages robbed. I knew that the robber wasn't you, though he tried to convince us that he was—but I also know that it wasn't Bramwell Caulder."

"Then it has to be someone who is working for him," Clay insisted. "Somehow, Caulder is behind all this. That's the only way I can explain why he would try to convince everyone that I was the one who held up your father's stage."

"I had the same conversation with Bramwell this morning," Stacey said.

"And?"

"And he was trying to convince me that you are the one behind it all."

"*Trying* to convince you?" Clay asked, looking at

Stacey with an expression of hope, and a suggestion of joy on his face. "Stacey, what do you mean he was *trying* to convince you? You mean it's possible—barely possible—that you might *believe* me? You are ready to concede that I might be innocent?"

"I don't know," Stacey confessed. "Oh, Clay, I *want* to believe you. But Bramwell is so sure he saw you. And then there is the evidence."

"All right, let's talk about the evidence," Clay said, "for I have a few questions of my own, if you're willing to listen."

The road made a hairpin turn and Stacey negotiated it with skill, taking a moment before she answered Clay. "I'll listen."

"Consider Bramwell Caulder's story for a moment, will you? He claims that he knocked me out, then went for help. But when he returned with you and the posse, I was still there. Why hadn't I left? If I had just robbed the stage, do you think I would wait around for the posse to return?"

"I don't know," Stacey said again. "Maybe you had just come to. Or maybe you were so groggy from the blow that you didn't know what you were doing."

"Then what about the strongbox?"

"The strongbox?"

"Yes. The one with the money."

"Maybe you just took the money and left the strongbox."

"There are a couple of things wrong with that," Clay said. "Three-fourths of that money was in coin. I know, because I watched them count it and put it in the box. Do you have any idea how bulky seventy-five hundred dollars in coin is? There was no way I could have secreted that much on my person. I would have had money bags hanging all over me, but as you remember I had nothing. Also, if I took just the money and left the strongbox, what happened to it? Why hasn't it been found yet?"

"So what does that mean?" Stacey asked.

"It means that whoever *did* do this, took the strongbox with him," Clay said.

"But you say Bramwell did it," Stacey protested. "You forget, I saw Bramwell that morning too. He didn't have the strongbox with him. And if it were as heavy as you say, he wouldn't have carried it away on foot."

"That doesn't mean anything," Clay said. "He probably had confederates working with him."

"Did you see anyone else?"

"No, Stacey, I did not. I wish I had. I wish to God I had, for then I would have been much more cautious. Perhaps I would even have been cautious enough to prevent Caulder from slipping up on me."

"But it couldn't have been Bramwell," Stacey said. "Oh, Clay, it just couldn't have been. Did you actually *see* him slip up on you?"

"No," Clay admitted.

"Maybe someone slipped up on the stage after you stopped. He could have climbed up on it, or jumped on the roof, just as you did, without being seen. Then he could have knocked you out, killed the others and taken the money. If he was about your size, Bramwell might have mistaken him for you, especially as he fled into the rocks on the side of the road after the stage stopped. Then, if he

248

thought you were the culprit, Bramwell sneaked up on you and knocked you out."

"Is that the story he tells?" Clay asked.

"Yes. Only he insists that it was you. He insists that there could be no mistake."

"I didn't do it," Clay said simply.

"Oh, Clay," Stacey said, her voice cracking with hope. "Is it possible that you didn't?"

"It's a fact, Stacey." Although Clay put a hand on Stacey's shoulder, her eyes never left the road until they came to a level stretch. Then she turned to look into his eyes. In that moment, it was if they were windows which opened to his very soul. She looked very, very deep, and saw no deception.

"Believe me," he pleaded, "I'm innocent."

"I . . . I do believe you," Stacey finally said. "The question now is, what are you going to do?"

"Do?"

"About proving your innocence," Stacey answered, her eyes back on the road. "Clay, you can't go on living the life of an outlaw forever, you know."

Clay laughed a short, bitter laugh.

"Darlin', the truth is there's nothing I can do. I hoped against hope to be able to convince you of my innocence, and now I did. But there's scant chance of anyone else believing me—especially with someone hell-bent on making me into the criminal of the century. If I so much as show my face anywhere, people will shoot first and ask questions later. The only thing I can do is just stay out of sight."

"Clay, why don't you leave the area?" Stacey asked.

"No," Clay answered. "I'm looking for someone. A person named Barney."

"Oh, yes," Stacey said. "I remember now. Because of your family's murder."

"Yes, that's why I went to Portland. I heard of a gambler there who fit the description: a well-educated, smooth-talking dandy. They didn't say anything about his hands, but I figured him being a gambler, his hands would have to fit the description."

"His hands?"

"Yes. They are small hands, with long fingers and clean, smoothed off fingernails like a woman's."

"Was the gambler your man?"

"No," Clay said. "That gambler was a foreigner of some kind. He talked smooth all right, but he talked with an accent. My man is from this part of the country. And I'll find him." He looked at Stacey, and the expression of anger and determination that had come to his face left, to be replaced with a smile. "In the meantime, Stacey, I shall take great comfort from the fact that you, at least, believe me."

As Stacey turned her head toward him, Clay suddenly kissed her, then, with the taste of her kiss still on his lips, he stood up, clambered across the top of the stage, and dropped off to the rear. The passenger, Phil, never knew he had been there.

Chapter Twenty-six

In less than a month Howard Mason's objections to Stacey being a driver dissolved. He went from being an obstacle in her path to being her greatest supporter, and promised to "take it to the highest authority" if ordered to dismiss Stacey because of her gender. His enthusiasm was well-founded; Stacey's trips were always completed on schedule. She was well liked and courteous to her passengers, and the number of passengers increased, just to be able to say they had ridden with Wells Fargo's "beautiful lady driver."

There was another reason for Stacey's success as a stagecoach driver. Stage robberies, which were occurring at the rate of three a week within other areas of Mason's responsibility, were not happening on Stacey's runs. Speculation as to why she was being spared ran rampant, but the most commonly accepted reason was that Beau Bandito was too much of a gentleman to stop a stage driven by a lady driver.

Stacey did see Clay, though, and she saw him quite often, for he would drop in on her as he did on her very first trip. In fact, she began looking for him and was sometimes disappointed if a trip went by and he didn't show. But there had been no more nocturnal visits, and though Stacey by now would have welcomed such a visit, she had not yet acquired the courage to convey that message to Clay.

There would be little chance of Clay running into unwanted company should he decide to call upon her in the night, because shortly after Clay started dropping in on her she terminated her assignations with Bramwell Caulder. She wasn't sure why she began turning him away. She found herself wondering, more and more, if, as Clay claimed, Bramwell could be behind the efforts to frame him. If so, that would make Bramwell Caulder guilty of her father's murder too, and she could not consider intimacy with a man who might have killed her father.

Stacey's relationship with Caulder remained friendly, but proper. At first Bramwell couldn't believe that Stacey, who had once welcomed him to her bed, could grow so cool to his advances. Despite his persistence, however, Stacey stood firm, and the issue was subsequently dropped.

Stacey continued to live in the hotel suite, though now at her own expense, and she still enjoyed an occasional dinner with Caulder, or shows, lectures, or lantern projections with him, when such entertainments were available. There were even times when she would take dinner with him in his living quarters behind his law office, and listen to him play the piano. He was an excellent pianist, and she liked to watch his slim hands and long fingers fly over the keyboard. It was as if his hands were designed especially for such a talent, and she marveled at his skill.

Stacey was bringing a run into Sky Meadow, and remembering a concert she had attended the night before, had been humming Chopin for most of the drive. The way station would come into view as soon as she rounded the next bend.

She never failed to get a strange feeling at seeing this place which had been her home for so many years, and one of the pleasures she derived from driving was traveling the route which took her to her old homeplace.

As she urged the team into a brisk trot for the final thousand yards, she noticed that the three o'clock stage from Winchester was already there. Curious about why it was there so early, she was nevertheless pleased for her passengers, as it meant that they wouldn't have that long wait until three o'clock in the afternoon to make their connection.

Melissa, the station agent's daughter, met Stacey's stage as she pulled in. Melissa was fifteen years old, and Stacey saw herself in the pretty young girl, and was secretly flattered by the fact that Melissa saw herself in Stacey. Melissa too, wanted to be a coach driver, and seeing Stacey succeed had given Melissa hope for such a future for herself.

"You're twenty minutes early," Melissa said, climbing up the wheel to speak to Stacey. Melissa had long, straw-colored hair which she wore in pigtails, and eyes the color of Colorado columbines.

"*I'm* early?" Stacey asked. She pulled the huge braking lever and secured the trace lines to the rung in front of her seat. "What about him? He's about five hours early, isn't he?" She pointed to the other stage.

"Oh, that's not the regular stage. There was only one passenger in that stage, and she knows you. In fact, she said she was going to MacAllister to see you!"

"Folks, this is Sky Meadow," Stacey called to her passengers. "You'll change coaches here."

The three men and two women opened the door and climbed down, then began to stretch and work out the kinks from the trip. Stacey walked around to the boot of the stage and opened it, then she and Melissa began setting the passengers' luggage out on the ground.

"Did you say she was going to MacAllister just to see me?" Stacey asked.

"Yes," Melissa said. "Oh, Stacey, you should see her. She's beautiful, and she's wearing the most beautiful dress I have ever seen. She came from Denver and she says she knows you."

"Denver, you say?" Stacey asked, looking toward the house. "Who is she, do you know?"

"Her name is Yolinda Sinclair," Melissa said. "Why don't you go on in and talk to her? I'll close up the boot."

"Thanks, Melissa, maybe I will," Stacey said.

Oh, Stacey thought, why did Yolinda have to see her here, like this? She looked at her hands and saw the calluses from driving. She was wearing men's pants and a man's shirt, and an old felt hat to keep the sun out of her eyes. Yes, Yolinda would have her laugh all right.

But wait a minute, Stacey reasoned. This isn't Denver. Yolinda is on my ground now. She'll be as helpless here as I was when I first went to Denver. Stacey smiled at the thought, then realized that Yolinda must have known that too. Why then would she subject herself to this? Unless . . . Good Lord, perhaps something had happened to Aunt Pricilla or Uncle Tobias?

Stacey ran the remaining distance to the house she knew so well, jumped lightly onto the front porch, then pushed the door open and walked inside. The passengers she had just brought were ordering coffee and making arrangements to continue the journey. Sitting quietly on a sofa in the corner was Yolinda Sinclair. She smiled at Stacey, a wan, hesitant smile.

"Yolinda, what is it?" Stacey asked quickly. "Are my aunt and uncle all right?"

"Mr. and Mrs. Prescott?" Yolinda asked innocently. "Yes, of course,"

"Well, I was just surprised . . . I mean, to see you . . . Yolinda, you didn't really come to see *me*, did you?"

"Yes, I did," Yolinda said.

Stacey looked at her for a moment, unable to mask her surprise, and then she settled onto the couch beside her. "Why, Yolinda? I wasn't one of your favorite people back in Denver."

"Oh, Stacey, I do hope you can forgive me for all that," Yolinda said. "I must say that since you left, we have missed you. Besides, I feel as if I have grown up in the last couple of months. All that seems so . . . so girlish now."

Yolinda's words sounded genuine to Stacey, and she smiled and put her hand out to touch Yolinda's gloved one. "Of course I forgive you," she said. "And I shall be glad to have you as a visitor."

"When I inquired of the station agent if he knew you, he said you were driving the stage," Yolinda said. "Are you really?"

"That I am," Stacey replied with a smile. "And unless you've hired that private rig to take you all the way to MacAllister, you'll ride in with me."

"I had hired it for the distance," Yolinda said. "But if there is any way I can let it go back, I'll be glad to ride with you."

"Just sit there for a moment," Stacey said. "I'll take care of it for you."

Stacey talked to the station agent and worked out a plan whereby the passengers' fares from Sky Meadow to Winchester were paid to Yolinda for the use of the private coach, and they were able to cut five hours off the trip. Since the coach had been rented from Wells Fargo in the first place, it all worked out, and no one lost money.

"Papa and I will load the luggage," Melissa said. "You can talk to your friend."

"Thanks, honey," Stacey replied.

Yolinda laughed nervously. "I . . . I had no idea what to bring to wear, so I'm afraid I brought just about everything. That was one reason I hired a private coach. That, and the fact that I know nothing about the territory out here. I could see myself lost at some out-of-the-way Indian trading post. My, Stacey, this is certainly rugged country out here."

"Perhaps so," Stacey agreed. "But it's beautiful."

"It becomes you," Yolinda said. "If anything, you

are even more beautiful now than you were in Denver. And God knows, I was jealous enough of you in Denver."

"Oh, I'm sure I am," Stacey said, laughing. "Look at me—men's pants, shirt, and these hands. I'm a mess."

"I don't think you are a mess," Yolinda said. "And neither would Marcus."

"How is Marcus?"

"He's fine," Yolinda said.

"And Cynthia and Mary?"

Yolinda looked at the floor for a moment before she answered. "I do have some bad news for you," she said.

"Bad? What is it?"

"I know how much you liked Mary. Indeed, we all loved her. She was such a dear girl."

"*Was?*"

Yolinda looked up again, and Stacey saw tears sliding down her cheeks. "Mary is dead, Stacey. She caught some sort of strange fever and died in a matter of days."

"Oh, no," Stacey said softly. She thought of the plain, gentle, soft-spoken girl, and a lump came to her throat. Her eyes filled as quickly as Yolinda's had, and Yolinda handed her a clean, fresh handkerchief.

"I'm sorry to have to be the one to tell you," she said.

"Mary helped make Denver bearable for me," Stacey replied.

"She was a much finer person than I was, I'm sorry to say," Yolinda said.

"Oh, I was just as bad," Stacey replied. "It's all part of the game."

"That's just it," Yolinda said. "It was a game. Here, in this magnificent country, it doesn't seem real. I can't imagine playing a game out here."

"You can't?" Stacey asked, the inflection of her voice rising on the last word. "Then why are you here, Yolinda? I mean why are you *really* here?"

"I'm sorry," Yolinda said with a nervous laugh. "I guess you caught me there. In a way, I am playing a game now. At least, sort of a game. But I really have changed, Stacey, and I really am sorry for the awful way I acted when you came to Denver. And. . . ." she let the last word hang.

"And?"

"And I need your help."

"How?"

"It has to do with Marcus."

"What about Marcus? He's all right, isn't he?"

"Yes, he's fine," Yolinda answered quickly. "That is, I think he's fine. But I have a feeling there is something you can tell me about him that I don't know."

"What makes you think that?"

Yolinda sighed. "Stacey, I won't beat around the bush with you. Marcus and I are going to get married."

"Congratulations," Stacey said with genuine enthusiasm. Then, "Oh, Aunt Pricilla said that one doesn't congratulate the bride."

"In this case perhaps congratulations are in order," Yolinda said. "It was no secret from anyone that I had my cap set for Marcus. That was why I was so ugly to you when you first came to Denver. I saw you as competition. But now I've got him . . . I think."

"What do you mean, you think?"

"That's where you come in," Yolinda said.

"Yolinda, I consider Marcus Tremain a very good friend, and nothing more," Stacey said. "I have no matrimonial designs on him. If that's what you are worried about, you needn't."

"It isn't that," Yolinda said. "It's something else. Something that is so personal, that Marcus won't talk to me about it. He asked, in fact he *insisted*, that I come talk to you."

"Oh." Stacey suddenly realized what it was all about. Marcus had put the burden of telling Yolinda about his impotence on Stacey. "I see."

"Do you know what it is?"

"Yes," Stacey said. "I know."

"Marcus wanted me to talk to you. He said that if I still wanted to marry him after I returned, we would get married. Stacey, what is it? What is he talking about?"

"Stacey, you're all loaded up and ready to go," Melissa called from the porch.

"Do I have any more passengers?"

"One, the schoolmarm. She's waiting by the coach."

Stacey stood up, then looked back toward Yolinda. "Yolinda, this is something best discussed in complete privacy. I'll tell you what. We'll have dinner in my apartment tonight, and we'll talk about it there."

"Then you don't mind talking to me about it?" Yolinda asked.

Stacey smiled, a small, sad smile, and thought of the pain and suffering Marcus must have gone through before he decided to send Yolinda to see her.

"No," she said. "I don't mind."

Chapter Twenty-seven

The Texas Kid had spoken to no one since arriving at the Bull's Knee saloon in Winchester. He sat at the end of the bar, nursing his fizzwater and lemon, and looked in the mirror at the bar patrons. There were only seven customers in the saloon, one bartender, and a woman in her late thirties who was named Jeanine. Jeanine was trying to hustle drinks from the customers, but she had little to work with. Age and dissipation lay heavily on her, and made her a caricature of the bar girls Tex had seen in the Portland saloons.

Tex signalled the bartender for another fizzwater and the bartender complied. Tex would have preferred something stronger, but he knew his weakness with whiskey. He had a very low tolerance for it, and when he got drunk he got mean. Three of the twelve people Tex had killed had been shot while he was mean drunk, and he didn't even recall any of it when he sobered up.

Tex was talented with a gun. In fact, he believed, and Brewster and Athens backed him up, that no one, anywhere, was any faster. And that included Clay Conway.

Tex had an edge that served him well; he liked

killing. It was more than the challenge, or the excitement of actually facing death; he *enjoyed* killing, whether in the heat of a battle or in cold blood. And that included the cold-blooded murder of the two women who had been on the first stage he had robbed early in the spring. Tex had never killed a woman until those two. Barney had set up the robbery, but Tex did the work. That job netted him a share of ten thousand dollars, but when he thought back on it, it wasn't the money he remembered; it was killing the women. Killing those women, even the old, ugly one, had created in Tex the greatest sexual arousal he had ever known.

One of the women, he recalled, had mistaken him for the shotgun guard who was unconscious on the front seat. Tex hadn't known then who the man was. Now, knowing that the guard had been Beau Bandito—Clay Conway—he regretted not waiting until Conway regained consciousness so he could face him down.

Beau Bandito, Tex thought angrily. He was getting sick and tired of hearing about him. Everywhere he went he heard stories of how fast Beau Bandito was, and now, because of Barney's insistence that everything be done in Clay Conway's name, Beau Bandito's legend was growing. He was helping Clay Conway build a million-dollar reputation, Tex thought, and that wasn't fair. The reputation rightly belonged to the Texas Kid, and he longed to hear the name Texas Kid spoken with the same awe and respect as Beau Bandito.

Tex had assumed the name Texas Kid when he left Wyoming and abandoned his real name. He was hiding from Big Tom Fenton, the marshal of

Mustard Flat, Wyoming, who had sworn an oath to track Tex down, no matter where he went. And all because of some pipsqueak of a schoolmaster Tex had killed during a drunken spree.

There were times when Tex thought he should stop running and face up to Big Tom, despite the marshal's reputation. And he did have a reputation equal to that enjoyed by the Earps, Pat Garrett, Bill Hickock, and others. In fact, his life was the stuff from which legends are made, and even Clay Conway was not as famous as Big Tom Fenton. Rumor had it that Big Tom had once ridden a crooked path. Whatever his past, though, he had taken his role of guardian of the peace to heart and outlaws gave him a wide berth or fell before his deadly gun. It was said that the man who incurred his wrath would curse his mother for bearing him.

It was funny, Tex thought. Here he was, anxious to build his reputation, when all he had to do would be to face down Big Tom Fenton and his reputation would be assured—or he would be killed. And as Tex had known Big Tom all his life, and had seen him in action, he knew what the older man could do.

Perhaps it was a premonition of sorts, or the sixth sense men on the run often develop, but whatever it was, it caused Tex to glance up at that moment to see a man standing just inside the double swinging doors, looking over toward him. The man was at least six feet, six inches tall, and probably weighed 260 pounds. He had dark gray-flecked hair, piercing blue eyes, a weather-tanned face, and a scar across one cheek. A well-worn pistol belt was wrapped around his waist and the sheath hung low on his right leg. A .44 stuck out from the holster and the wooden handle of the pistol had a large chip missing.

Tex gasped, then said, "Hello, Big Tom." His heart was pounding fiercely, and he made fists of his hands to keep them from shaking.

Big Tom stepped up to the bar and ordered a whiskey. "Anything for you, Arnold?" he asked Tex.

"Whi . . . whiskey," Tex said, having to start the word twice. "And I don't use that name now."

"They tell me you call yourself the Texas Kid," the marshal said.

"That's right."

Big Tom laughed. "I suppose that's as good a name as any. But it's made it hard to find you."

"I didn't expect to see you here," Tex said. He drained his whiskey quickly, then signalled for another. The bartender refilled his glass, then started away, but Tex grabbed the bottle and held it.

"No, I don't reckon you did," Big Tom said.

"How did you find me?"

"It don't matter," Big Tom said. "The point is, I did find you. I got a message for you from your mother. She's worried about you."

"When has she ever not been worried?" Tex laughed. "That's always been her trouble. She worries too much."

"Your mother's a fine woman."

"Sure, and my dad's a fine man," Tex replied bitterly.

"He tries to be."

"I suppose I was a disappointment to him."

"A great disappointment."

"I've only tried to make him proud," Tex said.

"How? By killin'?"

"Like father, like son, they say."

"No," Big Tom said. "That's not the idea and you know it." He sighed. "I'm gonna have to take you back, you know."

"Not alive, you ain't," Tex replied. He stepped away from the bar and held his arms out, his right hand dangling just over the butt of his gun.

Tex's ominous words caused the others in the bar to dash for the far wall, out of the line of fire. The bartender moved to the opposite end of the bar.

"I might have to kill you to take you back," Big Tom conceded, "but I will if I have to. I guess that means I'd better get a bite to eat now. I missed my lunch."

"Eat?"

"Yeah." The big man gave Tex a laconic grin. "You know, killin' always dulls my appetite, so I won't be able to eat later."

"What if I kill you?" Tex wanted to know.

The grin didn't leave Big Tom's face. "Then it won't matter, will it?" he said. "What you got around here to eat?" he asked the bartender.

"Eggs, bacon, some beans," the bartender replied nervously from the other end of the bar.

"That sound fine. Throw in a cup of coffee, and I'll be sittin' at that table over there," Big Tom said. He looked over at Tex. "Care to join me?"

"No," Tex said nervously. Then, "Why are you houndin' me? You've followed me across Wyoming, Idaho, and Oregon. Why?"

"Because you killed a fine man," Big Tom said simply.

"I was drunk. I didn't know what I was doing."

"He's still dead."

"I'm sorry about that."

"Sorry isn't enough."

"Listen, are you crazy? Do you know how many men I've had to kill since then? What the hell difference does one man make?"

"Every man's life is important," Big Tom said. "Maybe if I'd stopped you earlier, there wouldn't have been any of the others."

The bartender walked over and put a cup of coffee in front of Big Tom, then stepped back out of the way again, quickly. Big Tom thanked him and picked it up.

And then Tex saw it—Big Tom's hand was shaking as he held the cup! Why, he's frightened too, Tex realized. Whether he was afraid that he was about to be killed, or afraid that he was going to have to kill Tex, it didn't matter. The point was, Big Tom was frightened.

Tex knew that the opportunity would never be better and he went for his gun at that moment, yelling at Big Tom as he did so.

Big Tom had taken the coffee cup in both hands, and when he saw Tex start his move he dropped the cup and dipped his hand to his own gun. He fired a shot off just seconds before Tex, but at the last minute he had made a decision to try to wound, rather than kill. It was a fatal error.

Tex felt the bullet pass through his shirt sleeve and burn a brand across his arm. He pulled the trigger and watched the expression on Big Tom's face change to surprise, then pain, and finally a kind of sadness, as he began to slide down in his chair. A dark red patch of blood began widening on the marshal's shirt, and his gun fell to the floor.

"You shouldn't'a come after me," Tex said, his voice shaking. "You should'a stayed home where you belonged."

"No," Big Tom replied, coughing. "You were my responsibility."

"I left your damn town," Tex said bitterly. "I quit being your responsibility then."

Big Tom coughed up specks of blood. "You could never stop being my responsibility," he said. "As long as I was the marshal—and your father—I was responsible for you."

"My God!" a man against the far wall whispered, "he just killed his own father!"

Big Tom rolled out of the chair onto the floor and lay there, still and quiet. Tex looked down at him for a moment, then looked at the others. "You all saw it," he said. "Anybody sayin' it wasn't a fair fight?"

"It was fair enough, I reckon," one of the men said.

"Mr. Fenton," the bartender said.

"Don't call me that," Tex said.

"But didn't he say he was your father?"

Tex looked down at the body on the floor. "Yeah," he said. "He was my ol' man. But I go by the name of Texas Kid now. When you tell this story, you tell 'em it was the Texas Kid that shot Big Tom Fenton." He smiled broadly. "And you tell it good, you hear?"

"Yes, sir," the bartender said. "The Texas Kid."

"How about you others?" Tex asked, looking at the men and Jeanine, who now, cautiously, re-

267

turned to their seats and nodded in silent agreement.

People had been coming in from the street after the shooting stopped, and by now the saloon was nearly full. Among the newcomers was a newspaper reporter.

"Bartender," Tex said, smiling broadly, proud of his moment of glory. "Set 'em up for everybody. Folks, drinks are on the Texas Kid."

"Did you see it?" the reporter asked one of the men who had been there.

"Yeah, I seen it. Why the kid there was purt' near as fast as Beau Bandito.

Tex overheard the comment, then smashed a whiskey bottle down angrily. The babble of excitement stopped and all eyes turned to him.

"Now get this, everyone," Tex said. "And get it straight. My ol' man, who's lyin' stiff on the floor here, was faster than Clay Conway ever dreamed of bein'. And I took 'im. Now, if I can take Big Tom Fenton, don't you think I could take Beau Bandito?"

No one answered.

"Well?" Tex yelled, looking directly at the reporter. "Do you think I could take Beau Bandito?"

"Yes, sir," the reporter answered. "I'm certain that you could, sir."

"You're damn right I could take him," Tex said. "Now, you write that in your paper. You tell Beau Bandito that I challenge him, man to man, right here in Winchester."

"Yes, sir!" the reporter said, smiling broadly. "Yes, sir, I'll do that and put it in big headlines."

"You put my name first, you understand?" Tex

challenged. "You make it read the Texas Kid challenges Beau Bandito!"

"Yes, sir, I'll do it just like you say," the reporter said.

Tex took a drink and looked at his father's body again, and smiled a satisfied smile. He'd always thought his old man was the fastest there was, but he had beaten him fair and square.

Finally he said to the room at large, "He was always afraid that he might get killed in some town far away from home, and he was right, 'cause that's just what happened." Tex laughed, as if enjoying a tremendous joke. "Only thing is, I bet he never thought it would be his own son who would finally wind up killin' him."

He was still laughing as he walked out of the saloon, and to the shocked patrons of the Bull's Knee, his laughter sounded like howls from all the hounds of hell.

Chapter Twenty-eight

"Ummm," Yolinda said, patting a napkin against her lips. "You must promise me you will never tell anyone you saw me eat so much. I can't *believe* I was so *ravenous*," she said, emphasizing the two words in a way that brought memories of Denver back to Stacey.

"It's the clear mountain air," Stacey said. "It makes you hungry."

"It may be. It could also be the meals I've been forced to endure since leaving Denver. My dear, you wouldn't *believe* some of the things I've had to eat."

"Yes, I would," Stacey said easily. "I've made the trip myself, remember?"

"Oh, of course. I must say, Stacey, I admire you tremendously. I'm afraid I'm just not as strong as you are. Thank you for taking me in. This is a perfectly divine apartment. A little surprising, for a town like this, isn't it?"

"I suppose it is," Stacey said. "As you can see, there is a bathroom and a separate dressing room, as well as the bedroom and parlor. It belonged to a friend before I took it."

"She must have been quite a good friend to give

it up for you," Yolinda said. The tone of her voice indicated that she didn't believe for a moment that Stacey's friend had been a woman, but Stacey didn't take the bait. Instead she got right to the point.

"Tell me about Marcus," she said. "Is he all right?"

"Yes," Yolinda said. "I suppose he is, but Marcus is . . . well, I guess you should know better than anyone, Stacey, he's strange."

"In what way?"

"You know what I mean, don't you? He's detached from everything. He never seems to talk to you without giving you the impression that he's thinking of something else."

"Yes," Stacey said. "I know what you mean."

"Even when he asked me to marry him, it was as if the words were an afterthought."

"And yet he did ask you to marry him," Stacey said. "I'm pleased for you, Yolinda. Genuinely pleased. Tell me about Marcus. How has he been?"

"Well, after you left Denver he became very distraught. He was in love with you, Stacey. But of course, I'm sure you know that."

"No, I didn't know," Stacey said, surprised by the revelation.

"Oh, come now, you can't tell me you didn't know," Yolinda said. "Everyone knew how much he loved you."

"But that's not true," Stacey protested. "We were just friends. I considered Marcus a very close friend, perhaps the best friend I've ever had. I loved him that way, yes, and I'm sure he loved me the same way. But not as you think."

"Yes, as I think," Yolinda said. She looked at Stacey with surprise on her face. "It's true then, isn't it? You really didn't know that he loved you madly?"

"Oh, poor Marcus," Stacey said. "No, I didn't know that. Oh, Yolinda, I'm afraid I treated him so shabbily. I'm glad that he loves you now."

Yolinda's eyes suddenly darted toward her plate, and she sat there for a long moment before she answered.

"I said he was going to marry me," Yolinda said quietly, "but I didn't say he loved me."

"But of course he loves you," Stacey said. "He wouldn't have asked you to marry him otherwise."

"I'm not so sure," Yolinda said. "You see, he had two blows, one right on top of the other. First you left, and after that, he started keeping company with Mary."

"Marcus and Mary? Oh, how wonderful for her!" Then, "Oh, forgive me; that must sound awful to you."

"No, you were Mary's friend, I know that," Yolinda said. "I don't know how she managed it, Stacey, but Mary took over right where you left off. She and Marcus went everywhere together, and did everything together. You should have seen her. She was positively radiant. Stacey, I swear, as plain as she was, she was almost beautiful. And then . . . ."

"What happened to her, Yolinda?"

"The doctors don't know," Yolinda said. "She came down with some sort of chills and fever. She was terribly sick for about eight days, and then she . . . she died." Her voice cracked on the last word. "I went to see her just the night before. I had no idea she was that sick, but she knew. She said that no matter what happened now, she would have no regrets. She said it had been a summer of happiness, and then she said something about you. Something I couldn't understand.

"What?"

"She said, and let me see if I can remember it, 'Stacey started it all by what she did at the Cinderella Ball. Marcus didn't say anything about it, but I know it was Stacey.' What was she talking about, Stacey? Was she talking about you shooting at Beau Bandito?"

"No," Stacey said.

"Do you know what she meant?"

"No," Stacey said. She knew that Mary was referring to her insistence that Marcus buy Mary's dress, but she said nothing. "I guess whatever it was will be Mary's secret forever."

"Ah, yes, secrets," Yolinda said. "And that brings me to the purpose of my visit. After Mary died, I tried to comfort Marcus. And I was genuinely trying to comfort him, Stacey. For the first time in my life I wasn't doing anything devious. I was concerned only about Marcus, and not about whether or not he would see me as a possible wife. In fact, when Mother suggested that my chance had come, I almost called it off entirely, lest Marcus misunderstand the first good thing I had ever done. But Marcus did understand, and, then, to my surprise, that which I had tried to bring about through subterfuge for so long, finally fell into my lap when I was least expecting it. Marcus asked me to marry him."

"Then why do you say he doesn't love you?"

"Because I've not only become honest with others, Stacey, I've become honest with myself. Marcus has been badly wounded and he wants to retreat from it. In fact, he wants to retreat from life itself. And he asked me to marry him as a way to close the door on everything else. But, even in this, it seems there is something else I must face, something that Marcus couldn't speak about, but that you know. What is it, Stacey? Why did he send me here to talk to you?"

"Yolinda, earlier tonight you said that Marcus always seemed detached," Stacey said.

"Yes. Does that have something to do with what he wants you to tell me?"

"I believe it does."

"Stacey, I'm a grown woman," Yolinda said. "I know that men sometimes sow a few wild oats, as they say. Are you trying to tell me that Marcus and you . . . that the two of you . . . uh, how can I put it?"

"Are you trying to ask me if Marcus and I have shared a bed?" Stacey asked.

"Yes," Yolinda replied softly. "Because if that's what it is, then I don't mind. Really I don't, and I told Marcus that."

"What did Marcus say?"

"He just smiled that same, sad smile, and told me to talk to you. Stacey, for God's sake, what is it? Surely his conscience can't be bothering him that much. So you made love, so what?"

"But we didn't make love," Stacey said.

"Stacey, believe me, I won't be upset by it," Yolinda replied. "I'd welcome a little clearing of the air. I told you I was being honest with others, and I was being honest with myself. Why can't you and Marcus be honest with me?"

"I am being honest with you," Stacey said. "Marcus and I have never made love—Marcus has never been to bed with *any* woman."

"Oh, come now," Yolinda said. "It's whispered all over town that he has visited bawdy houses. Even my mother has heard that. She told me it was to be expected of men. So why are you telling me such a thing?"

"Because it's true," Stacey said. "Yolinda, Marcus sent you to see me because he didn't want to face you with the truth himself. He's never made love to any woman because he can't—he's impotent."

"But I don't understand. Marcus has always . . . I mean, his reputation!" Yolinda cried.

"It's unfortunate, but it's true," Stacey said. "He can't . . . he's unable to . . . ." Stacey stumbled over her words, looking for a delicate way to say it.

"My God, doesn't he have what other men have?" Yolinda asked finally.

"Yes, he has," Stacey said, "but it doesn't—work."

"But that can't be true. All men have to fight to keep their terrible urges under control," Yolinda said. "That's a well-known fact."

"That's what we are taught as little girls," Stacey said. "But it simply isn't true. Marcus suffers from this affliction, not only by not being able to make love, but in his own self-esteem. He doesn't consider himself a man, Yolinda. And that's why he acts as he does."

"And all because he's impotent?" Yolinda asked.

"Yes."

"I see. I wonder why he could tell you, and he couldn't tell me."

"He didn't tell me," Stacey said, letting the statement drop there.

"Well then, how did you know if he didn't tell . . . oh!" Yolinda put her hand to her lips as she suddenly realized what Stacey meant.

"I suppose he wanted you to know before you found out on your wedding night," Stacey said. "Assuming that there will still be a wedding night, now that you know."

"Of course there will be a wedding night," Yolinda said. "Why shouldn't there be?"

"Yolinda, haven't you been listening to what I just told you? You and Marcus could never have a normal married life."

"Of course we could," Yolinda said. "We just won't bed together. But to my way of thinking, that's all the better. That's certainly not the part of married life that I would look forward to anyway. It doesn't get you anything but a passel of kids, and I don't want any."

Stacey looked at Yolinda in surprise. It was obvious that Yolinda meant what she was saying. But how could she mean it? How could she willingly deny herself the pleasure a man could provide? In that moment, Stacey wondered anew whether there was something wrong with *her*. Was she suffering from some monstrous quirk of nature, betrayed by her body as Marcus was by his? Was she cursed with unwomanly passions, as surely as Marcus was cursed with impotence? If that was true, what a strange twist of fate it was.

"What's wrong?" Yolinda asked seeing the changing expressions on Stacey's face.

"Nothing," Stacey said quickly. "Nothing is wrong. I guess I had just assumed that you would want children, that's all."

"Well I *don't* want them" Yolinda said, and smiled. "I guess that would make me the perfect wife for Marcus, wouldn't it?"

"I suppose so," Stacey said, still disturbed by the way Yolinda took the news. One of them was wrong, she knew. But which one?

Chapter Twenty-nine

When Stacey returned from her trip to Sky Meadow the next day, Mason asked her if she would take the overnight run as well. Pete Johnson normally took that one, but he had sent a message that he was sick and unable to make it. There was no one else to go, Mason explained.

"But I have a guest in town," Stacey protested. "She came all the way from Denver to see me."

"Stacey, I don't have any choice," Mason replied. "I've got passengers and a shipment which must go out. After all, you wanted to be a stage driver."

Stacey rubbed the back of her hand across her forehead and smiled. "All right," she said. "I'll be back in time for the afternoon run. But I need to go to my apartment and explain things to my guest. Also, I want to take a bath and change clothes."

"Why?" Mason asked in surprise. "You're just going right out again."

"You don't understand," Stacey said. "I hold the thought of that bath in front of me, like a carrot on a stick. It's what gets me through the last three hours, and I'm not going to deny myself its pleasure, even if I do have to go right back out. By the way, who's going to take my six o'clock run in the morning?"

"Pete will," Mason said. "He'll be okay by then. And when he returns, he'll go right back on his own run. You'll get back to your regular schedule within a couple of days."

"Have Jack take care of changing the team, will you? Tell him I won't be back in time to help, I'll just barely make it for departure. Now, if you'll excuse me, I must hurry."

"Thank you, Stacey. You don't know how much I appreciate this."

Stacey looked at Mason and saw that he was genuinely relieved that his problem had been solved. She smiled. "Ahh, I don't mind. After all, you said it. I did want to be a stage driver, and you've got to take some of the bad with the good. Don't worry about it, I'll be back in time. You just have Jack take care of the team and you handle the loading, that's all I ask."

Stacey hurried along the boardwalk, headed for the hotel and a hot bath. As she thought of it, the idea became more acceptable to her. In truth, she had no idea what she could do to entertain Yolinda, though she had the feeling that she should do something. This would at least postpone it for one more day. Perhaps by then she would think of something they could do.

Stacey thought of the upcoming trip. It was called an overnight run because the stage would arrive at Sky Meadow too late to return on the same day. The driver and passengers generally spent the night at Sky Meadow, and the passengers went on through the next day while the driver brought the stage back, picking up new passengers who were going in the opposite direction. The prospect of spending a night at Sky Meadow again was actually a pleasant one.

As Stacey stepped into the lobby of the hotel a waiter from the dining room saw her and hurried over to her. "Miss Pendarrow, do you wish your usual table for lunch?"

"No, thank you, Sam," Stacey replied. Stacey had made a habit of taking a light, mid-afternoon lunch, as she didn't eat during the trip. The late lunch usually meant a very late dinner, but that, too, was to Stacey's liking. "By the way, have you seen Miss Sinclair today?"

"She took her breakfast quite late," Sam said, with just a hint of disapproval in his voice.

"I see. Well, she may not want anything either. I must take another run right away so I won't have time to eat."

"You are going right back out?" Sam asked.

"I'm afraid so. Pete's sick."

Sam smothered a cough. "He's intoxicated, you mean," he said. "He goes on these two-day binges from time to time."

Stacey smiled at Sam's use of the word "intoxicated." Sam considered his position as a waiter to be the badge of a gentleman and he strove to express that in his choice of words. "Sick or intoxicated, it's all the same," Stacey said. "I've got to take his run for him."

"Perhaps you would like lunch sent up to your room?" Sam asked.

"Yes," Stacey replied. "Yes, thank you, Sam, that

would be nice. Send David up in about five minutes, would you please?"

"Of course, Miss Pendarrow," Sam replied.

Stacey glanced over into the dining room as she climbed the stairs, but she didn't see anyone she recognized. She was just as glad because she wanted a quiet, leisurely bath, and that meant she would have to get into the tub right away and not waste time talking.

Tex and Brewster were in the dining room. They had come into town for supplies, but Tex insisted that they stop to "eat a steak that ain't saddle-broke." After all, he wanted to know, what good was the money if they didn't spend it on things like women, whiskey, and steak?

They had just taken their seats when Brewster happened to glance in the mirror and see the reflection of Stacey climbing the stairs.

"My God!" he said, "it's her!"

"Who is her?" Tex asked.

"That girl, climbing the stairs, she's the one Lorin . . . uh . . . Athens and I had a run-in with back in Denver."

"Run-in, huh?" Tex said. "Ram-in was more like what I heard. I didn't get a chance to get a good look at her. It may be I might want to try a little of it myself."

Brewster was studying the mirror to see if she'd seen him. Evidently she hadn't and he breathed a little easier.

"You'd be better off leaving her alone," Brewster said.

"Why?"

"She's a hellcat," Brewster said. "I don't want her to ever see me again."

Sam walked back into the restaurant from the lobby, and saw Tex and Brewster sitting at the table. He approached them with a practiced smile. "Would you gentlemen care to order?"

"Yeah," Tex said. "I want the biggest, best steak you got. And you tell the cook that if it's tough, I personally am gonna come into the kitchen and settle accounts with him."

"Our steaks are not tough, sir," Sam replied haughtily, as if offended that anyone would even suggest such a thing.

"That's what they all say," Tex said. "And I've eaten in better joints than this."

"I daresay that is difficult to believe," Sam said, taking pleasure in the fact that he considered himself to be cutting this uncouth boor to the quick.

"Yeah, well it's true," Tex conceded. "But as long as me 'n you got an understandin', I'm not gonna worry about my steak."

"That's good, sir."

"I'm not gonna worry ," Tex went on, " 'cause I figure you and the cook will do the worryin' for me. Especially seein' as who I am."

"Who *are* you, sir?"

"I'm the Texas Kid."

"The Texas Kid?" Sam repeated, setting each word apart. "Is that supposed to be meaningful, sir?"

Brewster laughed.

"Are you tryin' to tell me you never heard of the Texas Kid?" Tex asked in amazement.

"I'm afraid not, sir," Sam replied.

"Where you been, Sam?" a young man asked. He had been busy clearing tables, nearby, and now walked over to their table, drying his hands on his towel and staring at Tex. "Are you really the Texas Kid?"

"That I am," Tex replied, beaming under the recognition.

"Gee, I read all about you in the papers. You shot Big Tom Fenton, didn't you?"

"Shot 'im dead," Tex said, smiling proudly.

The young man finished drying his hands, then stuck one of them out toward Tex. "I'm awful pleased to meet you, Texas Kid. My name is David Banks."

David's hand hung in mid-air for an awkward moment, then he brought it back.

"Boy, you got a lot to learn," Tex said. "You never shake hands with a gunfighter."

"Oh, no, I . . . I guess not," David said sheepishly.

"You see, now that I've killed Big Tom Fenton, why there ain't no question at all as to who is the fastest gun around," Tex went on. "I'm the fastest, and that means the others are going to come lookin' for me, tryin' to build 'em up a reputation. I can't take no chances on havin' my gun hand tied up."

"I see," David said.

"My gun hand will always be free," Tex said, loudly enough for everyone in the room to hear him. "And I'm ready to take on anyone, at any time."

The others who were in the restaurant either studiously avoided looking at him, or observed him only with the greatest of caution lest they do something to provoke him into challenging them to a gunfight.

"Is it true that you challenged Beau Bandito?" David asked. "Or was that just newspaper talk?"

"That's true," Tex said. "Beau Bandito is a phony, and I aim to prove it. I already have, seein' as how he ain't answered my challenge."

"David, would you run up to Miss Pendarrow's room and take her order please?" Sam asked, thankful for an excuse to remove young David from the presence of this gunfighter.

"Is she back yet? I haven't seen her."

"She just went up the stairs," Sam said.

"Isn't she going to come down here and eat at her regular table? I've already put fresh flowers in the vase."

"You may take the flowers up to her if you wish," Sam said. "And I shall see to your steaks," he added, to Tex and Brewster grateful for the opportunity to withdraw from the table.

"So, her name is Pendarrow," Brewster said when they were alone. "And she's the same girl Barney said would come in helpful later on."

"Yeah, she drives the stage," Tex said. "Hey—I know her. She was the passenger who knew I wasn't Beau Bandito. Yeah, she was a pretty thing, all right. Maybe we should pay a visit to her."

"No, if she recognized me now it would ruin everything," Brewster said.

Tex laughed. "You're afraid of a woman? That's the damndest thing I ever heard of."

"Oh, am I ever so glad to see *you*," Yolinda said when Stacey stepped into her apartment. "I have

285

been absolutely *bored* to *death*. What is there to do in this dreadful place?"

"Not very much," Stacey replied. "But, after all, this isn't Denver."

"I agree with you there. This certainly isn't Denver," Yolinda said.

"The hotel has a few books," Stacey called back from the bathroom. "It isn't exactly a lending library, but they will let their guests borrow them. Perhaps you can find something interesting to read tonight."

Steam rolled up from the water, and Stacey began stripping out of her pants and shirt.

"Tonight? But surely we are going to do something tonight other than sit around this dreadful room?" Yolinda's disappointment was obvious.

"I'm sorry, Yolinda," Stacey said, coming out of the bathroom to talk to her. "But I've just found out that I have to drive the evening stage. You'll have to entertain yourself tonight."

Yolinda gasped. Stacey was totally nude and she stood there talking to Yolinda as casually as if they were both fully dressed and standing in the hotel lobby. "Stacey!" she said, "you're naked!"

"I'm about to take a bath," Stacey explained.

"But you don't have on any clothes!"

"I don't usually wear my clothes in the bathtub, do you?" she asked, not as a joke, but on the basis of Yolinda's reaction.

"Well, no," Yolinda said. "But I would never let anyone see me that way."

Stacey smiled. "We're both women," she said. "I don't guess your looking at my body is too much different from your seeing your own."

"But I never look at my body either," Yolinda explained.

"What?" Stacey asked, totally flabbergasted by the announcement. "But surely you do. You just said you bathe in the nude."

"I don't take my robe off until the last moment," Yolinda said. "Then I slip into the tub as quickly as I can. I try not to catch my reflection in the mirror."

"Are others like you?" Stacey asked curiously.

"Of course they are. At least proper ladies are," Yolinda said. "Why, Stacey Pendarrow, your aunt would be absolutely shocked if she saw you like that."

There was a light knock at the door at that moment, and Yolinda jumped. "Heavens, who could that be?"

"It's probably David," Stacey said. She grabbed a towel and wrapped it around her. "He's from room service. You can let him in."

"You are going to receive a caller dressed like *that*?" Yolinda asked, almost in total shock.

"He's not a caller. I told you he is with room service. And yes, I'm going to receive him. I'm hungry and won't get an opportunity to eat anything until late tonight."

Yolinda started for the bedroom.

"Where are you going?"

"I'm going to wait in here until you've ordered," Yolinda said. "I'm too embarrassed to be in the room with you like that, and with a man in here."

Stacey laughed. "He's not a man, he's only a boy," she said. But even as she spoke she realized that David was as old as she. Their years were the same, but what a difference in their ages!

Stacey ordered cold chicken and a salad, then closed the door behind David as he left. She unwrapped the towel, then on an impish impulse, walked into the bedroom where Yolinda sat on the edge of the bed. Stacey was again totally nude.

"He's gone. You can come out now," Stacey said. "You were right about receiving him in the towel. It came loose and I didn't know what to do, so I just left it there."

"You mean like that?"

"Well, what could I do?" Stacey teased. "Once I dropped the towel he saw me anyway, so I just pretended that nothing happened."

"Oh, I would have been mortified."

"Mortified? Oh, no, I was flattered," Stacey said, her eyes twinkling in merriment over the joke. She left Yolinda with shock still showing in her eyes, and went in to settle into the bathtub. It felt so good that she wished she could stay there for the rest of the day. But she couldn't; there was a four-hour stage drive ahead of her tonight.

Chapter Thirty

When Stacey returned to the Wells Fargo depot she saw the stage standing there with the team already hitched. There were four passengers getting on, if they could be called passengers, for all four were men far into their cups. They were singing raucous songs and passing a couple of bottles around.

"I'm sorry about this," Mason said. "They are cattlemen, and they just closed some sort of big deal. They've been celebrating all afternoon."

"Well," Stacey said, "maybe they'll get so drunk that they'll pass out and sleep for the whole trip."

"Maybe they will," Mason agreed, hopefully.

"Hey, fellas, lookit what we got travelin' with us. Little lady, you can sit on my side of the coach," one of the men said.

"Naw, she ain't gonna sit on your side. She's gonna sit on my side."

"If you gentlemen will kindly board, we'll get underway," Stacey said.

"Lissen to the little lady give us orders," the first one said. "Little lady, you're a pretty thing, but you don' give ol' Diamond Dan orders. No one gives Diamond Dan orders," he admonished, waving his finger at her, though barely able to maintain his balance, so besotted was he with drink.

"If you want to reach Sky Meadow on my stage, you'll do as I say," Stacey said. "Now please step into the coach."

"Your stage?" Diamond Dan said. He looked at the others with surprise on his face. "Well, would you lookit this? Damn if I don't believe she intends to drive this stage."

"That's exactly what I intend to do."

"I don't want to ride with a woman stagecoach driver," Diamond Dan said. He looked back at Mason. "Hey, what is this? Don't you have any other drivers?"

"Our regular afternoon driver is ill," Mason said. "Miss Pendarrow is our morning driver, and she has kindly agreed to take this run. She is our most accomplished driver," he added. "I'm certain that you will enjoy your trip."

"If you've no wish to ride with me you can wait for tomorrow's coach." Stacey said. "And believe me, I've no more wish to carry you, than you have to ride with me."

Diamond Dan's traveling companions laughed at him. "I guess she got you told off pretty good there, Dan."

"Come on," one of the others said. "It might be fun to ride with a lady driver."

Diamond Dan looked at Stacey, then smiled a lecherous smile. Stacey had seen many such smiles in the past and she was pretty adept at gauging their intent. Had Diamond Dan not been drunk, his was the type of smile that would have put her on her alert. As it was, she figured he would be asleep in a short time, and would offer her no trouble.

The four men climbed inside and Stacey shut the

door. Their baggage overflowed the oxhide boot, and the surplus was lashed down on top of the coach. The stage was heavily loaded and Stacey knew that the horses would be getting quite a workout on this trip, so she walked along the hitch, speaking soothingly to each of them. Finally she returned and started climbing up to the driver's seat.

"I put the mail bag under the seat," Mason said. "At least you don't have to worry about any money tonight. Just a few letters."

"That's good," Stacey said, taking the reins in her hand. "I'll see you tomorrow, but only to turn this stage back in. After that I'm going to take the whole day off."

"You will have earned it," Mason assured her.

Stacey snapped the lines and the horses leaned into their harness. She pulled them around and the stage made a wide U-turn in the street in front of the Wells Fargo depot, then rolled past the outskirts of town at a fairly good clip.

For the first few minutes, Stacey could hear the cacophony which the four drunks passed off as song. But, as she had figured, it didn't last long, and on the flat, straight stretches of the road where the stage rolled smoothly and quietly she could even hear snatches of snoring. She set the pace for an uneventful trip.

It was nearly two hours later when she reached the pullout and brought the team to a halt to allow them to catch their breath from the long climb. She tied the lines off, then climbed down and stretched her legs and looked into the coach. The four men were sleeping in various positions, mouths open and spittle drooling. It was a most unattractive sight and she decided to let them be, rather than inform them of the rest stop.

Stacey felt her own need for the stop, and she walked off the road and along a path through the rocks to a spot which she knew would provide her with privacy. She took the bullwhip with her, the one she used to control the team, because although she had yet to see a snake during one of these stops she felt safer if prepared for one.

Stacey was an expert with the whip and she used it liberally on the teams without ever inflicting actual pain. She could pop it with the report of a pistol shot, placing it by the ear of whichever animal needed attention, and if a greater impression were needed, she could cause the end of it to snap against the animal's flesh with an attention-getting sting, though falling far short of brutality. It was this expertise with a whip which would allow her to pop the head off a rattler, should the occasion ever present itself, so she always carried it with her when she left the road.

Stacey found a private spot and had already started back when she saw Diamond Dan, leering from his vantage point in the middle of the path. She gasped, and her face burned red in embarrassment.

"What are you doing here?" she asked.

"I came to make you a little proposition," Diamond Dan said. "I'm willin' to pay for a little fun, if you know what I mean."

"What? Get out of here! How dare you follow me down here!"

"Now come on, honey, don't get so huffy. I mean after all, you're drivin' a stage, ain't ya'? That's not exactly a schoolmarm's job, is it? You know what it's all about. I'll bet you entertain men passengers all the time when the price is right. Well, honey, I got me a terrible need, and I'm willin' to meet the right price. You just tell me what it is."

Diamond Dan began opening his pants and walking toward her.

"I told you to get away from me" Stacey said. She took a hesitant step backwards.

"Come on, honey, what are you worried about? The others are dead to the world. You'll prob'ly have to wake 'em up when we get to the way station. But me, why, I'm ready for a little fun."

Diamond Dan suddenly lunged for her, and Stacey, having seen him staggering around when he got onto the stage, was surprised by his quickness. Before she could react he was upon her, with his hands clawing at her shirt. In an instant the front of her shirt was ripped open, and one pink nipple peeked out. She twisted away quickly, darted around him, then started back up the path toward the stage.

"Come back here, you little bitch!" he called. "Who do you think you are?"

Stacey ran along the path until she reached the turnout where the stage stood. Then with enough room to work, she turned and faced Diamond Dan, holding her whip poised above her. "Stop right there," she called.

Diamond Dan stopped, then laughed. "What do you think you can do with that little ol' switch?" he called. He took another step forward, and Stacey flipped the whip out, snapping it painfully but not severely across his shin.

"Hey!" he cried out. "Put that thing down, slut, and I'll go easy with you when I get you."

He took another step, and this time Stacey snapped the whip just across his chest.

"Now cut that out!" Diamond Dan bellowed. He grabbed for his gun, but it was no sooner out of its holster than she snapped it out of his hand, sending it careening toward the nearby rocks. He let out a sharp exclamation of pain and grabbed his wrist.

"If you take one more step toward me, I'll fix you so that you'll never be interested in any woman again," Stacey said quietly.

"What do you mean?" Diamond Dan asked, much of the wind taken out of his sails. "You couldn't do that."

"If I can hit your belt buckle, I can hit anything I want," Stacey replied. She threw the whip out again, and the tip of it snapped against the man's belt buckle. "Do you see what I mean?"

"No!" Diamond Dan cried, covering himself now with his hands, crouching in fear before her. "No, don't do it, please!"

"Get back on the stage," Stacey said.

"I'm going, I'm going," he whimpered, scampering for the stage, holding his arms out to ward off any further blows.

Stacey couldn't resist popping the whip with a pistol-like report just by his ear as he climbed back into the stage. The others had snored through it all.

By the time Stacey returned to the driver's seat she was smiling. She had come face to face with the thing which had always bothered her. How, she had often wondered, would she handle a male passenger who might become mean? Well, she met that challenge today, and she believed she had overcome it

Meanwhile, dirty gray piles of clouds began stacking up over the mountains, and Stacey knew they would collect enough rain to cascade through the canyons and fill the washes. It was good that she was on the last leg of the trip, because these roads were dangerous at any time, but much more so in the rain, and extremely hazardous in the rain at night. And it would be dark before Sky Meadow was reached.

The sun began dying in a brilliant display of color, and the dark blue of the eastern sky moved across the heavens, as if pulling a shade down over the world. Soon the last vestige of the sunset was gone and the night turned black. The evening breeze carried moisture in its breath, and Stacey knew that it would be a race as to whether they reached Sky Meadow before the rain reached them. She quickened the pace of the animals, and then gave a sigh of relief when she saw the rock formation she used as a sign of when to blow the trumpet.

Stacey gave a few bleats on the horn, and looked through the darkness to try to pick out the cluster of building that was Sky Meadow. By the light of day she knew they would be clearly visible from here. Now she had only the golden points of light to guide her.

The rain hit in the last five hundred yards, but by then the worst of the road was behind her, and she kept up the pace of the team so that one minute later she was braking the coach to a stop in front of the way station.

"All right," she called out, as she hopped down from the seat. "We're here. Everyone inside; you'll have to make arrangements for the night."

When Stacey went inside, she saw the surprised look on Melissa's face

"What are you doing here?"

"Pete's sick," Stacey said. "I had to take his run."

"Oh, no, how are we going to handle this?" Melissa asked.

"Handle what?"

"I mean, where are you going to sleep?" Melissa asked. "The other stage has six passengers, and all the beds are taken — in fact, they're doubled up. I thought Pete would be here, so he was going to sleep with Pa. I've already got two other women with me."

"Don't worry about it," Stacey said. "I'll sleep in the barn."

"Oh, no, I don't want you to have to do that."

Stacey laughed. "You'd be surprised at the number of times I've done that in the past. I don't mind, really I don't. The barn is very dry and sort of cozy, I'll be fine there."

"Why don't you take my place and *I'll* sleep in the barn?" Melissa offered, genuinely concerned over Stacey's well-being.

"No, thank you," Stacey said. "I used to live here, remember? I know what it's like to share your bed with passengers. Believe me, if I'm going to drive back tomorrow, I'd better get a good night's rest, and I can do that better alone in the barn. Besides, unless things have changed drastically around here, you're going to have to get up early and fix breakfast. I know I always had to."

"Nothing has changed here, that's for sure," Melissa said, making a funny face for Stacey.

"I thought so. Well, we all have to start somewhere, and that's where I started too. Now, if you'll find a pillow and a blanket for me, I'll get along perfectly."

"Do you want supper?"

"Uhmm, absolutely," Stacey said. "I'm starved. And I don't get a chance to eat your cooking that often, so I intend to take this opportunity. Tell me, what are we having?"

"Stagecoach stew," Melissa said.

"We would be," Stacey replied, making a face. Stagecoach stew was the common term for leftover hash. It was the most universally served, and the most thoroughly cursed, food along any of the Wells Fargo routes. But the Wells Fargo fare budget dictated that it be served often.

Melissa laughed. "I was teasing. Tonight we're having roast beef."

"Roast beef? Now that's more like it," Stacey said. "I'll be right back in after I've stabled and fed the team. And if you let the passengers eat all of it before I get back, I'm going to eat yours," she teased.

"I'll hold enough back for both of us," Melissa promised. "And we'll eat together."

After Stacey helped unhitch the team she led the horses into the barn where she fed them, then stabled them. She looked around to see that there was a stall with fresh hay for her own bedroll, found a nice dry one, then returned to the main house for her meal.

Melissa's father, the driver of the other stage, and the passengers were still sitting around the great table, having just finished their meal. There were two plates set at the small kitchen table for Melissa and Stacey, and a crackling wood fire in the cooking stove, which made a comfortable addition to this wet, cool evening.

"Now, isn't this nice?" Melissa asked. "Just the two of us."

"Yes, it is," Stacey said. She poured herself a cup of coffee, then sat down.

"It just isn't fair," Melissa said a moment later.

"What? What isn't fair?" Stacey replied, surprised by the pronouncement.

"The railroad," Melissa said. "They are going to have the railroad built from Medford all the way to MacAllister before I'm ever old enough to drive the stage."

Stacey laughed. "This isn't the only stage route, you know."

"I know it isn't. But it's the one you have, and I wanted to be just like you."

"Well, don't forget—when the railroad is built, I'll have to find another route for myself as well."

"Yes, that's right, isn't it?" A smile brightened Melissa's face. "Maybe it will work out after all. Oh, Stacey, you've no idea how badly I want to drive a stage. I want it more than anything, but nobody can understand that, except maybe you. Do you think I'm crazy?"

"Yes," Stacey said. "I think you're crazy."

"Really? But *you're* doing it."

"I know," Stacey said. She smiled broadly at Melissa. "But I'm crazy too."

Chapter Thirty-one

That night, after she had eaten and talked for a while with Melissa, Stacey donned a waterproof poncho, took the blanket and pillow, and darted through the rain to the barn, there to make her bed. The stall she had selected proved to be an excellent choice as it was dry and warm despite the rain, and the straw was fresh and pleasant smelling.

After her bed was made Stacey walked over to the side of the barn and peered out through a window to look at the streaks of rain slash down out of the night sky, and watch the flashes of lightning illuminate the range of mountains across the valley. After each lightning flash she heard the thunder roll, and after one particularly loud burst of thunder she heard the horses move about restlessly. She spoke soothingly to them to reassure them.

As she stood in the window some of the rain blew into her face but she made no attempt to escape. She loved the rain. It blanketed all sight and sound and formed a curtain behind which her soul could exist in absolute solitude. Only those with whom she really wanted to share could penetrate it.

The door to the barn opened and closed, but Stacey didn't look around. "Melissa, are you still worrying about me?" she asked.

"I'm not Melissa, but I worry about you," a man's voice answered.

Stacey felt a quick thrill course through her body, for she recognized Clay Conway's voice. She turned quickly. "Clay, what are you doing here?"

"I'm getting in out of the rain," Clay said. "What are *you* doing here? I thought you only took the morning runs."

Stacey explained about Pete's illness and the arrangement she had made with Mason. Then she asked, "What do you mean you are getting out of the rain? You mean you come here often?"

Clay gave a sheepish grin. "Yeah, I do," he said. "I have to stay somewhere, and I sort of like it here. It was here that I first met you, if you remember."

"But isn't it dangerous for you?"

"Honey, everywhere is dangerous for me now," Clay said. "So I might as well find a place that is comfortable, and that I like."

"Why hasn't anyone ever discovered you here? One of the drivers, or someone who is tending the horses?"

"Come up here, I'll show you," Clay said.

Stacey followed Clay across the floor of the barn, then up a ladder to the hayloft. Once there, Clay moved a couple of bales of hay, then held his arm out invitingly.

"Madamosel, may I offer you the hospitality of my quarters?" Clay asked, faking a dandy's cultured accent.

Stacey had to bend over to walk through the space, but once inside it was pitch dark, and she could sense that she was in a large cavern-like area.

"I'll light a lantern as soon as I close the door,"

Clay said, pulling the bales of hay back to conceal the entrance. "Now, from out there it looks just like a stack of hay. But from in here. . . ." Clay let the sentence hang as he struck a match to a lantern.

A golden light flared out from the lamp, and Stacey was able to look around her. Clay had ingeniously constructed a room from the bales of hay, complete with a bed made by stretching blankets over straw, a small table, a wash basin, and even a few changes of clothes.

"You . . . you actually *live* here, don't you?" Stacey said, fascinated by her surroundings.

"Yes," Clay said. He pulled a loose board out from the wall. "I bank here too," he added with a smile. "This is where I keep my ill-gotten gains."

Stacey looked down inside, and saw a small sack.

"Count it," Clay said.

"What?"

"Go ahead. Count it. It'll make you feel better."

Stacey laughed. "I don't need to count it," she said. "The fact that you were willing to let me count it is proof enough . . . if I still needed proof."

"You mean you don't?"

"No," Stacey said easily. "I don't need proof anymore."

Clay put his arms around her and squeezed her, then whirled her around, laughing happily.

"Clay, put me down!" she said. "You'll take my breath away."

"I can't help it, girl," Clay said. "You don't know how happy you've made me!" He let out a yell.

"Clay! You must be quiet!" Stacey warned.

"Don't worry. This hay deadens the sound. And it's a long way to the house, and the rain is making a noise to beat the devil. There's no danger of anyone hearing us."

"Oh, the light. How about it?"

Clay walked over and opened a window. "Look," he said, "this window opens over the edge of the mountain. There's nothing out there for twenty miles, and if anyone ever happened to be out there and saw the light shining at night, why they would be so far away that they couldn't tell whether it was coming from the barn or the house. And on this side, it's not visible from the house, or anywhere on the grounds." He smiled. "I lit it one night and walked all over the place for the better part of an hour, trying to see if it could be seen. It can't be, I'll promise you that." He started to close the window.

"No, don't close it, please," Stacey said.

Clay smiled and left it open.

"I'm glad you came tonight," Stacey said. "And I'm glad you showed me your room. I wish . . . I wish we could . . . oh, never mind. That's silly, I suppose."

"You wish what?" Clay asked.

"I wish we could just stay here, just like this, forever. The rain outside, us dry and cozy inside."

Clay smiled, then stepped up to her and kissed her. He pulled her to him tightly, and her lips opened under his. She ground herself against him, enjoying the feel of his strength.

"Oh," she said, when at last the kiss ended. "Clay, you're so wet. You're going to catch a cold if you don't get into something dry."

"That's why I keep a change of clothes up here," Clay replied. He began unbuttoning his shirt, and

Stacey walked over to get a blanket from the bed. She draped it around him as he removed his shirt, then a moment later he handed her his trousers from beneath the blanket. He clutched the blanket about him like an Indian, then, smiling, began dancing around and whooping.

"Clay, what are you doing?" Stacey asked, laughing.

"Uhmm," Clay said. "Me Indian chief. You young maiden. I think maybe I capture you, take you to my teepee, make you my squaw woman."

"Oh, Big Chief Hokum, I'm just a common maid. Surely you want a princess," Stacey said, going along with the game.

"Uhmm, no, Princess Moon have'm face like'm cow. I no like her. I like you."

"I don't know. What gift do you bring me?"

Clay smiled. "How about nice Indian blanket?" he asked, coming toward her and opening his blanket.

Stacey went toward him, and he closed the blanket around her, pulling her against his nude body. She could feel the muscles of his bare chest and arms, the powerful thighs, and the unmistakable thrust of his manhood, as she leaned into him. They kissed, long and deep, and then Clay began removing Stacey's clothes. A moment later her clothes were in a pile on the floor, and Stacey and Clay stood together, bare flesh against bare flesh.

Stacey broke off the kiss, smiled up at him, then stepped out from under the blanket and walked over to the bed. "This time," she said, "I want it to be perfect."

"It was perfect last time," Clay replied. "It could never be anything but perfect with you."

Stacey lay down on the bed and her smooth skin shone gold in the light of the lamp. Her amber eyes were wide and glowed with an inner light, and her tongue darted across her lips, leaving them soft and shining.

Clay was to her in three quick steps, then dropped down onto the bed beside her. She held her arms out to him, welcoming him to her, taking him into her, losing herself in the dizzying ecstasy of the moment. She surrendered herself to him, and their flesh became as one flesh. Fulfillment hung in explosive potential, easily attainable but postponed to prolong the delicious agony of the quest. When it finally did arrive, there was much more than the momentary physical pleasure. Clay had touched the deepest, innermost part of Stacey. Now she felt as he felt, thought as he thought, and for a brief instant in the continuum of eternity, time stood still and they were one.

They lay side by side in the soft light of the lantern, without touching and without speaking. The window was still open and the rain made music. It was perfectly orchestrated, from the rhythmic percussion and harmonic bass notes of the large booming drops to the delicate trills and melodious tinkling of water which ran off the roof and cascaded across the eaves and sill of the window.

They didn't speak, because they wanted to preserve this moment and lock it forever in their hearts. And the pure truth was that Stacey and Clay were in love.

Chapter Thirty-two

Brewster tried to keep Tex from drinking too much but his efforts were futile. When Tex was determined to do something, there was very little that Brewster, or anyone else for that matter, could do to stop him. Especially as Tex told him in no uncertain terms that one more comment about his drinking would be all the excuse he needed to close Brewster's mouth forever.

So, under Brewster's watchful but impotent charge, Tex drank heavily, grew intoxicated, and Brewster walked on eggshells to keep from saying or doing anything that would set off the volatile young man. Thus it was that when Tex suggested they spend the night in town rather than return to their mountain cabin through the rain, Brewster readily agreed.

The rain began just after nightfall and when Tex and Brewster left the saloon (only because it closed for the night), the rain was falling in a deluge. Brewster suggested that they bunk down in the livery stable with their horses but Tex wouldn't hear of it.

"We got money to spend, don't we? We'll stay in the hotel."

"But it's so late, Tex," Brewster protested. "The clerk has probably gone to bed already."

"Then we'll get his ass up," Tex said. He took another swallow of the bottle he had brought with him. "Come on, let's do this in style."

Tex didn't wait for an answer. He lunged straight toward the hotel, nearly falling off the boardwalk into the mud of the street, then lurched through the driving downpour, staggered across the street and onto the boarded walk in front of the hotel.

Brewster ran after him, wishing that Athens and Barney were here to help him control this idiot, wishing also that he had the courage to just shoot the son of a bitch and get it over with.

The clock over the bar had said midnight when the bartender closed up, so Brewster wouldn't have been surprised if the front door to the hotel had been locked. But it wasn't, and Tex pushed it open, then stepped into the lobby with Brewster right behind him.

A kerosene lantern stood on the front desk, its flame turned low to emit only a very subdued glow. There were no other lights in the lobby, but the sofa, chairs, and tables were revealed in stark black and harsh white by the frequent streaks of lightning which flashed through the windows, as bright as the magnesium flares in a photographer's flash.

Tex stumbled into a table, then angrily shoved it to one side. He walked over to the desk and banged his hand down on the little bell. There was no response to his summons.

"Let's go on back to the stable," Brewster suggested.

"Hell no. Why sleep in wet hay when we can sleep in a dry bed?" Tex replied. He banged the bell again. "Hey, you!" he shouted. "Get your ass out here!"

There was no answer.

"I said get your ass out here before I start shooting up the damn place!" He banged the bell again.

A door opened from a room just behind the desk. A man who had obviously been asleep emerged, placing his glasses on his nose carefully. He was wearing a long nightshirt and a nightcap, the tassle of which dangled across one shoulder.

"I'm sorry, sir," the clerk said. "I was sleeping."

"Yeah, well that's what we want to do," Tex said. "Give my partner and me a couple of rooms," Tex demanded.

"I have only one room left, I'm afraid. You'll have to share it."

"That'll be all right," Tex said. "Give me the key."

"You'll have to register first, sir," the clerk said. "And the rate is seventy-five cents, in advance."

Tex slapped the money on the counter, then spun the book around. He picked up a pencil stub, wet it with his tongue, then very laboriously printed 'the texas ked,' disdaining capitals and misspelling the word kid. At the very top of the page he saw the neatly written name Stacey Pendarrow, and he noticed Stacey's room number, 206.

"All right, Brewster, I signed us in, let's go," Tex said.

"Gentlemen, your room number is 203," the clerk said, handing Tex a key. "Please remove your boots before you go to bed," he added, noticing the mud tracks the two men were leaving on the floor as they started for the stairs.

Tex lurched about on the stairs, once falling against the wall, but they finally made it to the next floor, then found their room. Tex couldn't fit the key in the lock so Brewster took the key from him and tried himself. As Brewster was unlocking the door Tex looked down the hall and saw the door to Stacey's room. He thought of the girl he had seen climbing the steps earlier that evening, and remembered her from the stage he had robbed. He thought of Brewster with her, and the thought gave him an erection. He tipped the bottle up for another long swallow of whiskey.

"There it is," Brewster said, finally turning the key. He opened the door and pushed it open. It smelled musty. "Whew," Brewster said. "We would have been better off in the barn." Brewster felt his way to a table, found a matchbox, and lit the lamp. There was only one bed in the room, along with the bedside table, a chair, a dresser, a water pitcher and a basin.

"We're going to have to share the bed," Brewster said. "Which side do you want?"

Tex walked over to the chair and plopped down without a word. He took another drink from his bottle.

"You don't have a choice?" Brewster asked. "Then I'll take the side next to the wall. I'm going to hit the sack now and that way you won't have to crawl over me."

Tex took another swallow, but said nothing.

Brewster sat on the edge of the bed and removed his boots, dropping them one by one at the foot of the bed. He rubbed his feet and sighed. "Damn, there is nothing that feels better than taking off your boots."

"Yes, there is," Tex said, speaking for the first time since they'd reached the room.

"I'd like to know what it is," Brewster said.

"You oughtta know," Tex said. He smiled a wicked smile. "Didn't you tell me you had a little of that girl we seen climbin' the stairs?"

Brewster smiled and said, "Yeah, you're right, Tex. That felt better than taking off my boots."

Tex took another swallow of whiskey and looked toward the direction of Stacey Pendarrow's room.

"Are you coming to bed?" Brewster wanted to know.

"Yeah, in a little while," Tex said. "I want to finish my whiskey. Also, I gotta take a leak."

"You can just go out the window," Brewster said.

"Ain't this hotel got one of them indoor outhouses?"

"Yes, but it's way down the hall. It'd be a lot easier to just go out the window."

"Uh, uh," Tex said. "I don't get a chance to use one of those indoor outhouses all that much. I'm gonna use this one."

Brewster chuckled. "Suit yourself," he said. "Mind if I turn out the light?"

"Naw, go ahead," Tex said.

Brewster reached over to the lantern key and twisted it. The flame was snuffed and the room grew dark.

Tex sat in his chair for a few more minutes, drinking his whiskey and listening to Brewster breathe. After a few moments Brewster's breathing changed to snores, and Tex knew that he was asleep.

Tex drained the rest of the whiskey, then walked over to the window. He opened the window and tossed the bottle outside, barely hearing the tinkle of glass as it shattered below. He started to relieve himself through the window, then remembered the bathroom so he closed the window and stepped out into the hall.

When Tex left the bathroom a moment later he looked toward the door of Stacey Pendarrow's room. A picture of her came into his mind again, and he felt himself growing aroused. It wasn't fair, he thought. It wasn't fair that Brewster had her, and maybe even Barney had her, while he, who was more of a man than any of them, had been left out.

Brewster seemed afraid of her, though, and Barney insisted that she was going to be of use to them later on. Use? Tex thought. The only use she was to them was to go to bed with Barney. Well, to hell with them having all the fun.

Tex walked down the hall to the door, then looked at it for a moment. The chances were that the door was locked anyway. And if it was locked, he couldn't get in without breaking it down, and that would be so noisy that it would bring everyone in the hotel down on him.

Tex started to leave, but on impulse, tried the door knob.

It was open!

Tex stepped inside and closed the door behind him. He was quiet for a moment, listening for the girl's breathing. A flash of lightning illuminated the room and Tex saw with some surprise that there was no bed. What kind of room was this? Another flash showed some doors leading off the room and Tex suddenly realized that this was more than just a regular hotel room.

The last lightning flash had revealed a table lamp and matchbox. Tex lit the lamp and looked around. There were two doors leading off this room, which appeared to be some sort of sitting room or parlor. Tex walked over and opened one of the doors cautiously. It was a bathroom! Here in the same room was a bathroom! Tex had never seen such a sight and he stared at it in awe for a few moments. Then he remembered why he was here, closed the door and backed out into the sitting room again.

There was only one door left and Tex knew that the girl had to be in there. He opened it quietly, and looked inside. There she was, on the bed.

Tex stood in the doorway for a moment, listening to her breathe. As he looked at the shadowed form on the bed his need grew great, and he felt a pressure in the front of his pants. He walked over to the bed and looked down at her. Her face was in shadow and he could see very little of it, but that didn't matter. He knew what she looked like, and that drove him on.

The palms of his hands were sweating and he picked up the spare pillow, and when he shoved it down onto her face he felt his heart pounding violently. The girl tried to scream but the scream was muffled by the pillow. She pushed at the bed-clothes, but she was so well covered that the blankets worked almost as a restraint and her fighting was ineffectual.

Tex increased the pressure on the pillow and his breathing came in gasps. He felt a building up of pressure inside him, then, to his surprise, he spilled his seed without ever touching her or himself. The front of his pants felt warm, wet and sticky and he gasped aloud at the pleasure which flooded through him as the girl struggled her last, feeble struggles. He held the pillow over her long after she stopped, then released the pressure and sat on the edge of the bed to recover the strength he had felt oozing out of his body at the moment of his most intense pleasure.

Finally the weakness passed, and Tex stood up, looked down at the still body with the pillow over its face, then turned and left to go to his own room and bed.

Brewster was still asleep when Tex reached the room, so Tex just stretched out on the bed beside him, still wearing his pants and boots, and fell into a drunken, exhausted slumber.

Chapter Thirty-three

Stacey was awakened by a tender kiss, and she opened her eyes to see Clay Conway looking down at her. She had slept in his arms, her head on his shoulder, feeling his body next to hers during the too short night hours. Now the soft glow of a brilliant pre-dawn moon silvered the inside of the little room, and clean, rainwashed air greeted the arriving morning.

"You're still here," Stacey said softly. She smiled, and squeezed him tightly. "I'm so glad you aren't just a dream."

Clay reached down and pulled a few pieces of straw from her hair, then brushed it away from her forehead. He returned her smile. "You're beautiful when you're sleeping," he said.

"Hmm, how do you know?" Stacey asked. "You were sleeping too."

"No, I wasn't," Clay said. "I didn't sleep a wink."

"You didn't? Why not?"

"Because I didn't want to waste a moment. I wanted to look at you, and touch you, and feel you in my arms for the entire night."

"But aren't you tired?"

"Not a bit," Clay replied. He finally let go of her

and sat up, watching her while she removed bits of clinging straw, and arranged her clothes. "I just wish that we had four more hours until dawn."

"Oh, what time is it?" Stacey asked, suddenly remembering where she was.

"I figure it's about one hour 'till dawn," Clay said. "Melissa will be out here in about thirty minutes to feed the horses. And, no doubt, to awaken you."

"Oh, you know Melissa's schedule, do you?" Stacey teased. "And have you hidden in the straw to give her a good morning kiss as you once did me?"

"No, of course not," Clay said seriously.

Stacey laughed. "I was just teasing. But let me catch you doing such a thing and my teasing will stop."

"Oh, ho, so you are the jealous kind."

"Jealous? No, I'm not jealous," Stacey said. "Why would you say such a thing?"

"In that case," Clay replied, "It's good that you aren't, for you would no doubt be upset by the number of women I've been forced to kiss while leading my life of crime."

"Women you've kissed?"

"Of course— I'm Beau Bandito, remember?"

"Oh, pooh, that's just newspaper talk."

"Most of it is," Clay admitted. "I certainly have committed nothing like the number of robberies they've credited me with. But the other thing, kissing the women . . . well, that may be a different story."

"What do you mean?" Stacey asked, an edge of concern in her voice. "Surely you haven't kissed as many as they say."

"No . . . ." Clay said seriously.

"I thought not," Stacey replied with a smug smile.

"I've kissed more," Clay teased, grinning broadly.

"Oh, you . . . you . . . ." Stacey said, striking out at him with her fists.

Clay fended off her attack, trying to stifle his laughter. He finally collapsed under her continued assault and then, still laughing, grabbed her and pulled her to him, ceasing his laughter only when his lips were sealed with her kiss.

Clay rolled over so that Stacey was beneath him, and the laughter and frivolity fell away, to be replaced by a burning need, one for the other. They separated, and without a word began removing their clothes, their eyes locked on each other.

The moon, still shining brightly and sailing high in the early morning velvet sky, spilled its iridescence through the small window, bathing Stacey in a soft, shimmering light. Her body was highlighted and made all the more mysterious and intriguing by the subtle shadows and lighting of the night. Her skin was cooled by the soft breeze, but the heat within flamed unchecked, needing much more than a cooling breeze to be subdued.

"I love you, Anastasia Pendarrow," Clay said as he came to her, and Stacey, waiting for him, joyfully gave herself to him. They made love again, and as it had been the night before, it was as rich and fulfilling, as strongly physical and immensely satisfying—but it was much deeper. It was as if their emotions were perfectly orchestrated to move in harmony.

Afterward they lay together, watching the graying of the sky. Stacey could feel Clay's hand on her naked hip, cupped lightly over the sharpness of her hip bone and the soft yielding of her flesh. His hand lay there in a proprietary manner and Stacey enjoyed the good feeling of being possessed. Finally Clay interrupted their quiet reverie.

"Melissa will be out soon."

No sooner had he spoken than they heard the barn door open, and Melissa called out to Stacey.

"Stacey, time to wake up. Stacey, where are you?"

Stacey pushed one of the hay bales to one side. "I'm up here," she called down. "I'll be right down."

"Up there? Why are you up there? I thought you were going to sleep in one of the stalls."

"I just decided to come up here to sleep," Stacey said. "I'll be right down."

As Stacey spoke, Clay moved his hand along her still nude body and lightly cupped a breast. He tweaked the nipple, making it stand out hard, and Stacey felt a flood of renewed arousal coursing through her, heightened by the exquisite edge of danger in knowing that discovery was so close, and intensified by the delight of sharing such an intimate secret.

"I'll come up to see where you slept," Melissa said.

"No, no, I'm coming right down," Stacey said quickly. She reached desperately for her clothes, which Clay, laughing quietly, pulled just out of her grasp.

Melissa started climbing the ladder, and at the last minute Clay handed Stacey her clothes, then bounded quickly over the barrier of bales to get down out of sight.

"Oh," Melissa said as she saw Stacey trying to get into her clothes. "No wonder you came up here to sleep. I didn't know you slept without your clothes."

"I, uh, just spread them out to get dry," Stacey said. "I was afraid I'd catch my death if I wore them wet, to bed."

"Oh, yes, of course," Melissa said. "Well, coffee's on and breakfast'll be ready soon."

"Thanks," Stacey said. "Coffee sounds awfully good right now."

"Also, papa has an important message for Mr. Mason," Melissa said. "It's awfully mysterious. Do you have any idea what it might be about?"

"I haven't the foggiest notion," Stacey said.

"Me neither," Melissa said. "And papa won't even let me see it. Will you tell me what it is when you get it? I'm dying of curiosity."

Stacey laughed. "If it's a sealed message, the chances are that I won't know what it's about either."

"Oooh," Melissa said in exasperation. "That's not fair. People should know better than to send secret messages. They should know that it just makes other people curious. Doesn't it make you mad?"

"You'll learn to live it as you get older." Stacey said, still able to feel the impression of Clay's hand on her breast. "In the meantime, let's get some of that coffee, shall we?"

Stacey finished dressing and the two girls climbed down the ladder, gave the horses their morning oats, then went inside the way station to drink coffee and prepare breakfast.

Stacey had an uneventful trip back to MacAllister. One of the passengers had insisted upon riding on the seat beside her, and as the company policy allowed such a thing, there was very little she could do about it. It meant, though, that Clay would be unable to drop onto the roof during the trip back, and for that she was sorry, because she would have enjoyed his company.

Stacey thought of the night just spent, and recalled the two times she and Clay had made love. Even the memory of it was enough to send a tremble of ecstasy through her body. It was, she realized now, an exchange of love—the kind of love a woman can know for a man when thought and reason are set aside and pure, unrestrained truth can surface. She smiled at the knowledge that she didn't enjoy Clay because of the act of sex, but that she enjoyed sex because of Clay.

She had fought against the feeling from the beginning, from the soul-stirring kiss in the barn that morning months ago, to the kiss at the Cinderella Ball; through the episode in the hotel room when they first made love, until last night when she had fought no more and enjoyed Clay for the pleasure he could bring her. She was in love, and the man she loved was Clay Conway.

"Clay," she said, speaking the word softly.

"Whazzat? You say somethin'?" the man beside her asked. He had been dozing with his head leaning forward on his chest, and the sound of her voice awakened him.

"I just said it was a nice day," Stacey said quickly.

"Oh, yeah, yeah," the man said, letting his head fall forward again.

"And I love him," Stacey said aloud.

"Yeah, yeah," the man mumbled.

Chapter Thirty-four

The sheriff was waiting at the Wells Fargo depot in MacAllister when Stacey returned. She greeted him cheerfully, then followed the passenger down from the high seat.

"What are you doing here?" she asked the sheriff, curiously.

"Stacey, how about stepping into Howard's office for a moment?" he replied evading her question.

"Sure, I'll be there soon as I get the stage unloaded."

"I'll take care of that, Stacey," Howard Mason said gravely. "I think you'd better go with the sheriff."

"All right," Stacey said, her bewilderment growing now because both men were acting so strangely. "Oh, here is a message that I'm supposed to deliver to you personally," she added, handing the sealed envelope to Mason.

Mason put the message in his pocket and saw to the unloading of the stage while Stacey, still wondering what was going on, followed the sheriff into the office.

"I'm afraid I've got some bad news for you, girl,"

the sheriff said as they stepped behind the partition that separated Mason's office from the rest of the depot.

"What type of bad news?" Stacey asked. Suddenly she gasped and put her hand to her mouth. "Clay hasn't been killed?"

"Clay?" the sheriff asked in sudden surprise.

Stacey realized almost at once that she had made a blunder and she attempted to cover it up. "It's just that I . . . I don't want anything to happen to him before justice is served."

"Oh," the sheriff said as if understanding, though still eyeing her suspiciously. "No, I'm afraid this is about your friend."

"My friend?"

"The girl who came to visit you. What was her name?"

"Oh, you mean Yolinda Sinclair," Stacey said. "Why, what about Yolinda, did she . . . ." Stacey suddenly stopped in mid-sentence. "Did you ask what *was* her name?"

"Yes," the sheriff said. He cleared his throat nervously. "I'm sorry, Stacey, but your friend Yolinda is dead."

"Dead? But how? What happened?"

"It appears that she was murdered," the sheriff said. "She was found this morning with a pillow over her face. The doc says she was smothered."

"My God!" Stacey cried, her mind reeling. "I don't understand. I don't understand it at all. Who would murder her? Unless it was the work of some fiend . . . was she molested?"

"No," the sheriff said, wishing he were somewhere else. "She was lying peacefully in her bed.

Only the pillow over her face and the blue color of her skin showed any signs of foul play."

"Was she robbed?"

"We can't be sure until you check the room thoroughly," the sheriff said. "But from the looks of it, I would say no. There is money in her purse, nearly one hundred dollars, in fact. And from the footprints it looks like someone just walked in, did it, and walked out."

"Footprints?" Stacey was weeping now, and the sheriff shifted awkwardly from one foot to the other.

"Yes," he replied. "Whoever did it had been out in the mud last night. His tracks lead from his room, to the bathroom, then to your apartment. Once in the apartment they wander a bit on your sitting room carpet, though not as if he was searching for something to steal, more like he was trying to find his way into the bedroom. There the tracks go right to the bed and then come straight back."

"You say they came from his room? Then you know who did it."

"Not exactly," the sheriff answered. "But we have a pretty good idea."

"Who?"

"It was either a man named Brewster, or someone called the Texas Kid. Have you ever heard of them?"

"No," Stacey said. "I don't think I have. Why?"

"Well, since there was no robbery, and no rape— uh, excuse the language, Stacey—then there can be only one motive."

"What would that be?"

"The killer thought it was you in the bed, and he set out to kill you."

"But why?" Stacey asked, wide-eyed. "Why would anyone want to kill me?"

"I was hopin' you might know that."

"No, Sheriff, I don't," Stacey said. "I'm sorry, but I'm afraid I can't help you at all."

"Well, I guess we just got us another one of them mysteries," the sheriff said easily.

"Where is Yolinda now?"

"She's down at the undertakers," the sheriff said. "I found a man's name in her purse, a fella named Marcus Tremain. We sent him a wire and he wired back that he's comin' in on the Midnight Flyer. I guess he'll be here on the afternoon stage tomorrow."

"He'll probably be here earlier than that," Stacey said. "If I know Marcus he'll hire a team."

"Then you know him?"

"Yes. He is . . . was," she corrected herself, "Yolinda's fiancé."

"I see," the sheriff said. "Well, it can't be a pleasant trip in front of him then, can it?"

"It hasn't been a pleasant summer for him either," Stacey mused. She ran her hand through her hair. "I think I'll go to my room now if you don't need me any more."

"No, go right ahead," the sheriff said. "I'm sorry I've greeted you with such sad news. But seein' as how we got a good idea of who done it, you can at least comfort yourself with the knowledge that he'll pay for it."

"Yes," Stacey said with a sigh of resignation. "Though I've learned that's scarce comfort."

Stacey left by the back door of the office and walked through the alleyway toward the hotel. She felt sick at heart over the senseless death of Yolinda, and saddened at the increased burden Marcus would be forced to bear. And she felt a nagging sense of bewilderment, as she wondered why anyone would do such a thing.

Shortly after Stacey left the office, Howard Mason finished with the passengers and came back to talk to her. He found the sheriff still there, but Stacey was gone.

"Where did she go?" Howard asked.

"Back to her apartment," the sheriff said. "She was upset by the news. I guess she just wants to be alone for a while."

"I guess you're right," Howard said. "Anyway, we've plenty of time tomorrow to discuss this money shipment."

"Money shipment?"

"Over one hundred thousand dollars," Mason said. He held up the message Stacey had given him. "That's what this letter was about. Wells Fargo is transferring that money to the bank here, to provide funds for the railroad. There'll be a special stage run tomorrow."

"I see," the sheriff said. He took the note and looked at it, and as he was studying it, Bramwell Caulder came through the front door.

"Where's Stacey?" Bramwell asked anxiously.

"She went to her apartment," the sheriff said. "She was pretty upset by what happened to her friend."

"And well she should be," Bramwell said. "I only

just heard of it myself, having just returned from Portland. My God, Sheriff, do you have any idea who might have done such a thing?"

"We've got a damn good idea," the sheriff said. "It was either a fella named Brewster, or another loud-mouthed kid who calls himself the Texas Kid."

"What?" Bramwell asked, visibly shaken by the news.

"It has to be them," the sheriff said, noticing Bramwell's reaction. "They stayed at the hotel last night and muddy footprints lead from their room to the girl's room. Say, look here, Bramwell. You act as if you know those fellas."

"I do," Bramwell said.

"You do? Well say, this is a fine break. Where do those scoundrels hang out? I'll get a posse out and we'll go get them!"

"I don't know," Bramwell said. "I don't know them that well."

"But you do know them by sight?"

"Yes."

"At least we'll have another means of identification," the sheriff said. "Sam, David, and the clerk at the hotel can also recognize them. We shouldn't have too much trouble."

"Sheriff, in the meantime I've got to make arrangements about this," Howard said, reaching for the note. "I want to go over the details with Stacey first, but I'm certain she'll want an armed escort. Perhaps you can help us there."

"Yes, of course," the sheriff said, handing the note back to Mason. But just as Mason reached for the note the sheriff drew it back. "Wait a minute," he said. "Mason, there's somethin' been botherin' me for the last few minutes."

"What?"

"It's about the girl, Stacey. Are you sure you want her to drive that special coach?"

"Yes, of course. Sheriff, I must admit that even I had my doubts at first, but Stacey has long since put those doubts to rest. She is the best driver on the route, perhaps on the whole line. If there is a special coach, then the policy is to let the best driver take it, and that would be Stacey."

"No, you don't understand," the sheriff said. "I'm not criticizing her driving. It's something else."

"What else?"

"I can't quite put my finger on it," the sheriff said. "But it was somethin' she said a while ago. Somethin' about Clay Conway. She acted real upset when she thought I was talkin' about Conway instead of her friend from Denver."

"What are you getting at, Sheriff?" Mason asked.

The sheriff rested his chin on his hand for a moment, and crossed his arms across his chest. "Let me think out loud for a minute, will you?"

"Go on, Sheriff," Bramwell put in, to join the conversation and thus be included in any information which might be forthcoming. "What are you thinking about?"

"Have you noticed that of all the stages that have been robbed, not once has she been hit?"

"Well, yes, you can't help but notice that," Mason said. "She's been very lucky."

"Luck may have nothin' to do with it," the sheriff said. He looked at Caulder. "You've been spendin' quite a bit of time with her, Bramwell. Answer me

327

this and answer it truthfully. Could it be that she's in cahoots with this Clay Conway character?"

"Sheriff, you don't know what you're saying," Mason protested quickly. "You don't know how she hates the man who killed her father."

"That's just it, Howard," Bramwell said quietly. "She doesn't think Conway killed her father."

"What? How can she not think that? My God, you *saw* it happen. Didn't you tell her?"

"Sure, I told her," Bramwell said. "But it didn't convince her. She believes that someone else did it. She thinks Clay Conway has been made to suffer the blame."

"Then that confirms it," the sheriff said. "Mason, you can't let her drive the special stage tomorrow. Don't you see? If she is involved with Clay Conway, all she has to do is tell him that she's bringing in over one hundred thousand dollars, and he'll hit it. It's pure and simple."

"Then that leaves me between the rock and the hard place," Mason said quietly. "Pete is just too damn undependable. But I don't guess I have any choice."

"Maybe you do," Bramwell said.

"How?"

"Why don't you send Pete on the special coach, complete with armed escorts and everything, but leave the money in Medford?"

"I don't get it. What will that accomplish?"

"It's simple. Since Pete is taking the special coach, you'll have to send Stacey on in to Medford with the regular coach run. Have the money back here on her coach."

"What? Are you kidding? You expect me to ship

328

over one hundred thousand dollars without any precautions at all?"

"But that is your best precaution," Bramwell said. "Don't you see? Not even Stacey will realize that the money is in the normal shipping pouches. That way she can't get word through to anyone."

"He may have a point there, Mason," the sheriff put in quickly. "And what better way to protect the money than to let Stacey bring it in? After all, she hasn't been robbed yet. We could sneak the money in before anyone knew it was coming."

"I don't know," Mason said doubtfully. "Maybe you're right. But I must confess feeling awfully uneasy at sending over one hundred thousand dollars on an unprotected stage."

"Don't worry about it," Bramwell said. "I assure you that this will be best for all concerned."

Chapter Thirty-five

"You fool! Just what the hell did you think you were doing? Didn't you know the muddy footprints would lead right back to your room?"

"I'm sorry, Barney. I didn't think about that," Tex said.

"You didn't think. Of course you didn't think. And you, you're just as bad as he is," Barney charged, directing his wrath at Brewster. Barney, Brewster, Tex and Athens were in the single room of the small mountain cabin, Barney having ridden out there as soon as he could get away from Mason and the sheriff.

"I swear to you, Barney, until you came in here with the news this minute, I knew nothing about it."

"And why didn't you know anything about it? Your job was to keep an eye on him. Why did you let him drink in the first place?"

"He insisted on drinking. I'm just one man. There was little I could do to stop him."

"But you didn't have to go to sleep and let him go out and murder a girl. My God, something like that could have ruined all my plans. And you still haven't answered me, Tex. Why did you do it?"

331

"I thought it was Stacey," Tex said sheepishly.

"Well, that's even worse. I told you I had plans for her."

"Yeah, I know what kind of plans," Tex said leered. "You and Brewster were havin' all the fun with her while I was gettin' left out. Well, I wanted a little fun too."

"Brewster? What are you talking about?" Barney asked. Barney looked at Brewster with the question reflected in his eyes.

"I, uh, knew the girl in Denver," Brewster said.

"What?" Athens asked quickly. "Who is she?"

"It's the same girl, Lorin." Brewster said. "You know the one with Tremain?"

"Would you kindly explain all this?" Barney asked again.

"Brewster and Athens raped her," Tex said smugly. "Brewster told me all about it. It was when they was in Denver. They tied the girl down and raped her while her boyfriend watched."

"I didn't have anything to do with it," Athens protested. "It was him!" He pointed at Brewster. "His real name is Billy Miles and he's the one who couldn't keep away from her. Her boyfriend put up a reward for us, and that's why we left Denver."

"A fine lot of morons I have to work with," Barney said disgustedly. He sighed. "Very well, what's done is done. And it looks like the event I've been waiting for is going to take place tomorrow anyway, so with any luck we can take our money and then, gentlemen, and believe me I use that word advisedly, we can terminate our relationship. You sicken me—all of you."

"What do you mean, take our money?" Tex asked. "What's supposed to happen tomorrow?"

"Wells Fargo is transferring over one hundred thousand dollars by stage coach from Medford to MacAllister," Barney said. "And we're going to rob that stage."

"What's the plan?"

"It's a simple plan," Barney said. "Tomorrow morning a special stage is going to go from MacAllister to Medford, pick up a locked box, and then, under armed guard, return to MacAllister."

"The plan can't be too simple then," Miles said. "The armed guards will make it dangerous."

"That's just it," Barney said. "We won't rob that stage."

"What? Why not?"

Barney smiled. "Because, my dear fellow thieves, the money won't be on that stage. It's simply a ruse. The money will be on the following stage, an ordinary Medford to MacAllister coach, driven by our friend Stacey Pendarrow, and guarded by no one."

"Are you positive about that?" Billy Miles asked. "That makes no sense at all. Why aren't they protecting the money?"

"Oh, they *are* protecting it," Barney replied. "They're protecting it with the armor I suggested for them."

"What was that?"

"Stealth," Barney said. "They figure that transporting the money in such a fashion will thwart any potential robber, because the robber won't be aware of the money's presence."

"Oh, yeah, I get it," Tex said. "They're gonna surprise anyone who might try and rob the stage."

"Precisely." Barney said. "But the surprise will be on them." *And on you,* he added to himself.

Stacey could only speculate about the special stage which left about an hour before she did the next morning. It had a shotgun guard on board, and four armed outriders going with it. There had been rumors for some time that a rather large shipment of money was being transferred from Medford to MacAllister, and Stacey assumed this was to be that shipment. She also assumed that the secret message she carried the day before had something to do with that shipment, but she didn't dwell on it. She couldn't, as she had her own trip to prepare for. She was waiting outside the office when she saw Bramwell approach.

"Good morning, Stacey," he said, tipping his hat.

"Good morning, Bramwell," Stacey replied. "I thought you were going to get back to town yesterday."

"Yes," Bramwell said. "I was going to return but unexpected business came up and I was delayed a little longer. I didn't return to town until this morning."

"Then you haven't heard about Yolinda?"

"Yolinda? No, I haven't. What about her?"

"She was murdered night before last," Stacey said. "It was an awful thing to happen."

"Stacey, I'm terribly sorry to hear that," Bramwell said with the proper amount of shock. He put his hand on her shoulder. "Listen, I know things haven't been the same with us of late, but perhaps you will have dinner with me tonight after you return from Medford?"

"Yes," Stacey agreed. "Yes, I'll have dinner with you tonight. But it will be the last time, Bramwell, because I've something I feel I should tell you."

"Oh, I hate to hear you say it will be the last time," Bramwell said, smiling ruefully. "But, whatever you decide, I shall honor and respect your wishes. I want only your happiness."

"Thank you Bramwell," Stacey said.

"I must say, I already miss hearing you call me Bram. But, so it goes. Do you have time for breakfast?"

"I've already eaten, thank you," Stacey said. "I'm about to get underway. I'll see you when I return."

"I'll be looking forward to it," Bramwell said. He touched the brim of his hat and took his leave, while Stacey went inside to get the shipping orders from Mason.

As she was taking care of the last-minute details prior to leaving, she suddenly thought of something Bramwell had said. She looked up at Howard Mason with a puzzled expression on her face. "How would Bramwell Caulder know I was going all the way to Medford this morning?"

"He found out yesterday afternoon. Mr. Caulder has been very cooperative," Howard replied. "He helped the sheriff and me work out the special stage route, and suggested that you take the regular coach run to Medford."

"Did you say yesterday afternoon? That can't be.

He didn't return from his business trip to Portland until this morning."

"Oh, no, he was here yesterday afternoon, don't you remember? Oh, wait a minute, I believe he came along right after you left. Yes, I can see why you wouldn't have thought he was here yesterday, if you didn't see him."

Or if he told me that he wasn't here, Stacey thought. But the question in her mind was, why? Why had he lied to her? It couldn't be just to avoid her; in fact it was he who continued to press the relationship between them. *But*, she decided, *what difference does it make?* After tonight, when I intend to tell him about my love for Clay Conway, he will know exactly where he stands, and there will be no need for further discourse between us.

The MacAllister to Medford run was the same route as the MacAllister to Winchester run as far as the Sky Meadow way station. Beyond Sky Meadow the road forked, going west to Medford and east to Winchester. Therefore the first part of the trip was like all the other trips Stacey had been taking, and when she arrived at Sky Meadow she was greeted enthusiastically by Melissa.

"Pete came through this morning on a special stage," Melissa said. "I'll bet that it was what the message was all about."

"It could be," Stacey said, climbing down from the stage. "I've only got one passenger, and he's a through passenger for Winchester. Is there anyone here headed for Medford?"

"No," Melissa said. "Are you going to Medford?"

"Yes," Stacey said. "Three more hours there, then three back to here."

"Good, then you'll be spending the night here on your way back," Melissa said, happily. "Only this time you won't have to sleep in the barn."

"Oh, but I enjoy it," Stacey said remembering. "Really I do."

"Pooh, you're just saying that, I know. But I'm going to have a special place prepared for you by the time you come through tonight. Oh, I'm glad you'll be staying here. It's so nice to have someone to talk to."

Stacey smiled at the eager young girl. How well she could relate to Melissa's desire for outside companionship, though she would have much preferred staying in the barn tonight. That way she knew she would see Clay again. But of course, she could not let Melissa in on her secret.

"All right," Stacey finally said. "I'll sleep in the house tonight."

"Oh, wonderful, we'll have a fine time, you'll see."

"Melissa, would you take care of the arrival details for me? I think I lost a locket the other night and I want to go have a look around for it."

"You lost a locket? Oh, how awful. I'll come and help you search," Melissa said anxiously.

"There's no need," Stacey said quickly. "It was a very inexpensive locket but I liked it. I'll just have a quick look and if it's not there I won't bother about it. You take care of things for me here and I'll be in shortly."

"All right," Melissa said, "if you're sure I can't help."

Stacey gave Melissa the shipping orders to log in, then she went into the barn and climbed the ladder to the hayloft. She hadn't actually lost a locket, but it was a good excuse to visit the barn in the hope that Clay would be hiding in the little room he had built.

Clay wasn't there but Stacey had prepared for that by writing a note before she left MacAllister, and now she opened the note and reread it before leaving it for him.

Clay,
You have told me that you love me, and though at first I willed my ears not to hear, my heart listened. Now my heart can also speak, and it speaks of love. My love for you, for it is true, my darling, I do love you. I am taking the regular stage run to Medford, and will be back through here tonight. I hope that you are here waiting for me, and my love.

Your own,
Stacey

Stacey folded the note and propped it up against the oil lantern so that he would not miss it. Then she left the hayloft and returned to the main house.

"Did you find your locket?" Melissa asked.

"My locket?"

"Yes, the one you went to look for."

"Oh, uh, no, I didn't," Stacey said. "It doesn't matter. As I said, it was inexpensive anyway." Stacey took the shipping orders from Melissa. "Well, I've got a lot of miles to cover so I'd best be getting on my way. I'll see you tonight."

"I'll have a surprise for you when you return," Melissa promised.

"Good," Stacey said. "I like surprises. Though the prospect of spending the night here talking to you is pleasant enough."

Melissa beamed under the compliment. She had resolved to turn the hayloft upside down if necessary, to find Stacey's locket. That would be her surprise.

Chapter Thirty-six

Stacey pulled the team to a halt and set the brake, then climbed down from the stage and looked around. She was in Medford twenty minutes ahead of schedule, having driven harder in order to make a good impression on this, her first run to Medford. She walked into the depot and over to the station agent's cage. He was intently studying a time schedule, and he had a pencil stuck behind one ear. He looked up as Stacey approached.

"Yes, miss, can I help you?"

"I'm Stacey Pendarrow."

"Yes?"

Stacey realized then that the agent didn't know who she was. "I'm the driver of the stage that just came in," she said. "I'm here for shipping orders."

"Oh, oh, yes, I believe I was told that there would be a . . . lady . . . driver," the agent said, setting the word 'lady' off from the rest of the sentence. "Well, it's good that you're here. I have six pouches for you. If you would sign here, please?" He pushed a form across the counter to her and took his pencil from behind his ear.

"Six? Isn't that a little unusual?"

"No, not too unusual," the agent said. "Why do you ask?"

"I've never carried more than one mail pouch and it was seldom full. And now I have six."

"Yes," the agent said. "Please sign this and let me get them aboard for you. I don't want to keep them any longer than I have to." The agent appeared uncomfortable.

"Why are you so nervous about them?" Stacey asked. "What's in them?"

"What's in them? Why, I don't know," the agent said briskly. "I don't ask questions and neither should you. Just sign here and I'll get them aboard."

"Very well," Stacey said. "It's probably just old newspapers and circulars anyway. If it had been something important it would have gone on the special coach with the money."

"How did you know about the money?" the agent asked.

Stacey smiled, then signed the form and slid it back to the agent. "I just guessed. Why else would they send a heavily guarded coach on a special trip?"

"You shouldn't guess about things that don't concern you." The agent took the form and put it on a spindle by the window. "Well, I'll just get these loaded now, and post a guard by them until you're ready to leave. Will you be pulling out soon?"

"Right away," Stacey said. "Do I have any passengers?"

"One," the agent answered. "A man. I think he's back now; he stepped across the street to have lunch. You're early, you know."

"Yes," Stacey said smugly, "I know."

"Oh, here comes your passenger now," the agent said. "You take care of him while I'll load these pouches."

Stacey turned to look at the passenger and recognized him with a quick beat of joy. He raised his arms and she ran into them.

"Mark! But I thought you would hire a team."

"I tried to," Marcus said hugging her. "There are none available. The railroad has preempted every mode of transportation, no doubt to force people to ride their trains. That would be fine if the train went where you wanted to go. Unfortunately, there is no train to MacAllister."

"Oh, stop complaining and give me a kiss," Stacey said, smiling broadly at him. They hugged each other affectionately, oblivious of the stares of passers-by.

"I'm glad I couldn't hire a team," Marcus said. "I would rather ride with you. You're looking lovely, Stacey."

Stacey blushed. "Oh, I'm sure I am," she said. "Just look at me, this outfit, my hair, my hands. I'm a mess and you know it."

"No, you're beautiful," Marcus said.

"Oh, Marcus, I'm so sorry about Yolinda," Stacey said, acknowledging why Marcus was here.

"Yes," Marcus said. "Friendship with me seems to carry some sort of terrible curse, doesn't it?"

"Don't be ridiculous. I consider you my very dear friend, and nothing has happened to me."

"Stacey, nothing would dare happen to you. You're a person who commands fate. Who else but you could have realized such an unlikely ambition?

343

Here you are, a full-fledged driver for Wells Fargo."

"And you are my passenger," Stacey said. "You must ride on the seat with me, Mark. We have a lot to talk about."

"You mean it's all right for me to ride up there?"

"Sure," Stacey said. "Climb on up, I'll be right behind you."

When Stacey and Marcus were settled into their seat, Marcus noticed a large number of people standing around looking at them. "Stacey," he said, *sotto voce*. "Why are they looking at us?"

"They want to see if I can handle this team, I guess," Stacey said easily.

"Doesn't that bother you?"

"No, not any more. Generally, when I show them that I can, their curiosity is satisfied." Stacey untied the reins, released the brake, then snapped the whip over the heads of the eight-horse hitch, and they were off. As they rolled through the streets of Medford, several people waved at them. A handful of kids and dogs kept pace beside them for a few blocks, but the kids soon tired and fell behind. The dogs, yelping and snapping excitedly at the whirling wheels, followed for a bit longer but by the time the city limits were reached they, too, fell behind, so that the stage left town unescorted.

"I saw your aunt and uncle before I left Denver," Marcus said. "They're doing well, and they send you their regards."

"I must write to them," Stacey said guiltily. They rode in silence for several moments, then Stacey spoke again. "I was saddened to hear about Mary. She was such a sweet person."

"Her death was a great personal tragedy for me," Marcus said.

"I'm sure it was. Yolinda said that you and Mary were keeping company quite regularly."

"Stacey, I don't know how to explain it," Marcus said. "But there was something about Mary . . . something almost mystical . . . that made our relationship a truly satisfying one. I knew I had the problem of impotence, but somehow, with her, it didn't seem important. Mary taught me to live with it, to come to terms with it. It was only to help Yolinda adjust that I sent her to you. I have found an inner peace."

"Marcus, I'm glad," Stacey said. "You're such a good person, and you have so much to offer, you shouldn't spend your life worrying about—" Stacey's sentence was interrupted by the roar of a shotgun blast, and three riders suddenly appeared in front of the stage.

"Hold it!" the rider with the shotgun yelled. He leveled the gun at Stacey and she halted the team.

"Billy Miles!" Stacey gasped.

"So," Billy said, "we meet again. And Marcus Tremain! Fancy seeing you here."

"Billy Miles and Lorin Keefer," Marcus said. "I had hoped to be able to pay the reward I offered for you by now."

"Well, look at it this way," Billy said. "With us still moving around, you're saving money."

"What the hell is this, old home week?" Tex asked. "Get on with it."

"Oh, excuse me," Billy said. "Allow me to introduce the Texas Kid."

"The Texas Kid!" Stacey gasped. "You're the one who . . . ."

"Killed Big Tom Fenton? Yeah, that's me," Tex said proudly.

"No," Stacey said coldly. "I was thinking of Yolinda Sinclair."

Tex grinned. "Yeah," he said. "Yeah, I killed her too. I like killin' women. So you'd better do like I say, little lady, or I'll kill you like I did her."

"You . . . you killed Yolinda?" Marcus asked in disbelief. "Why? What kind of a fiend are you?"

"I'm the kind who could kill your ass like steppin' on a piss ant," Tex said. "Now, you just sit there like a good boy, and let the lady beside you do all the work. Miss, they tell me you're a good driver. You think you can take this stage down through that creek bed there?"

"Why would I want to do that?" Stacey asked.

"'Cause it might keep you alive a little longer," Tex said. "I'm gonna climb up on the top of the coach and keep this scatter gun about two inches away from your head. You're gonna follow your two friends down this here creek bed to a little camp we got set up."

"But what do you want with me?" Stacey asked. "I'm not carrying any money."

The three road agents laughed.

"It's the truth!" Stacey said. "I'm not carrying any money."

"You're carryin' over one hundred thousand dollars, Stacey," Billy said.

"No," Stacey said, "you're mistaken. That money was sent on the armed coach. It went through here this morning."

346

"Open one of the pouches," Billy Miles ordered.

"Open a mail pouch? Why?"

"Just open it."

Stacey picked up a pouch from the footwell, and unlaced the rawhide tie. When she looked inside she saw several stacks of money, neatly bound in bank bands indicating the amont of each stack.

"I don't understand . . . ." Stacey faltered.

"You don't need to understand," Tex said. "Barney figured it all out for us. All you gotta do is take this here stage down that creek bed like I told you."

Tex rode up to the side of the stage, then climbed from his horse to the stage roof. He settled in comfortably, and pointed the shotgun at Stacey's head. "And try 'n make it a nice gentle ride too, will you?"

Billy and Lorin rode off the road and down the dry creek bed. The creek bed was narrow and twisting and full of rocks, but it was wide enough and flat enough to allow the stage to pass, though it took all of Stacey's skill to keep from breaking a wheel or axle, and to manipulate the stage through the close area.

Stacey drove the stage through the creek bed for nearly an hour, when finally it flattened out into an area that was obviously a camp site. Billy and Lorin dismounted, led their horses to a tree, and tied them there.

"This'll do," Tex said. "Now, hop down."

"What are you going to do with us?" Stacey asked.

"You'll see," Tex said, grinning broadly. "Brewster, you and Athens," Tex started, then he stopped and looked at Stacey. "I'm sorry, you know these two galoots as Billy and Lorin, so I'll call them that to make you feel more at home."

"I know them as scoundrels and cowards," Stacey said.

"You got spirit," Tex said. "I'm going to enjoy it when the time comes."

"Enjoy what?" Stacey asked, fear creeping into her voice.

"Uh, uh," Tex said. "That's my little surprise. Now, Billy and Lorin, get these two tied up, and then go get Barney."

"There's no need for both of us to go after Barney," Billy said. "I'll stay here."

"Are you afraid that I'll take the money and go?" Tex asked.

"No, it's not that," Billy said. "It's just that I think we would be better off if one of us stayed with you."

"Well, it's good that you don't think I'll take the money," Tex said, "because if I wanted to take it, I would, you know. And you could do nothin' to stop me."

"I don't think you're going to take it," Billy repeated.

"Yeah? Well, I don't know. Maybe I will and maybe I won't. Whatever I decide, you won't have no say in it, you got that?"

"Yeah," Billy said, "I got it."

"Now, you, Lorin. You go get Barney, and you get back here quick. Tell him I'm thinkin' about takin' it all for myself. That'll get him here quick enough."

"Right," Lorin said. "What about these two?"

"What about 'em?"

"Barney said he didn't want anyone left alive."

"Well, Barney ain't runnin' this show out here; I am," Tex said. "And I aim to keep 'em alive for a while longer."

"Why?"

"Barney had his reasons for keeping them alive, now I got mine," Tex said. "You just fork your horse and ride."

Stacey, who, with Marcus, was now tied to a tree, listened to the exchange with anger and anxiousness. Who was this mysterious Barney, and why did he want them killed? What reason did Tex have for keeping them alive, and would he be able to do it? Her throat was dry and her heart was pounding, but there was nothing she could do for the moment but worry and wait. And though she wasn't given to too much prayer, she found herself praying the same thing, over and over: *please, God, let Clay find us here.*

Chapter Thirty-seven

Clay Conway moved through the dark shadows with the fluid grace of a cat, and climbed the ladder to the hayloft. Then he pushed the bale of hay away from the opening, and slipped inside. He lit a match, saw a white piece of paper propped against the lamp, then lit the lamp and read the note from Stacey.

"She's late," a girl's voice said.

The sudden voice startled Clay so badly that he whirled and drew his gun all in one fluid motion. There, sitting on his bed with her knees drawn up and her arms wrapped around them, was Melissa.

"What are you doing here? Clay asked, sheathing his gun.

"I'm waiting for you."

"Waiting for me?. What do you mean waiting for me? How did you know I would be here?"

"I found this room while I was looking for Stacey's locket," Melissa said. "And I found her note to you. So I knew you would be here. But she's late and I'm worried about her."

"Late? Late for what?"

Melissa explained that Stacey had taken the stage run to Medford, and was due back by seven.

"It's nearly ten o'clock and she hasn't shown up. I'm afraid something has happened to her."

"Maybe she decided to stay in Medford," Clay suggested.

"No. We had a rider stop to take supper with us. He left Medford after the stage did. He saw it pull out."

"Well, did he overtake the stage on the road?" Clay asked.

"He says he never saw a thing. Oh, Clay, I'm awfully worried about her. What if she went over the edge of the road or something? She could be lying in the bottom of some ravine somewhere, dead or dying. Please, go look for her!"

"Melissa, I have to be careful, you know that. I'll tell you what. If she doesn't turn up by tomorrow, you can notify the sheriff and he'll take a posse out for her. But I know Stacey, and I think she's probably all right. She's just holed up somewhere for some reason."

"No," Melissa insisted. "Something's wrong, Clay, I know it. I can feel it inside. Please, you have to go look for her!"

Clay sighed, and looked at the note again.

"Besides, you love her and she loves you," Melissa said. "That should be reason enough for you to go."

"Didn't anyone ever tell you it wasn't nice to read other people's mail?"

"It isn't mail," Melissa said. "It's only a note, and notes are meant to be read by anyone who finds them."

"Have you told anyone about finding this place?" Clay asked.

"No, not a soul," Melissa replied.

"It doesn't really matter," Clay said. "If you found it, others can find it. I guess I'll have to move my hiding place."

"Clay, please hurry! You have to go look for her."

Clay saw the intensity in the girl's eyes, and smiled. "All right," he said. "I'll find her. But I'm sure she's all right, so just don't you worry."

Melissa returned his smile. "I won't worry now," she said. "If you're going to look for her, everything will be just fine, I know it will."

Clay flashed a big smile and turned to leave.

"Clay?" Melissa said.

"Yes?"

"I thought Beau Bandito gave all the women a kiss?"

"And I thought you were Stacey's friend?"

"I am," Melissa said. "This will just be a kiss for luck."

Clay laughed, then walked over to the girl and tried to kiss her on the forehead but she tilted her head back quickly and offered him instead her soft, cool lips.

"Uhmm," Clay said, after he kissed her. "You're going to be a heartbreaker in a couple of years."

"Please," Melissa said satisfied now. "Find her."

"Don't worry," Clay promised. "By tomorrow morning everything will be fine."

Clay slid the bale of hay to one side and slipped through the opening, then crossed to the loft window, dropped down quietly to the ground, and ran into the shadows of the trees where his horse had been tethered for the night.

* * *

The moon floated high and silver, slanting down through the trees with beams as visible as sun rays, though much softer and with less illumination. The illumination was enough, however, for Stacey to see the two men who held them prisoner.

Billy walked over to the tree where Stacey and Marcus were tied. He was eating a piece of jerky.

"Are you hungry?" he asked.

"No," Stacey said coldly, though in truth she realized that she was, having missed lunch, intending to make it up at dinner.

"Suit yourself." Billy looked at her for a moment, and Stacey saw the same unmistakable signs of lust in his face that she had seen when he raped her in Denver. "Do you remember the last time we met?" he asked.

"Do you think I could ever forget it?"

Billy laughed. "How about you, Marcus? Did you learn anything from before? Or maybe you need another lesson?"

"You are an animal," Marcus said through clenched teeth.

"Yeah, that's me all right. I'm an animal. I'm an animal during the rutting season, and I think I just might have a little of this girl again." He started unbuckling his pants.

"Miles, if you lay one hand on her, I'll kill you," Marcus said.

"You'll what?" Billy asked, laughing so hard he could scarcely get the words out.

"I said I'll kill you," Marcus said again, his words as cold as ice.

"You know, I honestly believe you mean it. Hey, Tex, did you hear that?"

Tex walked over to the tree. He too was eating beef jerky. Spittle drooled down his chin and across his scraggly beard. He made no attempt to wipe it off.

"What do you want to know if I heard?"

"Marcus Tremain, the dandiest dude of Denver, has threatened to kill me if I touch this girl here."

"Well, why don't you just do her and see what happens?" Tex asked.

"I believe I will," Billy said. He walked over to Stacey and jerked her shirt open, sending the buttons flying. Smiling obscenely at her, he loosened her belt, then opened her pants and jerked them down to her knees. The inverted triangle of hair at the junction of her legs glowed blue-black in the moonlight.

"Now just where is it that I can't touch her, dandy? Here?" Billy asked, putting his hands on her breasts. "Or here?" he put his hand on the spade of hair between her legs.

Stacey made no attempt to fight. She knew that to do so would be futile and might even be an added source of pleasure for Billy. She had no wish to give him pleasure of any kind.

"Or maybe it's just *what* I touch her with that bothers you," Billy said, continuing to tease Marcus. "Maybe you don't want me to touch her with this?" He dropped his trousers, and took himself in both hands, wielding his manhood proudly in the moonlight.

"I'll kill you," Marcus said. "As God is my witness I'll kill you."

"We'll just see about that," Billy said. "Oh, pardon me, Tex, but I've already had the pleasure of knowing this girl once. Perhaps you'd like to be first this time?"

"Naw," Tex said, watching the scene unfold with eyes that were tiny and red. "You go ahead and do it. I like to watch. I'll have my fun afterward. I've got my own idea."

"If you're positive you won't mind," Billy said formally. He stepped up to the tree where Stacey was tied and planted his mouth over hers, trying to kiss her, but she bit his lip, bringing blood, and he jerked away.

"Oh, so you don't want a kiss, is that it? You want to get right down to business. Well, I guess I can accommodate you there."

Stacey's legs had been tied in a moderately open position, and though they were not spread far enough apart to facilitate easy entry, neither were they close enough together to allow her to deny him. She felt him thrust into her painfully, and with a sense of detachment realized that that which could be so pleasurable under the right conditions could be so painful under the wrong.

Billy pounded her, rough and hurting, and she was forced to suffer the attack, thankful only that she did not have to look at him. But when she turned her face away from Billy Miles, she was greeted with a sight that both shocked and revolted her. There, watching in lustful joy, was the Texas Kid and that which he held in his hand was not a gun. Stacey shut her eyes, to shut out the sight. In a way, seeing the Texas Kid abusing himself while watching her being raped was more horrible than that which Billy was subjecting her.

It was only when Billy grunted, sighed, shuddered, and then withdrew from her that she was aware that Marcus was still threatening to kill Billy Miles.

"You'd better shut up," Billy said panting, "or I'll let you have it right now."

"Give me a gun," Marcus cried, struggling against his bonds. "Give me a gun and I'll kill you."

Billy Miles laughed, then looked over at the Texas Kid. He noticed then what the Texas Kid had done, and his immediate reaction was similar to Stacey's.

"What are you lookin' at?" the Texas Kid asked.

"I'm not looking at anything," Billy Miles answered as the Texas Kid closed his trousers.

"I told you I've got my own way of doing things," Tex said. "It'll be even better when I kill her."

"Are you going to kill her?"

"Yeah," Tex said.

"I thought you were going to keep her around for some reason."

"I just did the reason," Tex said, laughing obscenely.

"Kill us both if you must," Marcus said. "But before you do, give me a gun and a shot at Billy Miles."

Billy Miles laughed. "Listen to him. He's crazy, ain't he?"

"I don't know," Tex said slowly. "He might have a pretty good idea."

"What are you talking about?" Billy asked suspiciously.

"I think I'll just give him a gun and see what he can do with it."

"Are you crazy too? Why take a chance like that?"

"I like taking chances," Tex said. He walked over to the saddlebag of his horse and pulled out a belt and gun. "This belonged to my old man," he said, holding the gun out. "I took it off him myself, right after I killed him." Tex opened the cylinder gate and began ejecting bullets. Finally, he spun the cylinder, squinted into the chambers, then put the gun back in the holster. "Untie him."

"Tex, you aren't serious."

"I'm very serious," Tex said. "Now untie him and have him strap this gun on."

"What if he gets lucky and kills me?"

"Then you'll just be unlucky."

"What if he turns the gun on you then?"

"He only has one bullet," Tex said. "So when he draws he has to decide which one of us he wants to shoot. I think it'll be you, don't you?"

"I—I don't want any part of this," Billy said. "This is crazy."

"I said untie him," Tex said coldly. "Do it now, or I'll kill you where you stand."

Billy measured the intent in Tex's eyes, and found it sincere. With a final protest he untied Marcus.

"Put this on," Tex said, holding the holster out toward Marcus.

Marcus put the gun on, strapping it high on his waist.

"No," Tex said. "Let that side hang low, you'll have a better reach for the gun."

"You don't have to give him lessons, for God's

sake," Billy said, his voice betraying a growing nervousness.

"It's a single action pistol," Tex went on, ignoring Billy's protests. "That means you have to pull the hammer the moment you draw the gun. When you get it level, its weight will cause the hammer to drop and it'll go off before you know it." Tex took the gun out of the holster and turned the cylinder. "Go ahead and try it a couple of times. You got a few empty chambers to work with. Practice."

"Tex, my God, what are you doing?" Billy asked.

"I'm teaching him how to be a gunfighter."

"But why?"

"I want him to kill you so I won't have to."

"Tex, come on, this isn't funny," Billy said. "What are you going to do with him if he does kill me?"

"Then *I'll* have to kill *him*," Tex said easily. He watched as Marcus went through a few practice draws.

"Tex, are you crazy?"

"Probably," Tex answered. "All right, you're ready to go," Tex said to Marcus. "Now remember, you got only one bullet. You're going to have to take your chance on which one of us you want to go for. If you kill him, I'll kill you. I don't intend to draw the first time, so if you decide you want to kill me you can probably get away with it. But remember that while you're killing me, he'll be killing you, then he'll be left alive. I think that makes it real interesting, don't you?"

"Let's get on with it," Marcus said coolly. He turned to face Billy.

"Shoot him!" Billy said. "Draw your gun and shoot him. I'll give you another chance."

"Draw," Marcus said.

"No, are you crazy?" Billy shouted.

"Draw!" Marcus said again, shouting the word.

Both men drew at the same time and the two shots sounded as one. When the smoke drifted away; Stacey saw Billy standing there with a triumphant grin on his face. Then, slowly, the grin faded and Billy toppled over. It was only then that she saw the spreading stain of dark on his shirt.

Marcus looked at the smoking gun in his hand for a moment as if bewildered over what had just happened, then he tossed the gun toward Billy's body.

"Now, gunfighter," Tex said flatly, almost bored. "How do you want it? You want me to give you another bullet and another chance, or should I just end it all for the two of you, quick and easy?"

"That won't be necessary, mister!" a man's voice suddenly called from the trees.

"Clay!" Stacey cried. "Oh, thank God you've come."

Clay stepped out of the shadows and into the moonlit clearing. His gun was still in his holster, and when Tex saw that he smiled broadly.

"So," Tex said, almost happily. "I finally get to meet Clay Conway."

"That's me," Clay said. "And who might you be?"

"I'm the Texas Kid," Tex said, stung by the apparent lack of recognition.

"That's a dumb name," Clay said. "No wonder I've never heard of it."

"What do you mean you've never heard of it? I'm the Texas Kid. Why, I killed Big Tom Fenton!"

360

"We all gotta go sometime," Clay shrugged. "I guess it was just his time. Now it's yours."

Tex's hand started for his gun, but Clay had his own out and booming before Tex could completely clear leather. The gun slipped out of his hand and fell back into the holster, as the impact of the bullet sent Tex back against a nearby tree stump where a coffeepot sat. Tex tried to sit on the vacated stump, but was too unsteady and slid off the stump and onto the ground.

"I wouldn't'a thought it," Tex said, unable to believe what had happened to him. "I wouldn't'a thought you could beat me." His head fell forward and he died.

"Stacey, are you all right?" Clay shouted now, running toward her. "Help me get her untied," he said to Marcus.

"Just leave her there," another voice interrupted, "or this scatter gun will go off."

"It's Lorin," Marcus said. "He's back."

"Yeah, I'm back," Lorin said, stepping into the clearing with the gun. "And I've got Barney with me. Come on out, Barney."

As all heads turned to look at the newcomer, Stacey gasped. Stepping out into the clearing was Bramwell Caulder!

Chapter Thirty-eight

"So, you're Barney," Clay said flatly.

"Yes," Bramwell said. "Barney is a name I used in my youth, and I found it useful to continue to use it in my extracurricular activities."

"I should have known it was you," Clay said. "Your mannerisms, your hands. But I never got a look at your face."

"No. I was outside, guarding the horses when your father was shot and your mother and sister raped. I couldn't take a chance on them identifying me, so it was necessary to kill them. I regret that, but it was a necessity."

"I have looked for you ever since," Clay said.

"I know you have," Bramwell said easily. "But you didn't know me, whereas I did know you, and that made it easy to avoid you. I also had the foresight to keep you alive when I robbed the stage you guarded. I figured I would have some use for you later on, and I allowed you to live as a cover."

"Oh, then it *was* you!" Stacey said slowly. "*You* killed my father."

"No," Bramwell replied. "I didn't kill him. He did." Bramwell pointed at the still form of the Texas Kid. "But it's all academic now. Unfortunately, I'm going to have to kill the three of you now. You, I'm afraid, are just an innocent victim, like the passengers in the first stage," he concluded, looking at Marcus.

"I can tell by your language, sir, that you are an educated man," Marcus said.

"Yes, I am. I'm a graduate of Yale, and I'm a lawyer."

"Then why have you entered a life of crime?" Marcus asked, stalling for time.

"The answer is quite simple. Greed. This is a growing country, and intelligent investments at the right time can make a man wealthy beyond imagination. I have the intelligence. Unfortunately I do not have the funds to make the proper investments. I have seen fit to acquire those funds in this manner."

"I see," Marcus said. "My name is Marcus Tremain. Perhaps you have heard of my father, Upton Tremain?"

"Yes," Bramwell said. "I've heard of him."

"Then you know he is a very wealthy man."

"So?"

"He's wealthy enough to make it worth your while if you set us free."

"How do I know you are who you say you are?"

"He is, Barney. I know him," Lorin said. Lorin still held the shotgun on them. "We were blackmailing him back in Denver until he put up a reward on our heads."

"Tsk, tsk, Mr. Tremain," Bramwell said. "It appears that you are not a man to be trusted. No, I'm afraid that what you propose is quite out of the question."

"No, you must listen to me!" Marcus said. "Please, I beg of you, for God's sake, spare my life! Kill the others if you must, but spare me, spare me!"

As Marcus begged for his life he fell to his knees and started crawling toward Lorin.

"Haw, look at 'im," Lorin said. "He hasn't changed a bit. He was just like this in Denver."

"Please," Marcus begged. "Please, kill them, but spare me!"

"You mean you want me to kill the slut?" Lorin asked.

"Yes, yes, if you must."

"Then say it," Lorin said. "Say kill the slut."

"Please," Marcus said, crawling all the way over to Lorin, and stopping just before him, "kill the slut."

"Naw, I think I'm going to . . . ."

"Now, Clay, draw!" Marcus yelled, lunging into Lorin and knocking him to the ground.

Clay, who had been looking for the chance he needed, drew his pistol and fired at Bramwell, then whipped it over toward Lorin who was trying to swing the shotgun around to shoot Marcus. "Drop that shotgun or you'll die this instant," Clay barked.

"I'm droppin' it, I'm droppin' it," Lorin shouted, tossing the shotgun to one side.

Marcus jumped up quickly, and ran over to untie Stacey. Clay, with his gun still in his hand, walked over and poked at Bramwell with his foot, but Bramwell was dead.

"Marcus, you were magnificent," Stacey said as she repaired the damage to her clothes.

"I'll say you were," Clay agreed. "What kind of move was that?"

"That was called a tackle," Marcus said. "It's used in a game called football."

"I've never heard of football," Clay said.

"The colleges back East play it," Marcus said.

"Well, all I can say is you must have been pretty good at it."

Marcus laughed. "Good at it? I couldn't even make the team."

"What are we going to do with him?" Stacey asked, pointing to Lorin.

"I'd like to kill him," Clay said. He cocked his pistol and pointed it at Lorin's head.

"No, no," Lorin screamed. "For God's sake, don't shoot."

Clay let the hammer back down slowly. "You give me one good reason why I shouldn't."

"I can get you off," Lorin said. "I know where all the money is hidden, and I can testify that it was Bramwell and Tex who killed the people in that first stage robbery."

"Clay, maybe this is your chance!" Stacey said.

"I don't know," Clay said. "I've pulled a few jobs myself, remember? They aren't likely to forget that."

"What if you paid the money back?" Marcus asked.

"I don't have all of the money. I've spent some of it to stay alive."

"Perhaps you would allow me to make up the difference," Marcus suggested.

"Mark, you would do that?" Stacey asked.

"Sure."

"I don't know," Clay said. "I don't like to be beholden to anyone."

"Why not?" Marcus asked simply. "I'm beholden to you for my very life. Surely my life is worth something?"

"Clay, don't be so stubborn," Stacey said sharply. "You let Mark fix things with Wells Fargo so we can get married."

"Married?" Clay said, looking at her in surprise. "Who said anything about getting married?"

"I said it. You *are* going to marry me, aren't you?"

"Stacey, you aren't supposed to ask me; I'm supposed to ask you."

"Who said?"

"Well, it's a man's job to ask the woman," Clay sputtered.

"Since when do I let things like that stand in my way?" Stacey asked. "Driving a stage is a man's job, too, but that didn't stop me."

"She's got a point there," Marcus said, laughing. "But if you don't want to take her up on it, I'd be willing to."

"I didn't say I wasn't going to take her up on it," Clay said. "I just said it should be me doing the asking."

"Well?" Stacey said.

"Well, what?"

"Well, ask me."

Clay looked at Stacey and smiled. "Will you marry me, girl?" he asked.

"I'll think about it," Stacey said.

Clay kissed her, full on the lips, pulling her

tightly to him. Finally, after several breathtaking moments, he let her go. "Well?"

"I . . . I need to think about it more," Stacey said, her knees weak from the kiss.

Clay kissed her again, then released her. "Well?" he asked.

"Yes," Stacey said. This time she kissed him. "A thousand times yes."

As they stood there, a small breeze whipped up, and carried on the wind was a tattered poster on Clay Conway, alias Beau Bandito. It plastered itself to one of the stage wheels, then blew away, carrying with it the storms of the past, clearing the air for the sunrise of tomorrow.

SPECIAL PREVIEW!

If you enjoyed *The Fury and the Passion* by Paula
Fairman, you will want to read her last novel, *Storm
of Desire*, about which *Publishers Weekly* said:

> When work begins on the Southern Conti-
> nental railroad connecting Albuquerque to
> Phoenix, romantic ties progress with the newly
> laid tracks. Three men with conflicting inter-
> ests court lovely, levelheaded Reesa Flowers:
> swart Ted Foster, the railway's founder; cun-
> ning Warren Leland, the sybaritic son of its
> financial backer; and suave Joaquin Mendoza,
> the Mexican whose land the line must cross.
> As Ted and his Chinese crew lay the tracks,
> both Mendoza and Leland attempt sabotage.
> The Mexican removes survey markers and
> Leland cuts funds. Before this tale closes,
> Reesa is robbed, kidnapped, married against
> her will and in a last climactic scene is almost
> killed in a thunderous rockslide. The pace here
> is streamlined, the subplots carefully con-
> structed and the balance between romance
> and the burgeoning railroad well apportioned.
> Fairman is the author of *Forbidden Destiny*
> and *In Savage Splendor*.

(*please turn page*)

Paula Fairman

Storm of Desire* *is the story of beautiful, high-spirited Reesa Flowers, innocent of the ways of the world, but beginning to feel the stirrings of her budding sexuality when the story opens. Both tempted and repelled by the woman-hungry men in the railroad camp where she lives with her telegrapher-father, Reesa is no match for the sophisticated city ways of Ted Foster, builder of railroads, a young man with a dream.*

Ted and Reesa will clash swords, wits, and passions, will love one another and hate one another, and Reesa will make a disastrous marriage, before she and Ted

370

reach the maturity that transcends their physical and emotional involvements with others.

Set in a tumultuous era, when a young country was feeling the growing pains of its adolescence, and a woman's life was directed by her father or her husband with no consideration for her own feelings, Storm of Desire *tells the story of one young woman who refused to become a pawn in men's games and a victim of her times.*

Following are the opening pages of the last novel by Paula Fairman (author of Forbidden Destiny *and* In Savage Splendor).

Had Miller Flowers but known the indignities to which his daughter was nightly subjected, he wouldn't have continued to send her with the crew orders for the midnight train. Reesa was a voluptuous young woman of eighteen, and she couldn't help the fact that men found her beautiful. She had black hair, the color of burnished ebony, coupled with green eyes to make a rather unusual but striking combination. Her face was dusted with a light spray of freckles, an effect which enhanced rather than detracted from her beauty. And as she pushed through the crowd to stand near the twin steel ribbons that connected Albuquerque with civilization, her full breasts and well-rounded derrière would attract awkward and seemingly accidental touches.

Miller Flowers, who had returned from the battle of Shiloh minus one leg, found that he was also a widower with an infant daughter to raise. He had been Reesa's sole parent since she was three months old, and he still looked upon her as a young, innocent child. Young she was, and thus far innocent as well. But Reesa was no child.

Despite the pinches and grabs she had to endure, there was an excitement to meeting the midnight train

371

that Reesa relished. There was always a carnival atmosphere about the crowd; laughter, good-natured joking, the constant cry of drummers who hawked their wares to midnight customers, and, usually, music from guitars or an occasional band.

What Reesa liked best, however, was the approach of the engine. The whistle could be heard first, far off and mournful, a lonesome wail that never failed to send chills through her body. Reesa would stare down the track, waiting for the train. The first thing to come into view would be the light, a huge, wavering, yellow disc, the gas flame and mirror reflector shining brightly in the distance. That sighting would be closely followed by the hollow sounds of puffing steam, like the gasps of some fire-breathing, serpentine monster. As if to add to the illusion, glowing sparks were whipped away in the black smoke clouds which billowed up into the night sky.

As the train pounded by, something inside Reesa's body throbbed in rhythm with the engine's powerful beat, and she felt herself drawn to it as a woman is drawn to her lover. When the train was completely still, Reesa would stand there for a moment, feeling her body bewilderingly alive, yet hauntingly hollow, as if craving something more. It was a bittersweet sensation, and she allowed herself to drift with its pleasurable waves, though a small, unheeded voice often cautioned against it.

After the train was completely stopped Reesa came out of her reverie and walked along the side, headed for the engine. Sam Norton was the engineer, and as Reesa approached his cab, she could see through the window the maze of pipes and valves that were Sam's controls.

"Hello, Miss Flowers," Sam called down.

"Hello, Sam," Reesa replied. "Did you have a nice trip?"

"Sometimes better'n fifty-five miles per hour," Sam said proudly. Then, "Do you have our orders, girl?"

"Yes, here in this envelope," Reesa said. She strained and stretched, reaching up to hand the envelope to Sam. The action brought her dress tight against her body, and those who were standing nearby took visible notice of the curves thus accented.

The envelope slipped from Reesa's fingers and bounced under the engine.

"Allow me, miss," a man's deep, resonant voice said.

The man who spoke was a stranger to Reesa. He was tall and dark, and well dressed in a russet-brown jacket and brown riding breeches tucked into highly polished boots. A ruffled shirt did nothing to hide his powerful chest, nor did the jacket detract from his broad shoulders. His eyes were a warm brown, and Reesa noticed with some surprise that they nearly matched the shade of his jacket. He had an easy smile and a handsome face, and Reesa couldn't help but feel a quickening of her pulse as she looked at him. Her reaction surprised and frightened her somewhat, and she found that for a brief moment she couldn't speak. Finally she found her voice.

"I fear I'll cause you to soil your clothes, sir," Reesa said.

"Then I shall wear the grime as a medal of honor for having served you," the man replied. He handed the envelope to Reesa, then smiled as she stretched to hand it up to the engineer.

"You are staring, sir," Reesa said, flustered.

"Yes," the man answered easily. "And I'm enjoying every minute of it. Fully as much as you are, I suspect."

"Sir, you are impertinent!" Reesa exclaimed indignantly, but her cheeks flamed in embarrassment, giving credence to the man's comment.

"I apologize; I meant no disrespect," the man said. "I was so taken by your charming ways, and meant only to speak honestly. Please forgive me if I offended you."

"Miss Flowers, this here is Ted Foster," Sam said from the cab of his engine. "He's goin' to build this here railroad clear on to the Pacific Ocean."

"You're Ted Foster?" Reesa asked. For she had heard of him, as had everyone in Albuquerque. The news that a new railroad, the Southern Continental, was going to connect Albuquerque with Phoenix and San Diego, was on everyone's lips. But that a man so young could do all this? Ted Foster couldn't have been over twenty-eight.

"I see you've heard of me," Ted said. "I also see that I don't come up to your expectations. You, on the other hand, are everything I was told you are."

"You've heard of me?"

"Of course," Ted said easily. "You are Reesa Flowers, the beautiful daughter of the man who is going to be my superintendent of station masters and telegraphers."

A yard worker approached them and stood back quietly, awaiting recognition. Ted saw him, smiled broadly, and stuck out his hand. "My name's Ted Foster," he said. "Who are you?"

"Arnold Blair, sir," the man replied, surprised that he had been asked. "I've come to tell you that your private car has been detached from the end of the train and pushed onto a sidetrack."

"Good; thank you, Arnold. I appreciate that."

Reesa was impressed with the way Ted spoke to the man. Many, she knew, would have barely acknowledged him. Ted had taken the time to introduce himself, learn the man's name, and use it.

"That was nice," she said after Arnold had left.

"It was nice of them to take care of it for me," Ted agreed.

"No, I meant that you took the time to speak with him."

"Friendliness is an investment, Miss Flowers," Ted said. "One which costs little, and often gives great returns. Like now, for example. I'd like to make a friendly gesture and invite you to join me in my car for a small drink before I turn in. Would you be interested?" Ted saw the shock in Reesa's eyes, and he laughed. "No? Very well, then perhaps some other time. In the meantime, Miss Flowers, I bid you good night."

Ted gave a small bow, almost mocking in its lack of movement, though made gracious by his style.

"Good night, Mr. Foster," Reesa said.

As Reesa left the train, the image of Ted Foster stayed with her. She could still see his broad chest and wide shoulders, and the even white teeth that smiled at her from the tanned, handsome face.

Reesa's innocence went as far as her virginity. No man had known her, though there were many in Albuquerque who had privately vowed they would pay any price for the privilege. Reesa, though still a virgin, already knew herself to be a woman with a passionate nature. Sometimes, unbidden, erotic thoughts played their temptations in her mind. As she was completely without experience, there was no form or substance to these fantasies, but there was an insistent longing for something more.

There were even times when she secretly enjoyed the attentions of the men in the crowd, and their gropings, and took a measure of pride in the fact that she could stir men so. But such feelings were rare, and were always followed by a sense of guilt. Reesa was determined to dominate the sexual side of her nature. She realized that decent women were not ruled by their passions, but controlled by their minds, and she vowed to keep her lustful feelings in check.

But even as she thought of her determination to be

pure of thought, she found herself thinking of Ted Foster. The throbbing feelings in her body that were stirred by the arrival of the engine seemed, somehow, to intermix with thoughts of the handsome young man. She felt a spreading warmth in her body, and a weakness in her knees. No man had ever made her feel this way. What was it about this one that affected her so?

Reesa and Ted will soon come to know one another better, as lovers and as friends. But there will be others who come between them: Joaquin de Mendoza, fiery young Mexican rebel, who will fight to the death to keep the gringos off his family's land, and who wants Reesa in the way she wants Ted; Warren Leland, dissolute son of the banker who controls Ted's destiny by virtue of his financing, who sees in Reesa the perfect weapon to use against Ted; and beautiful Lyrica Montoya who, loving Joaquin, betrays Reesa.

In Storm of Desire *Paula Fairman has created powerful, flesh and blood characters whose strengths and weaknesses, good and evil, passions and lusts, are skillfully blended in an absorbing story that, once started, will be difficult to put down.*